ALSO BY KEVIN GERARD:

DIEGO'S DRAGON:

Diego's Dragon, Book One: Spirits of the Sun

El Dragón de Diego, Primer Libro: Espíritus del Sol

Diego's Dragon, Book Two: Dragons of the Dark Rift

CONOR AND THE CROSSWORLDS:

Conor and the Crossworlds, Book One:
Breaking the Barrier

Conor and the Crossworlds, Book Two:
Peril in the Corridors

Conor and the Crossworlds, Book Three:
Surviving an Altered World

Conor and the Crossworlds, Book Four:
Charge of the Champions

Conor and the Crossworlds, Book Five:
The Author of All Worlds

Visit the author's websites at:
www.diegosdragon.com
www.conorandthecrossworlds.com

For Kimberly —

Dragon Guide!

Kevin Gerard

DIEGO'S DRAGON
BOOK THREE: BATTLE AT TENOCHTITLAN

KEVIN GERARD

Crying Cougar Press ™

San Diego, California

Spanish word translations are located at the end of this novel.

Published by Crying Cougar Press
San Diego, California

© 2013 Kevin Gerard. All rights reserved.
First published in 2013.

Edited by the Penny Dreadfuls
Translations by Jose Jimenez
Cover art by Benito Gallego
Interior illustrations by Benito Gallego
Typesetting by Julie Melton, The Right Type

Congratulations to Starr Culwell from Desert Springs Middle School
for creating the winning subtitle for this book: Battle at Tenochtitlan

To every student who entered the contest, I offer my gratitude and appreciation.
Always nurture your creativity and enthusiasm, for they are pathways to your dreams.

Printed in the United States of America
ISBN-13: 978-0-985-98023-8
ISBN-10: 0-9859802-3-0

FOR ANYONE WITH A DREAM
DIE TRYING!

CHAPTER ONE
1519

With Poseidon's breath straining the sails, the ship's bow sliced unevenly through the briny water. As the heavy ocean pressed against its sides, the massive vessel groaned, the only sound accompanying the howling winds. The sea rose and fell rhythmically, sloshing against the hull like a glass of beer hoisted by a drunken sailor. No birds flew this far out into the ocean. No sea life, mammal or fish, rose from the depths to eye those on board.

The sleepy motion matched the routine of the men working quietly aboard ship. Those strung in the sails, like spiders tending their webs, paid no heed to the whitewater slapping against the ship. They tended the cloth lovingly, as if it were a baby's first diaper, for if the sails shredded, the boat and her crew might never see land again.

The crewmen on deck busied themselves with tasks important to the vessel's maintenance. Some honed heavy oak for future repairs, others scrubbed and greased riggings. The lower ranking men twirled lines or pushed heavy mops, fighting their endless battle against wear and tear caused by the sea.

A handsomely dressed man stood before the door to the main cabin. Sensing the sway of the ocean through heavy boots, he peered over the ship's wheel. Squinting, he sighted points of reference only a seasoned sailor would recognize. A gust of wind whistled over his ears, burning his cheeks for a moment. His deeply tanned skin had weathered many voyages, so he stood silently, allowing the sensation to pass.

"Three degrees starboard," he said without shifting his gaze.

"Three degrees starboard, aye," came the reply.

"Hold new course for two hours."

"Two hours, sir. Aye, sir."

Captain Francisco Pizarro looked out over the deck of his great galleon, the Asesino de mar. The largest of the Spanish Armada, it had been given to Pizarro with a commission he'd prayed for his entire life. With a half dozen ships following his lead, he would sail to lands yet unexplored by Spain. After befriending the native population, he would load his ships with treasure beyond imagination and claim the lands in the name of his home, España.

He lifted his chin to check the men aloft. The sails seemed to be holding well enough. If they maintained their present speed and the winds didn't stiffen beyond the mainsail's capacity, they would make good time.

Placing his left hand on the hilt of his sword, he scanned the deck. The men busied themselves with their respective duties. To a man they kept their eyes from the quarterdeck. Pizarro had hand-picked every one and instilled a healthy dose of fear and respect into all of them. They knew if he caught their eye he would deem them lazy and assign additional duties.

All looked to be in order. He inhaled deeply, enjoying the taste of the salty air.

"I'll be below. Disturb me only in case of emergency."

"Aye, sir."

After entering his cabin, Captain Pizarro pressed his shoulder against the warped oak door. He leaned forward until he heard the latch fall. Taking a key from the wide ring on his belt, he secured it, making certain no one could follow him.

Stepping down into his workspace, he removed his hat and tossed it aside. He shouldered his way out of the heavy captain's coat, draping it over the back of his chair. Before taking a seat at his desk, he drew his sword and scabbard and hung them on a hook next to the door. He made the sign of the cross above the hilt, asking his Holy Father to give him strength should he ever have to use it to take another life.

The ship pitched wildly as it careened over a huge wave, but he merely shifted his feet to compensate. To him, the surge in the seas was an answer to his prayer. God had used his mighty ocean to assure Pizarro of His care.

He removed a thick parchment from a case attached to the wall. After placing it on the table and unrolling it, he looked upon a map of the Americas and the seas surrounding the new lands. Using the tools of his trade, a mariner's quadrant and compass to plot his course, he calculated the distance from their current point to their destination.

Lowering his eyes, Pizarro ran his fingers through his thick, curly hair. "Seven months, at least," he said as he sat heavily in his chair.

A voice called out from the deep recesses of his cabin. "I can shorten the trip for you, if you wish."

Pizarro didn't look up. There would be no one to see. No other person, no human that is, occupied his quarters. Even so, he knew the voice well.

"No," he said. "We'll manage on our own."

"As you wish," said the voice. "You've done well, *so far.*"

A chilled breath followed the last two words spoken by the spirit. The icy gust crept forward, sliding slowly down Pizarro's back.

The captain shrugged off the sensation. "Play your games, elsewhere, spirit, I have work to do."

"Don't give orders to me, Captain. If it weren't for my influence in the Queen's court, you'd have been decommissioned long ago."

"I've said my thanks," said Pizarro. "You'll get what you want, whatever it is. Leave me to my work."

"I need only your assurance that my orders will be followed after we reach our destination."

"I must satisfy my Queen's commission. Afterward my army is yours to command."

"I care nothing for the gold you seek," said the spirit, hatred coating his words like hot wax around a wick. "You would not be sitting here, or commanding this fleet without me, Captain. Never forget what I've done for you."

"I haven't, and I won't. Now leave me be."

The spirit gazed at the creature sitting before him. He wanted to burn Pizarro, fry his skin so he could hear the terrifying screams that fueled his evil presence. He would strap the insolent captain to the bowsprit of his vessel during a violent storm, watching eagerly as he slowly gagged and drowned.

The thoughts of doing away with his latest servant gave him strength he hadn't felt since Vipero had failed him. Victory had been within his grasp, but Magnifico and his guide had snatched it away. For that they would pay a horrible price.

The spirit dampened his desire to annihilate Pizarro. He needed the fool a while longer, so he melted into the bulkhead behind him, enjoying the strength of the sea.

If only I could control the oceans. He would hurl a wave the size of an island at the captain's tiny fleet, smashing the boats into kindling. Then he would pour the might of the sea over and through the lands of the new world. The guide's people would be wiped away in one swift stroke.

"Continue your mission, Captain."

Pizarro didn't answer. For a second time he made the sign of the cross, this time gliding his finger across the beaded cloth of his uniform. His hand shook with the movement.

Lifting his index and middle fingers to his lips, he pressed them lightly against the soft skin. He closed his eyes, asking for protection for his wife and children.

He rolled up his maps, gathering them together neatly before returning the parchments to their secure hold. He walked a few steps, holding an overhead beam when a wave threw the ship portside. Standing with his feet wide before a wash basin, he dipped his hands into the cool, fresh water. He rubbed his face briskly before grabbing a rough cloth coated with soap. He dipped it, applied it to his face, then rinsed again. Without looking, he yanked a towel from a worn, brass ring. Finally satisfied, he ran his eyes up the wall and caught his expression in an oblong mirror.

His face showed what he expected, the rough, tanned skin of a life at sea. The hair, still thick and wavy, had accepted a few gray strands before the Asesino de mar set sail, but he could still summon the fierce scowl that had beaten back many a belligerent crew.

He blinked, staring at his eyes. At one time they'd glistened with a dark golden hue so brilliant even men fell under his spell. Women had no chance, even his beautiful Juliana. She'd fallen for him at their first meeting, although she played to his attentions with the perfect tone of detachment. He smiled, his mind drifting, and then caught his eyes in the mirror again. They had faded during the voyage, as had his faith. Always a man of unshakable belief in himself, his choices, and his savior, Captain Pizarro's insides had shriveled since the Asesino de mar set sail. The pale lifelessness of his eyes showed the sickness in his soul.

He wanted to pray, but the words wouldn't come. His sin would separate him from his faith for all time. He wondered how terribly God would punish him for striking a deal with a fallen angel.

CHAPTER TWO
PRESENT DAY

"It's the first light of dawn," said Racquel.

"The dawn of a new age," added Diego.

Beyond the small range of hills lay the Pacific Ocean, the gateway to the Americas over five centuries ago. The sky overhead still wore its midnight hue, but the horizon in the west had begun to cheer a little. The deep, reddish coloring preceding the sun's first kiss glowed on the hilltops like the embers of a freshly lit fire. Diego squeezed Racquel's hand, preferring the gesture to a spoken word. He glanced sideways without moving his head and noticed her breathing deeply with her eyes closed.

"You might not be able to enjoy it if you don't run home this minute," said Sullivan. He'd approached so silently neither Diego nor Racquel had heard him. The two teenagers looked around and saw him, hands in his pockets, staring at the ever lightening horizon.

"Your parents will be up and about in no time. I'd give good odds the first thing they'll do is check your bedrooms to wish you good morning."

Racquel's eyes went wide. "My bedroom? I haven't slept there in months!"

Diego looked at Sullivan and smiled.

"If I were you, I'd go now," said Sullivan. "Find your way to your room without disturbing anyone. Pull the covers up and nestle them around your neck. Remember what it feels like to sleep in a soft bed."

"And when my parents charge into my room asking a hundred questions at once?"

Diego turned his smile toward Racquel.

"What's with the silly grin?"

"C'mon," said Diego. "Let's go."

"I'll take Racquel home," said Sullivan. "You live right up the street, but she'll need a little help."

"Alright," said Diego, turning to Racquel. "Text me in a while. Let me know what happens."

"Okay," she said, puzzled. She looked up and met Sullivan's eyes. They looked kind but worn. When he smiled at her the lines beside his eyes stood out.

"Ready?" he asked.

"Yes," she said. "I want to go home."

Sullivan pulled his hands from his pockets as he strolled away from the horse club. He looked like a man taking a carefree walk by the ocean. Racquel fell in step beside him, looking at the light dancing on top of the hills.

A lone car turned a corner at the far end of the street. As he did every morning at dawn, the driver stopped every half block, hustling an armful of newspapers toward various homes. Half asleep and focused on his job, he barely noticed the man and the young girl walking toward him. If he'd worked a normal shift, or if he'd slept more than a few hours the night before, he might have noticed when the two strangers vanished into the misty dew of the morning.

CHAPTER THREE

Racquel snuggled under her covers, breathing deeply. The scent of her bed linens caressed her like an old friend. She ran her fingers along the embroidered edge of the comforter her grandmother had knitted for her. She felt every line, every bump, every twitch of her abuela es tiny fingers as the woman patiently increased the pattern. The warmth it provided always reminded Racquel of her soothing embrace.

Closing her eyes, she recalled her experience living with the Spirits of the Sun. Sol's strength had constantly flowed through her body, filling her with a sensation of endless energy. Remembering each face, she focused her thoughts toward the spirits. Try as she might, though, she couldn't establish the connection she'd made so easily before. Without knowing whether they'd receive the sentiment, she exhaled slowly, sending her most heartfelt wishes to them.

She tried to contact Estrella through their mind link. She waited to hear her dragon's lovely voice, but as with the spirits, no response came. She entertained a moment of alarm, but dismissed it. No doubt she and Magnifico were resting comfortably in the flames of Sol's eternal fire. She knew they'd enjoy their time together, soothing each other's souls, mending each other's wounds. Perhaps she would try and contact her later this week. For now, though…

"Racquel?"

She froze, wondering what might happen when her parents opened the door. Would they rush to her, smother her with kisses, tell her over and over how deeply they love her? Would her father storm to the side of her bed, demanding to know where she'd been for close to a year, why she nearly caused her mother to lose her mind with worry?

"Racquel, mi pequeño amor?"

The door cracked open a few inches. Her mother's face peeked in, all teeth and dimples.

"Time to get up, niña. You'll be late for school."

Racquel lay there, staring.

Her mother walked in and sat on the covers, snuggling in next to her daughter. "I know it's hard to leave such a warm bed." She smoothed the comforter a little. "I still have the blanket your great grandmother made for me."

Racquel beamed at her mother, threw the covers back and jumped into her arms. She hugged her so fiercely the woman cried out in mock pain.

"I missed you, too, niña." She hugged Racquel and then held her at arm's length. "Let's get moving. This is a big day for you. You're in the eighth grade now."

Racquel took her time showering and dressing. She couldn't believe it. Could her situation be explained away that easily? Estrella must have done something, or Magnifico, or perhaps Mr. Sullivan. Maybe all three, she mused, as she stood in front of the mirror, drying her face with a warm towel. She applied a tiny amount of makeup, only a little so her mother wouldn't notice. After stepping into her shoes, she grabbed her cell phone and typed a quick text.

Diego – Mama came in to wake me this morning. She acted like she didn't even know I'd been gone. What's going on?

"Breakfast is on the table, Racquel!"

She hit send, shoved her phone into her backpack, threw on a jacket and pulled open her bedroom door. She peeked out, looking down the hall toward the kitchen. She could hear her mother and father talking.

Swallowing hard, she turned into the hallway. The kitchen door loomed ahead like an entrance to another dimension. She felt nervous, scared even, ready for any reaction when she faced her father for the first time.

"Morning, Mama," she said, her eyes glistening. "Buenos Dias, Papa."

Her father looked up from his paper. At first his manner seemed stern, distant. Racquel felt her fears would be confirmed. She prepared herself for his questions.

"Mi corazón," her father said, dropping his newspaper and holding his arms wide. "Don't you want a big bear hug from el viejo oso?"

She ran to her father's arms. As she did with her mother in the bedroom, she dove into his embrace. "Oh, Papa, I missed you and Mama so much."

"Then maybe you'll stay here to attend school from now on."

"Y-yes," Racquel stammered. "I suppose I..."

"Tell us, poco angel," interrupted Mariana, her mother. "Would you go back to Sacred Heart if you aunt asked you to stay again?"

Racquel silently thanked her mother for her gabbiness. If she hadn't interrupted, she couldn't imagine where the conversation might have gone.

"I don't think so, Mama," she said, taking a seat at the breakfast table. "It was a great experience, but I'd rather be here with my family."

"You mean with that diablito, Diego, right?" said Arturo, her father.

Racquel smiled. Her cheeks burned hotter than the oatmeal she'd just spooned into her mouth.

"Hush, oso grande," said Mariana. "She's barely a teenager. What kind of thoughts will you put in her head?"

"No more than she probably already has," said Arturo. "Kids these days..."

"Racquel," said Mariana. "Don't listen to that old fool. He thinks he knows the ways of the world, but he can't even remember what I asked him to do yesterday."

"I remember how quickly Racquel's sisters grew up."

Mariana's mouth dropped open.

Valeria and Claudia walked into the kitchen, saving Racquel the embarrassment of watching her mother and father have an argument.

"Good morning, Mama, Papa," they said, sitting together.

Valeria looked at Racquel. "How is our spoiled little sister? Can you sit at the same table with us after being treated like royalty for a whole year?"

"Si," added Claudia. "Maybe we should serve you before we eat."

"Shut up," snapped Racquel, a little too quickly. She flashed a look at Mariana, catching her mother's expression of disdain.

"That's enough," ordered Arturo. "Valeria, Claudia, your sister's been gone almost a year, and this is how you treat her when she returns? You're both older. You should know better."

"Lo siento, Papa," said Claudia.

"Sorry, Mama," said Valeria.

Racquel waited until both Mariana and Arturo turned away. She looked up at her sisters, curling her mouth into a sneering, *'you got into trouble'* smile. The two older girls, seething, returned her gesture with nasty expressions of their own, letting her know they'd be looking for revenge later. Valeria tried her best to swing the toe of her boot against Racquel's shin.

"Girls?" asked Mariana. "Your cousin's quinceañera is in two weeks. I want you to call your aunt today and assure her you'll help in any way you can. She'll need all three of you now that the party is almost here."

"Okay, Mama," answered Racquel immediately.

"*Okay, Mama,*" said Valeria, mocking her sister's response.

Arturo's hand slammed down on the table. "I said enough of that. Is this why your mother and I work so hard to give you a good home? Is this how we raised you? You're a senior in high school, Valeria."

"But Papa, she..."

"I won't hear it. What other people do doesn't matter. How you react to it does. Do you understand?"

"Si, Papa." Valeria began eating her breakfast. Claudia did the same. Both of them kept their eyes on Racquel.

"You might not believe it, girls," said Mariana, "but some day the three of you will be best friends."

Racquel faked coughing up a bit of her oatmeal. She saw Arturo's eyes boring in from her left.

"It's true," said Mariana. "Do you think your aunts and I were always so close? As girls we competed for everything; boys, gifts, our parents' attention, anything at all. In fact, we never needed a reason to argue or fight with each other. We were sisters, and young girls. We needed to grow up, that's all."

"Women!" said Arturo, a small smirk twisting his face.

"Don't you start, *señor*," said Mariana, "as if boys never fight with each other."

"That's what we're supposed to do."

"You're excused because you're boys?"

"Men must grow up to be strong."

"And girls?" asked Mariana, forgetting about her three daughters. She clutched her fork in the palm of her hand, pointing it at Arturo. "If my mother hadn't taught us how important it was for boys *and* girls to be strong, I might never have earned my college degree. It took a great deal of courage for me to become the first in my family to achieve such an honor."

"Have I not always glowed when speaking of my wife's accomplishments? Look at the children you've raised. Three of the prettiest girls the world has ever seen, courteous, smart, good role models, except around here, of course."

Pride shined in his eyes as he looked at his daughters, his tres ángeles hermosos, as he referred to them. "You've given your girls someone to look up to, to model themselves after."

"Nothing I could have ever done without you, Arturo. You never once complained through the years when I had to study late, work past my appointed hours, or ask if we could postpone a vacation. You gave everything to me and to these chicas locas. They wouldn't be the women they are without your influence."

Arturo smiled at his wife.

"Te amo," said Mariana.

"Barf," said Claudia. "May I be excused?"

"Me, too?" asked Valeria. "I think I'm going to spew."

"Do you have food left on your plates?" asked Mariana. "You'd leave your fruit when your body needs nourishment? Do you know how many..."

Both girls devoured their grapes and cantaloupe immediately. With chins dripping, they looked to their father, the one they could sometimes depend on for mercy.

"Estás excusado," said Arturo. "Valeria, I want you to pick up Racquel after school today."

"Si, Papa."

Both girls rinsed their plates and silver before placing them in the dishwasher. They kissed their father's cheek, hugged their mother, and gave their sister a dirty look before racing out of the kitchen.

"After school, Racquel, I want you to write a nice, long letter to your aunt," said Mariana. "She acted generously toward you and our family. It's not everyone who gets to spend a year at a private school in a wonderful community."

"I will, Mama, I promise." She smiled, remembering her days on the sun, then dabbed her mouth with her napkin. "May I be excused?"

"Of course," said Mariana.

Racquel followed her sisters' lead, putting her dishes away. She hugged her father, kissing both his cheeks with undisguised affection. She threw her arms around her mother's neck and shoulders, breathing in the security of her embrace.

"I'm so glad to be home," she said.

"Not as glad as we are," said Arturo. "Now off with you. Make sure your room looks presentable. Your mother will be down the hall before you know it."

Mariana and her husband sat quietly, relishing a few seconds with each other. Soon the day's activities would begin, and their duties would pull them apart like drapes flapping in a strong breeze. Eventually, the wind would calm and the drapes would drift together again. Life would slow as the day ended, and they'd sneak a brief moment of peace before laying their heads down.

"She's changed," said Mariana.

"Of course she has," replied Arturo. "She's spent a year away from her family without running home. She's grown up."

"That's not what I mean. She's different. I know you sense it, too."

"She's a teenage girl. How can we know who she'll be at any given moment?"

"A mother can see things a father can't."

Mariana sipped the last of her coffee. She left the cup and saucer on the table along with everything else. She kissed her husband's forehead and walked through the door into her study.

Without watching where he placed it, Arturo set his mug on the table. He slid his finger around the rim, slowly, evenly. As his wife's words echoed in his mind, he stared down the hall toward his youngest daughter's bedroom.

Chapter Four

"Welcome," said the soothing voice.

Thousands of conduits circled the brilliance of Sol's spirit. Energy that bound every living being in the universe flowed through them, a force so pure and benevolent the conduits didn't immediately respond.

Nathan Sullivan's mind drifted, like a small strip of wood bobbing lazily in a river. Every thought of the past, future, or his present life wafted away like the last breath of air from collapsing lungs.

Within the soft cocoon of his meditative state, Sullivan's thoughts rolled lazily through the guides he'd mentored. On worlds too numerous to count, he'd placed hundreds of young guides with dragons. The pairings had been arranged long before either came into existence. The wisdom of the suns sought out each twosome, looking far into the future toward events yet to unfold.

The faces floated in and beyond Sullivan's consciousness. A sensation of calm soothed his spirit many times as he recognized certain guides. Some took to the role with ease, forming strong bonds without delay. Others, nursing powerful emotions of fear and doubt, kept their dragons at a distance far too long. He'd prodded them forward, gently, until he suspected they might never gain the courage to establish the link. In these instances he threw them literally into the fire. After conferring with the dragon, a training session ended with a guide atop the beast's shoulders, holding tightly and screaming to the heavens. After a few involuntary flights they finally overcame their fears. They joined with their dragons, combining heart, mind, and soul for all time. Sullivan warmed again, remembering that those who took the longest usually formed the most powerful bonds.

"The fifth sun is among us, my children," said Sol. "The brilliance of her spirit brightens the lives of countless billions in worlds beyond the Dark Rift. The force of her spirit flows through every one of you, and all life everywhere."

No one else but Diego could have served as Magnifico's guide. The great leader of the Sol Dragones would have run off any other choice within minutes. Diego had taken everything Magnifico dished out, beginning with trickery and concluding with a ferocious battle. Now in their third year as dragon and guide, he'd grown physically and spiritually. His courage could not be questioned; he'd fought Incendio, even Vipero, the enormous lord of the Rift Dragons.

Perhaps now was the time. He would approach Magnifico about the next level of training. Diego had mastered dragon fire. Sullivan felt he was ready to think like a dragon, to achieve a new degree of power. If they were to use the misty portals of the Rift to set right the evil Vipero had used to poison other universes, Diego would need these abilities. Sullivan meditated about this a while longer, letting his spirit drift.

"Rest, and find happiness among yourselves," continued Sol. "Let this be a time of recuperation and fellowship. I cannot measure the joy I feel having all of you here with me."

One by one they floated through the flames, and as they did so, their spirits took form again. Sullivan recognized images he hadn't seen in centuries.

"Nathan," called a delicate voice.

He turned. He'd hoped to find her. Only the sight of her surpassed the joy of hearing her voice.

"Jenna," he said, reaching out to her. "Let me hold you."

He felt her arms encircle his neck. Gliding his hands around the curve of her back, he drew her close. The flame of their spirits melted into each other's love, and they stood together, quietly, saying nothing. Sullivan nestled his cheek against the side of her head. He trembled as he held her, hoping never to move again.

Through every task, every assignment to a new guide, every triumph and downfall, Nathan had thought of her every day, counting the seconds until he could hold her again. He would cherish the moment for as long as she allowed.

"Please," Jenna said. "Let me look at you."

Reluctantly, Sullivan relaxed. Refusing to pull away, he allowed her to grasp his shoulders and gently push him back.

When their eyes met the universe dissolved. Even the suns' flames blinked out as if a priest had doused them with a candle snuffer.

"All the stars in the galaxy could never match your eyes, Nathan."

"Jenna," he said, smiling.

"Sit with me, my love. Tell me about Magnifico's guide."

"Certainly you've heard of his adventures. What more could I tell you?"

"About the boy, Nathan. I wish to know why my guide is so taken with him."

"Racquel?"

"Of course." She smiled, lightly brushing her fingers against his cheek. "Racquel would give her life for him," she said, allowing

Sullivan his playfulness. "I wish to know about him, who he is, what makes him strong enough to be guide to Magnifico."

"He *is* strong, and brimming with compassion and selflessness. He acts rashly at times, and he can be impatient when dealing with his dragon."

"Who wouldn't be? No wonder she loves him so much."

"He feels the same, but he is still a boy. At thirteen he struggles with the awkwardness of youth."

"As we all did," said Jenna.

"At home he feels secure. Having his brother back with him is a real comfort. Every boy should have a big brother they can turn to when the world presses in too closely.

"At school he and his friends are at the top tier as eighth graders. Sometimes Diego goes along with them when they act as if they're better than the other students, but not always. I'm certain he isn't comfortable playing that role."

"Then why should he allow his friends to influence him?"

"Most times he doesn't, but it's different there, Jenna. Their world is defined by their status, and as children everything that makes up who they are is important. Who their friends are matters, as well as what shoes they wear, how they carry their backpacks, what sports they play, or if they're involved in other activities, and are those pursuits considered to be acceptable in others' eyes."

"Such a strange world, Nathan. I always wondered why you requested to be its conduit."

"You are conduit to Racquel, is that not so?"

"Yes, but she didn't begin her life on earth."

"Yet she lives there now, and prefers it."

"Perhaps she sees what you do, my love."

"Probably," said Sullivan. "If not for Diego, I might have given up on them."

"He is different?"

"As different as Magnifico and the rest of the Sol Dragones. That's why I like him. He intrigues me and continues to surprise me."

"Tell me how."

"Diego is his own man. When kids his age stumble onto a new trend, he rarely follows. A new hairstyle, a twine around a wrist, a secret letter drawn on the inside of an arm, whatever type of fad pops up from time to time, Diego remains within himself. He's a leader, and others follow his example."

"Perhaps that is why Sol selected him to be Magnifico's guide."

"I'm certain of it. Diego is the light of the sun on earth."

"Certainly he has his flaws," Jenna said. "No one can claim allegiance with Sol that perfectly."

"Of course he does. He is prone to outbursts, as any earthling is, especially children. He can fall into a pit of selfishness like any other child, and at times he fights against an ego the size of Sol."

"As guide to Magnifico, what child wouldn't possess such an attitude?"

"The difference," continued Sullivan, "is that Diego checks himself. He takes time to control his outbursts, even apologizing if one slips out before he can stop it.

"Magnifico has seen this while gazing through the sun's fires. He watches Diego for hours at a time, learning everything he can about him. I've seen it as well during our time together.

"He's a good kid. He shows consideration for others' feelings, he respects his parents, and he's bright but isn't conceited about it. He spends a lot of time with the younger players on his soccer team."

"I'm sure he looks up to you."

"When he's not frustrated with his training, yes."

Jenna held a hand over her mouth and giggled. "Then he is much like his conduit, no doubt."

"Did I not also begin my life as a man?" asked Sullivan. "And you, as a woman of earth?"

"That was millennia ago, Nathan. We have evolved."

"No one escapes their beginning completely," said Sullivan. "Every conduit, no matter their origin, showed a certain level of disappointment at the start of their training."

"Some more than others."

Sullivan sat silently, remembering the early days.

Jenna held her fingers underneath Sullivan's chin. Smiling, she lifted her hand, raising his head until their eyes met. "That's one of the reasons I fell in love with you, Nathan, for your eagerness to learn. You focused so completely, I can still see the determined look on your face."

"I wasn't that bad."

"Worse," said Jenna. "I remember the time..."

Sullivan interrupted her. "It didn't help that you passed through the levels so easily. All of us were in awe of you."

"As I still admire and respect you," said Jenna. "Look what you've accomplished, and who you've gained as a close ally and friend."

"As long as he remembers his place."

Jenna smiled and looked past Sullivan, who turned around and found himself eye to eye with Magnifico.

"Eavesdropping on your conduit and his lady friend?" he asked. "I should think you'd have better manners than that."

"Are you questioning the leader of the Sol Dragones?"

"Greetings, Magnifico," said Jenna. "I am honored to see you again."

"The honor is mine, my lady. I am pleased to see you also. You're looking well."

"Why should she not?" asked Estrella, now standing abreast of her mate. "She's my hand-picked aide, conduit to the greatest guide since the first sun overtook the moonless night."

A low growl rumbled along Magnifico's belly. "You would place Diego beneath her?"

"I would never place either of them ahead of the other," said Estrella. "Men always cast everything into the realm of competition."

"Amen to that," said Jenna.

"Nathan," said Magnifico. "Perhaps you and I could find a quiet corner and have an intelligent conversation together."

"Amen to that," said Sullivan, smiling at Jenna.

"How is Diego, Nathan?" asked Estrella. "Has he suffered any ill effects from our battle in the Rift?"

"From afar I'd say he's fine. Both he and Racquel looked pretty drained when we left the horse club. I haven't had any close contact with him since then."

"You're not monitoring him, his movements, his well being?" asked Magnifico.

"Of course," replied Sullivan. "But as I said, only from afar. He deserves some time with family and friends."

"Yes, my love," added Estrella. "Let him live his life for a while, before we call him back to serve Sol again."

"What do you mean?" asked Jenna.

"Yes," added Sullivan, stepping in front of Magnifico. "Why should he be called so soon? Has not the fifth sun emerged? Are we not in an age of harmony, as the prophecy foretold?"

Magnifico blinked once, shifting his eyes to Estrella. A dense wave of dragon dust surged forth from his nostrils. Sullivan disappeared for a moment, enveloped in a thick cloud of Magnifico's frustration. Only his voice could be heard.

"Enough of your foolish games," shouted Sullivan. "Tell us!"

"The fifth sun calls to us," said Estrella. "We are to assemble in the grand hall of light."

"Magnifico!" said Sullivan.

"Nathan," cooed Jenna, "Sol will tell us all we need to know."

The dust cloud disappeared just as Magnifico's tail swept toward Sullivan. He ducked just in time, swatting the spiked tip as it soared over his head.

"Come, Nathan," said the giant dragon.

CHAPTER FIVE

"Diego!" said Racquel, her eyes wide with disbelief and excitement. "My parents didn't say anything. My mother came to my bedroom to greet me as she'd always done, and Papa, well, it was like nothing had changed."

Diego just smiled. "I don't really understand it myself, Racquel, but I'm beginning to come around."

"They did something, didn't they?"

"Oh, yeah. If I had to guess, I'd say Magnifico's been playing tricks with our parents."

"It couldn't be that easy."

"Why not? He lives on the sun with a mate just as mysterious as him. He commands a force of magical dragons with powers we could never understand."

Racquel nodded, smiling. "And I spent almost a year as a spirit living with them until Estrella invited me back."

"What about Mr. Sullivan?" continued Diego. "The guy appears out of nowhere two years ago, gives me a plaster statue and wham – look what's happened since then?"

"Es extraño," said Racquel.

"Pretty sick if you ask me," said Diego.

The bell sounded. Students began shuffling down the hallways toward their classes. Ricardo and Jose ran by Diego and Racquel.

"Beat feet, chico amante!" said Jose. Ricardo slapped his friend on the shoulder as they ran down the hall together.

"See you in history class?" asked Racquel.

"Save the desk next to yours, okay?" asked Diego.

"If Ricardo doesn't get there first," said Jose.

Diego flicked her ponytail, giving her the look she loved. Racquel's laughter danced alongside her as she jogged to her morning class. He watched her the whole way, forgetting about school, the Sol Dragones, Mr. Sullivan, and everything else.

"Better get to class, Mijo."

Diego turned and saw Hector, gordo y satisfecho, the school security guard. He was still Diego's favorite among the school staff.

"She's going to be a beauty," the big man said.

"Yeah."

"More than you'll be able to handle, eh, Mijo?"

"Look who's talking, gato gordo. I see the way you lower your head and shuffle whenever your wife visits you on campus."

"Careful, pequeño hombre. Words like that will get you carried down to the office upside down over my shoulder."

"C'mon, Hector, I thought we were cool."

"Vamos," said Hector, flicking the back of Diego's head with a huge finger. "We're cool."

Diego smiled as he ran his fingers through his hair. The final bell sounded across campus like an old fire alarm. Diego kicked it into high gear, ran past two buildings and turned right at the third. He ducked into his home room just as the teacher began writing on the board. He slid in beside Jose and Ricardo, watching them make faces, mimicking Diego's feelings for Racquel.

"Mr. Ramirez, I'll have something for you after class today. Please make sure to stop by my desk on your way out."

"Yes, sir."

Jose and Ricardo's faces shifted from lovesick puppies to mocking laughter.

"Please bring your friends with you when you report to my desk," Mr. Schneider said, facing his students.

After collecting their detention slips, the three boys walked quickly from the classroom and bolted straight across campus.

Diego watched the seventh graders milling about the sidewalks, looking for friends from their first year at school. If they recognized someone, they quickly huddled together, talked about summer, new video games, their newest cell phone apps, and their new teachers. When a pretty girl walked by a group of the boys, some of them stole quick glances. Others kept their eyes among the group, too embarrassed to receive a snub. If a large group of seventh grade girls saw a good looking boy coming toward them, a rally of whispered comments ensued, sometimes followed by a burst of nervous laughter. The girls stayed within their selective groups, rarely admitting an outsider. Truth be told, their biggest fear was to be excluded for committing some type of unspoken offense.

He shifted his gaze to the sixth grade students as they walked to their next classes in twos and threes. If other first year students passed by and they knew them, a nod of the head or a simple, "Hey," served as recognition.

Most of the sixth graders owned cell phones, given to them by their parents as a way to keep tabs on them. Nearly all carried them in their hands. When not reading texts or checking the internet, they responded to friends' questions in quick bursts. Most of all, they kept their focus on their next classroom.

Diego and his buddies stopped amidst the inner ring of lunch tables, where only the oldest students hung out. It was a privilege earned by their status as eighth graders, and they relished their standing in the campus pecking order. Dozens stood or sat around the tables, boys and girls alike. Over the first two years they'd established strong friendships in school.

"What's up with Schneider?" asked Jose as he waved to a few friends. "When did he get to be such a prick about tardiness?"

"Yeah," added Ricardo. "All the teachers are lame, but he's cool most of the time."

"I don't know," said Diego, juggling a few pebbles. "Maybe he had a rough morning or something."

"Hey, Diego," said Conor, as he walked through the crowd of students. "Hey Ricardo, Jose, what's up?"

All three exchanged the latest fist/hug greeting enjoyed by all the boys.

"Órale, Irish?" said Jose. "How's your leg?" He extended his hand, slapping Conor's away before embracing him.

"Still sore, but the doctor's got me repeating some stretching exercises three times a day. He says I should be ready for practice without delay."

"You mean, 'ready for practice, no problem,'" right?" asked Ricardo.

"Aye," said Conor, smiling. "That's what I intended to say."

Diego lowered his head and smiled. His body began shaking. He finally raised his face to the sun and laughed out loud. Jose and Ricardo joined him, unable to control themselves.

Diego backhanded Conor on the chest. "You're a crackup even when you're trying to be serious."

"That's grand," said Conor, clearly delighted with Diego's comment.

Everyone within earshot of Conor's last remark busted out laughing. The only thing louder than the students was the first bell for second period.

"Are we meeting after school today for an informal practice?" asked Conor.

"You mean are we going to kick the ball around some?" said Jose.

"Aye, I mean, yeah."

"Come to the field after sixth period," said Ricardo. "You don't have to bring your cleats. Coach just wants us to have fun for a while."

"Do you need help with the goals and gear?"

"Sure, Conor," said Diego. "Meet us in front of the locker room after school. We'll take everything out together."

"Alright," said Conor, beaming. "See you then." He trotted off toward the library, where he worked as an aide.

"C'mon, comodín," said Jose, pounding Diego on his thigh. Let's see if you can beat us to history class."

"If I get there first I'm sitting next to Racquel," said Ricardo as he raced away. Jose caught up to him and the two boys whizzed through the scattering students.

Diego ran as hard as he could, but Jose had been true with his fist. His thigh throbbed each time he landed on his left foot. "Payback sucks, amigo," he whispered as he pulled up and walked.

When he finally limped into the room he saw Ricardo sitting right where he said he'd be – in front of Racquel. She looked at him and smiled, then shrugged her shoulders. Diego looked at Ricardo, who ignored him completely, and then at Jose, who sat silently massaging his left thigh, as if trying to rub out a charley horse.

As he moved toward his desk, he stepped on Jose's foot, leaning down with all his weight. As Jose tried to twist his toes out from underneath Diego's body, Diego snapped his left ear with his middle finger. The contact was so loud half the class turned around.

Racquel and Ricardo smiled as they looked at Jose's face, and then nearly laughed out loud when Diego flicked his ear. Racquel had her hand around her cell phone, ready to take a quick movie in case something else happened.

"Class," said Miss O'Toole. "Please come to order. Today we begin our study of Spain's conquest of the new world. Open your textbooks to page one hundred twenty nine."

Diego reached down to pull his book from his backpack. As he rummaged through everything, his desk leaned far over to one side. The whole room began swaying with no particular pattern. It almost mirrored the few times he'd been out on his uncle's boat. During those short trips, though, the boat moved quickly, sliding up and over small waves along the coast.

Diego's stomach surged toward his throat. He gripped his desk with one hand, placing the other firmly on the floor. Everything centered on his chair, as though he were sitting at the helm of a huge sailing ship. Back and forth he moved, flowing with the tiled floor, which now resembled the rolling waves of a great ocean.

His nose twitched as he inhaled deep breaths of thick, salty air. His eyes watered as the wind carried the sea spray across the right side of his desk. Strands of hair whisked across his face as he lifted his hand from the floor to block the biting breeze. The wind blew through his outstretched palm as if it weren't there. He slapped it down again to keep from tumbling out of his desk.

The coloring of his face shifted a shade as he fought off a bout of sea sickness. Vomit gagged his throat, his head swirled like a top, and all he wanted was to step onto dry land.

The sensation repeated itself a few times, then stopped as quickly as it began. Diego blinked sweat and tears from his eyes and swallowed, driving the bile back down his throat.

"Diego," whispered Racquel. "What's wrong? Are you okay?"

He looked to his left to answer, but didn't see his girlfriend. Instead, he saw two heavy oak doors, which opened slowly to reveal a man leaning over at a sturdy table. Dressed in the style of the Spanish conquistadors, he poured over a set of papers held flat by brass weights. His posture reflected the captain's fatigue, but he worked carefully, mapping something with his instruments.

The cabin seemed well lit except for one corner by the door. Light seemed to dissolve there, and not from a shadow caused by a lack of lantern glow. The darkened beams swam with an eerie form of life.

Diego saw the wooden wall breathing, keeping a steady pulse. He measured it with the flow of the ocean's current. With a chill he saw that it was different, independent, alive.

Then it turned. Two eyes emerged, focusing on him. He barely saw them within the blackness of the spirit's body.

"Diego!" whispered Racquel harshly. "Open your book."

Jose kicked the side of his friend's desk. When he saw no response he shot his foot out again.

"Hernán Cortés sailed to the Americas for three main reasons," droned Miss O'Toole. "The most important had to do with the faith of his country, Spain. His mission was to spread Catholicism beyond Europe to the new world. Secondly, he would introduce civilization to the native peoples, freeing them from their savage ways. Finally, Cortés's mission would bring much needed gold back to Spain to finance wars of conquest and the expansion of the empire."

Miss O'Toole continued, her statements suddenly fading into the background.

"You *will* turn back, Captain," hissed a chilling voice only Diego could hear.

"The governor is a fool," said Captain Hernán Cortés. "He is a deskbound paper-pusher who couldn't identify the ocean if he stumbled over a gunwale and fell into the sea headfirst."

"I won't ask you again, Captain," said the spirit. Its form shifted to a darker shade of crimson. "My scheme requires neither you nor your worthless governor. I will exact revenge on my enemies, and you will not stand in my way. I order you to..."

Cortés wheeled around, sweeping his instruments onto the floor. "This is my vessel, spirit, or whatever it is you are, and I will determine the course of its destination."

A cylinder of flame overtook Cortés before he could utter another word. His uniform peeled away like paper thrown onto a roaring fire. He felt his skin bubbling away, his body roasting alive, torture beyond anything he'd ever experienced.

His hair caught fire, burning away in flash. His neck contracted, pitching his head back as his body locked in a spasm of unspeakable agony.

The spirit allowed Cortés to taste death's closeness. It relished the captain's shrieks of anguish. Fighting the powerful urge to end the man's life, it began pulling back the horrible spell.

Diego's eyes went wide with wonder and disbelief. He was aboard this captain's vessel, watching something evil slowly kill the man.

The flames receded. Captain Cortés fell, his skin sticking to the hardwood floor. He inhaled what seemed his life's last breath.

"Tell me, Captain," said the spirit softly, as if speaking to a small child. "Will you continue to disobey the orders of your governor and sail to the Americas?"

"We will turn back at once," spat Cortés, dragging ragged breaths into his damaged lungs. "The Americas will be left alone."

"Swear it," said the spirit, "on the souls of your mother and father."

"I swear, on the lives of Martín Cortés de Monroy and Catalina Pizarro Altamirano, that I will turn these ships around immediately."

"I am pleased, Captain, for you see, I have another fleet of ships on their way to the Americas as we speak. Their captain is not as disrespectful as you. He will do as I say, with mild objections only."

"Who?" asked Cortés. "Who would do your bidding so willingly?"

The scene shifted before Diego's eyes. The cabin looked similar, but the captain looked noticeably different. Cortés had disappeared, and in his place, another man poured over instruments, measuring their remaining voyage.

Diego leaned forward, peering closer at the man who'd replaced Cortés.

The doors to the captain's cabin slammed shut, breaking Diego's trance. He glanced over at Racquel. Her cheek rested in her left hand as she lazily took notes. Every few seconds she would flip a page in her textbook, looking ahead out of boredom. She caught his gaze, squinted, and shrugged her shoulders.

As she gazed at the next picture, Diego's eyes went wide. No longer in a daze, he sat upright, leaning toward her. After checking the page number, he grabbed his book and quickly flicked to the same picture.

He almost tore the page as he stared at a picture of Captain

Hernán Cortés, the man who conquered the Aztec nation. With his vision clear in his mind, he nearly vaulted out of his chair before remembering the rules.

"Miss O'Toole," said Diego. "May I have a hall pass? I need to visit the restroom."

"Can it wait, Diego?" asked the teacher. "We've only fifteen minutes left."

"Please?" he asked again, giving her his sweetest smile.

"Alright, the pass is hanging by the door. Don't be gone too long."

Diego leapt from his desk. "Thank you," he said as he grabbed the pass and slipped out the door.

Instead of walking down the hall to the boys' bathroom, he ran across campus toward the library. He figured he had about five minutes before his teacher sent Hector looking for him.

Diego thanked the Blessed Mother when Conor saw him enter the library instead of Mrs. Coble. He waved him over.

"What's up?" asked Conor. "Shouldn't you be in class?"

"I'm on a bathroom break."

"Not in here I hope," said Conor, smiling and backing away.

"Look," said Diego. "I need you to do something for me."

"Okay, as long as I get invited for dinner this weekend."

Diego smiled. Conor had come for lunch at his parents' home and eaten enough for three boys. Alejandra had gushed admiration for him, telling Conor he could visit her table anytime.

"I can't check out more than two books at a time, and I need every book you've got about the Spanish conquest of the Americas."

"Use your phone," said Conor. "Just do a search, you can find way more on the web than you'll find in here."

"Something's going on, Conor. I can't explain it right now. I need to look in the school's books, okay?"

"Aye, you've got it. Do you want me to leave them behind the building for you?"

"No, no, nothing like that. Just pass one or two to every eighth grade student that comes into the library today. Tell them to check them out and meet me after school by the benches. They'll know what to do."

"Shall I check two out for you, Diego?"

"If you want to come to dinner this weekend, you'd better."

"I'll do it with pleasure, then. Will you invite Jose and Ricardo as well?"

"Maybe," said Diego. "Or maybe I'll ask Racquel instead, and I'll ask her to bring Lea along."

Conor's eyes brightened. His cheeks reddened as well. "That would be grand, Diego."

"Conor? Who's out there with you?"

Diego pressed two fingers to his lips when he heard Mrs. Coble's voice. He slapped Conor's hand, then fist-bumped him. A second later he was gone, racing back to his classroom.

Most of the students snickered when they saw him reenter the room. Try as he might, he couldn't control his breathing. His forehead showed beads of sweat as well. He pulled his hand across his face, pushing the moisture over his head. He set the pass back on the rail and walked to his desk.

"The native peoples of the Americas engaged in barbaric practices," said Miss O'Toole as she watched Diego take his seat. "Human sacrifice was a common occurrence in their ceremonies, as was idolatry, and even cannibalism."

Jose stuck his hand in his mouth, pretending to chomp down on his fingers.

"If it weren't for the Spanish conquest, these rituals might have continued for many years. The people in these lands could very well have remained as they were for another century or two."

Ricardo and Jose made cave man faces and let their arms sag over the sides of their desks.

"In a way, the inhabitants of these lands owe a debt of gratitude to Captain Cortés. Had he not arrived when he did, they might not have learned the needed skills with which to better themselves."

The two boys sat straight up in their desks, hands joined and resting over their hearts. Their eyes rose to the heavens in thanks for their deliverer, Hernán Cortés.

"Conor," said Mrs. Coble. "Could you shelve this cart of books for me, please?"

"Aye, Ma'am."

"Thank you. I really enjoy having you as an aide."

Conor smiled. As he turned his head back toward the stacks, he marked the location of the history books. Scanning the spines, he spied a dozen or so showing the words "Spanish," or "Conquest," or both words together. As he glided through the stacks replacing the library books, he returned when he had available space and loaded the cart with the books Diego had requested. He concealed these in a rarely used corner of the room.

After finishing his task, he rolled the cart back to the front office. He saw Mrs. Coble transferring more books to a different cart.

"I can do that for you, Ma'am."

"Thank you, Conor. You're very kind. Are all the boys in Ireland as sweet as you?"

"Not all," Conor said, blushing. "We've our share of hooligans, like all countries."

"Well then, where did you get such impeccable manners, from your parents?"

Conor bristled for a second, then smiled. "My parents are wonderful to everyone, and yes, they instilled proper behavior in all their children."

"They should be commended. Tell me, where did you live in Ireland?"

"County Cork, Ma'am."

"Do you miss your friends?"

Conor smiled again, this time looking at the ground. "Aye, I miss a lot about my old life."

"Change is difficult, Conor, for everyone, but especially for the young."

The school bell seemed to know exactly when she finished her last remark. It rasped loudly, and both Conor and Mrs. Coble looked up at the clock.

"Five minutes to second bell," she said. "Go ahead and get ready for your next class."

Conor watched a line of students filing in the door. He walked calmly back to his cache and grabbed two of the history books he'd stashed. Placing them next to his backpack, he scanned the students moving into the library. He motioned to every eighth grader he saw, waving them over. To each he gave one or two books, asking them to keep them for Diego to collect later that day. When he'd given every one of them out, he grabbed his copies and walked to Mrs. Coble's desk.

"I'll be leaving now."

With the flurry of students coming in and leaving, she barely had time to respond. "You'd like to check those books out, Conor?"

"Aye, if you have the time."

Mrs. Coble flipped the first book up and glanced at the cover. "Suddenly everyone's interested in the Spanish raids during their conquest of the new world? You're the sixth student in three minutes to run this subject across my scanner."

"We're covering the period in our classes right now," said Conor. "I guess students want to get a head start on their papers."

"That'll be the day," she said, laughing. "Okay, Conor, you're good to go. See you tomorrow?"

"Aye. Bye, Mrs. Coble."

The second bell rang.

"Only students checking out books can stay in the library," said Mrs. Coble. "Everyone else, outside. It's a beautiful, sunny day."

The students filed out, saying their goodbyes. Most of them had met the librarian long before they became her "kids." She was well known in the community, having lived there most of her adult life. She and her husband had been involved with the school district for over thirty years. Two generations had passed them by, with mothers and grandmothers still dropping by to say hello or introduce a new family member.

Diego met his friends outside under the pepper trees. He sat as he always did, with his rear on the table and his feet drumming the bench. Students passed by him, the boys slapping hands and fist bumping, the girls smiling and saying their greetings.

Diego had grown quite a bit since seventh grade. He stood just over five feet eight inches tall, with a lanky but strong physique. Anyone who looked could tell he was an athlete. Even standing still he gave off an aura of balance and stability. When he moved, just walking or even turning his head, they'd see he could play any sport with little difficulty.

He'd become quite handsome as well. Esteban looked exactly like his father, ruggedly attractive, a bad boy appearance the girls seemed to love. Diego enjoyed some of his father's features, too, the thick, silky hair, strong cheekbones and jaw, but he'd been blessed with a masculine version of his mother's best traits as well. She'd given him her flawless skin, golden brown and warm. He also enjoyed her exquisite eyes, the kind no one can ignore. Without a spoken word, they conveyed his feelings to Racquel, to his friends, even to those who would challenge him, especially Magnifico. More than once his enormous friend had tried to intimidate him, only to have Diego stand his ground, forcing his dragon to look straight into his unblinking stare.

Neither Diego nor Racquel had ever mentioned a word to anyone about Magnifico, Estrella, Mr. Sullivan, or any aspect of their travels with the Sol Dragones. That world remained their secret, something they cherished together.

Who would believe them anyway? If Diego sat down and told Jose and Ricardo about the battle between the Sol Dragones and the Dragons of the Dark Rift, and how he'd led the way riding atop a magical creature that started out as a statue he'd won a couple of years ago, well, at least he'd give them a good laugh.

Could he tell his mother and father? They'd have him in a psychiatrist's office the next day, hoping the woman could save their son from his fantasy world.

Esteban was the only person who knew, and he'd kept his

mouth shut. After the night with Incendio, Nightfang, and Sharptooth at the stables, he hadn't mentioned a word to anyone. Even his co-workers at Monarch Market hadn't been able to get anything out of him. The police had questioned all of them, even threatening Eddie with jail time for misuse of the 911 call. Each of them told the same story about the huge shapes soaring over the donut shop, but the police weren't interested in fairy tales. When Esteban returned to work the next night, he kept quiet about his and Diego's adventure.

What would Racquel say to anyone? That she'd lived many lives, and her current incarnation as a middle school student served her dragon, Estrella, and in so doing, mighty Magnifico?

For the two of them, knowing glances would serve for now. When a fierce wind blew, their eyes would meet, and they'd share the same thought, that perhaps a dragon had just flown overhead.

The bell rang, ending their break. The older students waited until the sixth and seventh graders had left the quad before stirring. They said their goodbyes and walked toward their classrooms.

As he jumped from his seat on the table, Diego punched Ricardo in the shoulder. His friend elbowed him in the ribs and wrapped his arm around Diego's head. Diego worked his way free and slapped the back of his head.

He looked across campus and saw Conor waving. Diego smiled, waved back, and then saw Conor extend his arms, as if he was carrying a large box or something similar. Diego waved again, thanking his friend for putting the history books aside.

CHAPTER SIX

Nathan followed Jenna into the grand hall, an enormous, flaming valley. Voices rose and fell from every direction, dragons roaring and snarling as they jostled for position among their brothers and sisters. Sullivan saw hundreds, all standing next to their planetary counterparts, every one of them waiting to hear the soothing voice of Celestina, the fifth sun.

Gigantic gas plumes erupted from the sun's surface like cannon fire, calling the assembly to order. At first the explosions came in no particular order, but soon the suns settled themselves. The random aspect of the blasts ceased, and a majestic pattern emerged. Rows of fiery bombardment outlined the perimeter of the valley. The spirits of the two suns had united.

The conduits paced around their dragons, carefully grooming them. A stray scale, a piece of space debris, a scarred horn or tooth, nothing could be left to chance.

The dragons snapped at their aides, or brushed them aside with a nervous twitch of a sturdy wing. For an infinite number of generations, the Sol Dragones and the other clans had prepared for this moment. Stories had been passed from elders to young, explaining the significance of the suns in all of their phases. The long years of waiting, welcoming, and nurturing had finally come down to this introduction.

The eruptions ceased. The last remnants of Sol's power sailed away or settled back onto the sun's surface. A glorious light emerged, bathing the assembly with radiance never before seen or felt in the galaxy.

"Greetings, children of all suns. May your days be filled with infinite peace."

No sound emerged from the light. No voice called out, but the message came through, pure and immaculate.

"A terrible evil has escaped our grasp."

The grand hall buckled with a change in mood. The blissful feeling of the assembly fell away like an expired wave receding back into the ocean.

"Satadon has freed himself from the Xibalba. We cannot say how, and we don't know his current whereabouts, but the stars in every universe are searching for him. We cannot comprehend his intent as of now. We only know he is roaming freely, somewhere."

The dragons stirred, their anxiety overtaking them. It was everything the conduits could do to keep them settled.

"We must find him," said Celestina softly, evenly. "I cannot become whole unless the evil of the ancient cave is extinguished forever."

The entire hall stood still, the shock hanging over them like a heavy cloak. They had come millions of miles, through wormholes in space, some risking death or a life wandering through the stars. Gathering together with a combined sense of wonder and awe, they'd waited to hear of a new way, of pristine worlds where justice and peace would reign supreme. The conduits stared with mouths agape.

"Nathan," said Magnifico. "Go with Estrella and Jenna. I must confer with Sol. While I respected Vipero as a worthy commander,

I fear Satadon. The Dark Lord has powers that come from the time before the first sun."

"Perhaps I could..."

"Go, Nathan. I will join you when I can."

Magnifico turned and lumbered toward Sol's inner chamber. He passed dozens of his dragon siblings, touching each of them with a wing or a gust of fiery breath. He looked at every pair of eyes, seeing nothing but disappointment and despair. He tried to offer encouraging words, but as he continued to pass by dragons and conduits, he saw only lowered heads and shuffling steps. He mourned them, but he couldn't allow their sadness to dampen his soul.

He entered the chamber quietly, respectfully. This was his domain, granted to him when he agreed to lead the Sol Dragones. He'd brought Estrella here only once, so she could be christened his mate.

He padded forward, basking in the voice of his master.

"Sit, my son. Rest with me a while."

Magnifico did as Sol commanded. He lowered his body, belly flat, rear legs coiled, with his forepaws crossed over each other in his own relaxed manner.

"I am pleased you survived the battle in the Dark Rift."

"Many did not," said Magnifico, giving his warrior dragons credit.

"Yes," said Sol, caressing Magnifico's body with the energy of the inner chamber. "Do you mourn their loss?"

"Would you not?"

"No."

"They died serving you."

"Do you believe they are dead, that their spirits have disappeared forever?"

"I believe in the light," said Magnifico, "and in the infinite power of Sol."

"Then close your eyes and I will show you something wondrous."

Magnifico let his scaled lids fall. He saw a new world in his mind's eye, a world reborn, with fresh lakes, forests, and oceans, completely untouched or corrupted. As well as a dragon could, he smiled as he felt his body rise into the sky. He soared over the lands, taking in everything he saw.

It was the world promised by the entrance of the fifth sun. All creatures; predators, prey, meek or aggressive, roamed amidst each other peacefully.

He heard two voices call out. Turning his head, he rejoiced when he saw Sammavel and Nightslash fall from the heavens. Arcing on the currents of the winds, they soared through the sky, finally taking their positions by his side, flanking him as they would in a formation of the Sol Dragones.

"My friends," called Magnifico happily.

"My lord!" they replied.

Sammavel roared and banked toward the ground. Nightslash fell in behind him, beckoning Magnifico to follow. The two dragons led him through an immense canyon, with clear blue waterfalls spilling over the edges, and lush greenery spotting the hearty rock walls. The three of them spun, swooping wildly, playing as they used to while training. Magnifico snarled happily as his lieutenants took turns slashing toward him, snapping their jaws and swiping sharp wingtips across his scales. He responded skillfully, never giving his dragons the same move twice. A few times their games became so wild all three of them nearly crashed headlong into each other.

Finally, Sammavel pointed a tired wing toward a massive ledge off to their right. They coasted on an updraft for a few seconds before drifting down toward the ridge. Following centuries of training, Sammavel and Nightslash landed first, preparing a safe area for their lord. Each of them flapped their wings briskly as they brushed their scales with short bursts of fire.

Satisfied with his grooming, Magnifico addressed his dragons.

"How did you come to be here? You perished during the battle in the Rift, and yet you live."

"We don't know," replied Nightslash, looking to Sammavel, who nodded. "I felt my body explode when we attacked Vipero's forces, and afterward I found myself wrapped in some sort of cocoon. I wasn't alive, and I couldn't feel any type of physical body, but something had grabbed hold of me, pulling me away from death."

Magnifico shifted his gaze to Sammavel, who confirmed Nightslash's account with another quick nod. "Continue, please," he said.

"I felt it was me, but again, it wasn't me," said Nightslash. "It couldn't have been, for I saw the number of dragons we flew against in the battle. At least twenty of them shredded me with blasts of their electric fire. My last thought was one of total destruction. I couldn't have survived."

"I felt the same sensation of death," said Sammavel. "One second I was alive, the next I knew I'd been blown to bits."

Magnifico looked at his lieutenants, then up to the sky, where a flawless sun shone brightly. He smiled, then reared back and laughed, a big belly laugh, like a deep pool of water shaken by an earthquake. Two of his dragons had been reborn. Sol had made them whole again. Magnifico felt like a pup that'd discovered a new valley of fire in which to play.

"Thank Sol," he said to Nightslash and Sammavel. Afterward he closed his eyes, and the vision faded.

"It is you who deserves my gratitude."

Magnifico bowed his head low before the spirit of all light.

"We must work together again, my son, to locate the Dark Lord."

"How soon can we expect your summons?"

"We cannot say presently, but be ready, Magnifico. When we ask, you must answer immediately."

"My guide and I are always at your service."

"We may call upon others as well."

"Say the word and it shall be so."

"Go and reassure the others that all will transpire as it should, as it always has, as it always will."

"With your blessing I leave you," said Magnifico.

Sol's breath passed over him, massaging his muscles. One by one, like flowers opening to a new day's sun, his scales flared with every wave of warmth.

CHAPTER SEVEN

Diego's cheeks sagged between his palms. He'd been sitting at his desk for hours. Three of the library books lay open beneath his eyes. He read some text, scanned a few pictures, then turned to another book and did the same. He flicked the pages of two books at a time, soaking up as much as he could.

All of them contained information about the history of the Americas in the sixteenth century. After the bizarre occurrence in class, where his vision didn't match the picture in Racquel's book, he'd become obsessed with learning about the period and its importance to his people. He knew a connection lay there, somewhere, within the words, pictures, or both.

"Diego?" said his mother as she poked her head around the corner from the hallway. "How much homework do they give you in the eighth grade? It's only the beginning of school, and you're already locked to your desk. ¿Que pasa?"

"Nada, Mama," he said, turning and smiling. "We have a report due later this month. I just want to get a head start, that's all."

"Okay, Mijo, if you say so. It's so hot outside. I'd have thought you'd be in the pool with Esteban and Catalina."

Diego glanced to his right. He saw his brother playing with his girlfriend in the water. "Maybe later."

Alejandra snapped a towel in his direction and walked up the hallway toward the kitchen. She mentioned something about a special dessert that a certain someone might want to try unless he was too busy.

Diego looked toward his bedroom door. He took a deep breath, smelling the delicious muffins his mother had tucked away in the oven. He thought about running down the hall and grabbing a quick bite, but he knew she would want to talk. He checked his cell phone, seeing he only had another hour before dinner, and decided to stay with his project.

He turned to the start of a new chapter. It detailed the Mexica people, his ancestors from hundreds of years ago. He skipped ahead a dozen pages just to see the pictures. The outfits his people wore looked amazing, so much color and intricate design. Some of them seemed beyond bizarre, but when he read the captions under the pictures, he understood the reason for their costumes. He saw dancers, warriors, and what must have been people of great importance. He turned one more page and glanced at a great arena surrounded by temples and courtyards. The symbols and costumes were beyond colorful. The men looked majestic, the women powerful and stunning. He glanced at the arena again, then flipped the pages back to the beginning and started reading.

Halfway through the first paragraph his eyelids became heavy. He fought the waves of fatigue, but in the end they overtook him. Placing his hands one above the other on the books, he laid his cheek against his thumbs and closed his eyes.

He opened them and found himself walking in a city similar to those he'd seen in the books. He watched as people bought and sold goods in the center of a large courtyard. He saw everything for sale; clothing, food, furniture, games, animals, crafts, the size of the market overwhelmed him.

He walked around a corner and saw a small space with a few

items spread out on a thin, ragged blanket. He scanned them quickly, then started to turn away. His head snapped back when he saw a small dragon statue. Magnifico stood there in his silent, still form, black scales glistening. It looked exactly like the statue he'd won at school.

Diego pushed through the crowd, trying desperately to get to his dragon. When he finally side-stepped the last man in his way, he looked in horror at a boy holding Magnifico while talking with the owner of the stall. No doubt haggling over a price, when Diego saw the boy reach into his tunic for payment, he went crazy.

Rushing forward, he pointed at the statue, screaming that he'd double the price the other boy had offered. The stall owner stared at him, confused. The boy holding Magnifico did the same. Neither one of them understood a word he said.

Frustrated, Diego jammed his hand into his pocket, hoping to pull out a larger payment than the other boy could afford. His fingers grasped nothing.

The boy nestled Magnifico in his arms as he passed over some coins. When he left the stall, Diego watched as his dragon turned his eyes, and then his head toward him. As the boy walked quickly down a side passage leading away from the courtyard, Diego panicked. He took off after him, watching Magnifico's eyes the entire time. His dragon had come alive and climbed atop the boy's shoulder. He called out, a sick, lonely wail, begging Diego to save him.

The boy moved with uncanny speed. Dipping through buildings and racing around corners, he flashed by colorful stalls before disappearing into crowds of screaming shoppers. Diego ran with abandon, frantic about losing Magnifico. He reached out when he got close, straining and stretching his fingers, trying to grab the hair streaming along behind the boy's strong, tanned shoulders.

Seeing his guide so close, Magnifico howled his displeasure. His small claws pulled at the leather tunic as he climbed around the boy's shoulders. A single black talon bent out from the claw, a small hook Diego could use as leverage. He wailed again, pleading with him to hurry.

Finally, lungs pounding and muscles screaming, Diego lunged forward as the boy slowed to turn a sharp corner. They went down hard, rolling, kicking, and screaming in two different languages. Diego yanked the boy's hair, wedged his feet underneath his chest, and shoved him away. Shouting horribly, he grabbed his statue and ran for his life.

Rolling over and shaking himself, the other boy immediately took up the chase. He was remarkably quick, knew the streets well, and he understood how to run on the pathways of his city. Diego had no idea where he was, but holding Magnifico in his arms was all that mattered. Strangely, his dragon had gone rigid again, falling back into statue form. It made it hard for Diego to run, but run he did.

The other boy yelled something Diego didn't understand, but he could tell it was a cry for help. Villagers began craning their necks, turning their bodies to see the source of the outburst. A few called for soldiers in the marketplace to intervene. What began as a passing interest soon mushroomed into an intensive search.

Diego ducked into an innocent looking hallway. Swallowed by darkness immediately, he saw a small circle of light at the far end. He had less than a second to ponder where the tunnel might lead, because his pursuer dashed into the passageway behind him.

Like ghosts trying to escape a dream, they flew through the inky blackness. Every time Diego felt the other boy's hand closing in, he sensed Magnifico coming to life and biting his shoulder, urging him onward.

A blast of sunlight replaced the shadows of the tunnel. Diego ran blind, and in no particular direction. He'd entered a gigantic temple, or an arena of some sort. Completely deserted, but grand in design and scale, it obviously served as an important meeting place for the people of the city. As his vision settled, he took in the incredible designs cut into the stones.

He saw an exit and turned toward it. A smile creased his face as he thought for the first time he might outwit the other boy and escape.

A pair of imposing men stepped in front of the doorway. Diego's right foot skidded out from under him as he tried to dodge their grasping arms. Instantly, four more stepped from the shadows.

Eight strong hands grabbed Diego's arms and legs, yanking him off the ground. The commander of the soldiers ripped Magnifico from his grip. He held the statue high above his head, pointing it at the sky. He spoke words Diego didn't understand, but somehow he knew the man attached great importance to the sun *and* to his dragon.

The boy who had bought Magnifico yelled at the soldiers, screaming his side of the story. The commander paid little attention to him, all the while holding the statue out of reach. The boy tried desperately to retrieve it, but the soldier's height kept it away.

"Bring him," said the commander in an ancient language.

Diego shouted his innocence as the soldiers lifted him over their heads, using his wrists, ankles, and hips as grip points. They began singing a strange chant, and after two repetitions, Diego forgot all about his frightening situation. His mind swam as he listened to the very sounds and words he'd heard during his training sessions with Mr. Sullivan. The first time he'd successfully put up a frozen shield, he'd heard these voices, and they'd given him strength he'd never imagined. It was they who'd helped him see the true nature of the world, who'd allowed him to stop a ball of flame that would have reduced his father's truck to a melted hulk of twisted metal.

The soldiers' voices got louder. Diego couldn't imagine how so few could sound like so many. Turning his head, he saw the seats of the temple filled with people dressed in dazzling garments, some more flamboyant than others.

Their voices rose and fell with the different songs. The chanting rang true in Diego's mind, they were the ones he'd heard that day at the horse club by his house. Even though still a captive, he smiled as he looked around the temple at his people, the Mexica of the ancient lands.

The soldiers brought him to a stairway leading to an altar at the west end of the arena. They tossed him onto his feet, seeing if he would stumble and fall. Diego held his stance, placing one hand on the ground for support. When he rose, he gazed into the eyes of four men, so richly dressed he could do nothing but bow to them. He raised his head and eyes first before straightening his waist. The men wore fierce but fair looks. Diego could tell they held positions of great importance in the city. He opened his mouth to say something, but the commander of the soldiers cut him off.

"This one steals."

"Bring us a witness," said one of the four.

The soldier waved the other boy forward.

"It is true," said the boy. "I bought this statue. He chased after me and took it."

The noble looked down at Diego. He extended his hand to the commander, who placed Magnifico within his reach. He grabbed the statue gently, respectfully. Turning it a few times, he finally held the wings and stared into the dragon's eyes.

"Your name," said the noble, this time speaking English.

Diego froze. Incendio had asked who he was exactly the same way.

"Your *name*," he repeated.

"Diego, sir. Diego Ramirez."

The nobles flicked nervous glances at each other. The one speaking to him stepped forward.

"You have been charged with theft, young man. The penalty is death."

"What? This is my statue, *my* dragon."

"Can you prove this?" asked the commander of the soldiers.

The crowd roared with anticipation. Diego looked around the arena, locking eyes with thousands of onlookers. Then he fixed his gaze on the noble who'd asked him his name.

"I'll prove it right now."

The man set Magnifico on the dirt before him. Soldiers, nobles, and the boy who'd accused Diego backed up ten paces, but no more. If he made a run for it again, they would catch him and carry out his sentence.

The crowd fell into a soundless hush.

Diego crouched and stared at his dragon. At first he said nothing. He expected Magnifico to recognize him and rise into the heavens.

"He lies," said the other boy. "First he steals and now he speaks falsely. He's a demon and should be put to death."

The commander waved his hand sharply at the boy, silencing him. "This one needs to hold his tongue, but his words are true. The stranger is a demon sent to trick us. We will take him away and..."

"He will stay," said the noble, his eyes never leaving Diego. "Continue."

Diego bowed again, then returned to his dragon. "Magnifico, you know I'm the guide. Come to me, now. Show our people who I am."

The nobles closed ranks and murmured hastily to one another. The soldiers advanced, ready to strike Diego unconscious. The boy hurled insults at everyone, cursing them for allowing the stranger to fool them for so long. The crowd stirred, disturbed by what they'd heard.

Suddenly, everyone became quiet. The ground beneath their feet trembled. Every sound, every movement seemed to be coming from the area around the stranger and his dragon.

Diego smiled.

Magnifico's body shook. The plaster expanded, ready to burst. A faint, high-pitched whine streamed forth from his mouth. To everyone gathered in the temple, the little dragon seemed ready to come alive.

The statue wobbled once, twice, and then tipped over like a bowling pin. Diego reached out, his fingers cradled in disappointment. He knew without looking that every eye in the temple was watching him.

The sound of the crowd surged around the arena, a tidal wave of frustration. They'd believed in the stranger, and once again they'd been fooled.

"Seize him!" said the noble.

The commander repeated the order. Strong hands grasped Diego roughly. Again they raised him high in the air. The people in the stands stood, screaming their approval.

Diego looked over his left shoulder, into the eyes of the boy who'd chased him around the city. A strange grin appeared on his face. He recoiled as the expression changed from youthful innocence to devilish horror. Humanity melted away into a smoky, spiritual essence. The satanic smile grew until it consumed the boy's head. Soon nothing remained except a swirling mass of foul-smelling fog.

As a squadron, the soldiers vanished. Diego felt the coarse sand split his skin as he crashed to the ground. Looking up, he saw the commander's eyes a second before he disappeared as well.

The nobles went next, blinking out of existence without a trace. Diego sat up, scanned the arena, and watched every spectator dissolve into nothingness. He scrambled to his feet, stumbling awkwardly as he turned his head, trying to keep track of the audience members as they melted into their seats.

"Your name."

The voice, exhaled through a cloud of smoke, rasped as it whispered to him.

Diego turned. A swirling, filthy fog spun before him.

"You know who I am, Satadon."

"You are Magnifico's guide. Diego Ramirez."

"What happened to these people?"

"They are no longer."

"Answer me!"

"Their service to me has come to an end," hissed Satadon.

"You have no power. We defeated you in the Dark Rift."

"You conquered Vipero and his dragons. I remain. I will always remain."

"No. The fifth sun has risen. You couldn't have escaped the darkness."

"I am here. Is that not proof enough?"

"What do you want?"

"I came here to warn you."

"Right. What do you really want?"

"You have summoned the wrath of the ancients," said Satadon. "You and that fool Magnifico and the Sol Dragones disturbed the true chain of events."

"What are you talking about? Make sense, spirit!"

"Sol should have warned his servants, but he chose to keep them in the light. Shadows cannot exist within the brilliance of the sun. Sol kept the truth from everyone."

"What does this have..."

"Silence!" roared Satadon. "Perhaps Magnifico knew of the danger and kept it to himself, held it even from his lovely mate, Estrella. Perhaps he gambled with the lives of the Sol Dragones, and yes, even the life of his guide."

"Liar!" shouted Diego.

"Your people will perish, just as your ancestors died today. You won't know the time, or the place, or why it's happening. But they *will* die, and you won't be able to stop it. Not you, not Magnifico, no power known to Sol will thwart the ancients in their quest to right the wrongs done to them."

"You're the leader of a beaten army, that's all," said Diego. "You destroyed the other spirits in the Xibalba and took their powers, and yet you're nothing."

"You are wrong."

"Then what are you?"

"I am the guide, the guide to the ancients."

CHAPTER EIGHT

The Asesino de mar barreled over the fuming seas like a roller coaster gone wild. Huge waves crashed over the soaked railings, tossing the heavy mooring chains about as if they were toys. The ocean roared, but the sound of the waves paled next to the wailing winds.

Francisco Pizarro stood on deck with his crew, fighting the freezing sleet slicing across the ship's beam. A few times the ship almost capsized, but the men followed the captain's commands, saving their lives and their vessel.

Pizarro squinted against the storm. If they'd been a hundred yards from land he'd never have seen it. The rain and wind coated the sky, blinding anyone hoping to see beyond the ship's rails. He watched the sails mostly, and how tightly they'd been lashed to the yardarms. He almost expected to see them unravel and fly off into the night, like kites escaping their owners. He watched the material holding fast, his men had done their work well. Next he checked the masts. He looked at the tips, where the net ladders were only a foothold wide. The weathered wood leaned and twisted, bending to the will of the storm.

The ship shot skyward as it careened up the face of a massive wave. Pizarro made the sign of the cross with the medallion given to him by the queen. His stomach dove into his throat as the Asesino de mar crested the whitewater. The bowsprit split the wave, emerging into the night air before crashing down on the ocean again. The wave's energy embraced the stern, pressing it forward in a slingshot lunge that nearly took the crew's feet out from under them. The captain held fast to a winding hook, keeping his boots wedged against the mainmast and a set of cleats bolted to the deck.

"Five degrees port," he shouted. The ship's mate screamed the order, stretching his lungs beyond their limit. When the captain turned and looked at him, he repeated the order, even louder the second time. The howling wind fought back, trying its best to drown out the mate's command.

The crew snapped to their tasks as best they could. A quarter of them slipped when another wave washed over the port rail. They grabbed anything they could to steady themselves. Their fellows held the lines, fearing the captain's displeasure more than the loss of their lives. They grabbed onto their mates, straining, screaming as their muscles and tendons stretched to the point of bursting.

After ordering three additional men to the wheel, Pizarro jumped over the gun deck rail. Before hitting the main deck, he'd shed his jacket and torn his ascot from his neck. With the mate working beside him, he helped his crewmen gather their footing. When all had returned to their posts, Pizarro grabbed a line and pulled along with his crew. He and his mate shouted encouragement to the men, and they responded in kind. A rousing cheer rose up the masts of the Asesino de mar as its crew gained control once again. Slowly, with the effort of every man on board, the wheel turned and the rudder responded. Pizarro went from man to man, slapping their backs and promising extra food and drink after the storm.

The ship groaned like a drunken ogre as it changed course.

The mighty ocean slapped the sides of Pizarro's vessel, angry that it couldn't exercise its will.

It seemed as if Poseidon had decided to take the ship down himself. Lightning strikes blistered the darkness in the night sky. Crewmen looked to the heavens as waves of thunder rumbled around the dense clouds. In a wild demonstration of nature's power, the two forces collided together, exploding in a display unlike anything Pizarro had ever seen. The captain quickly looked round, checking for the other ships under his command, but the powerful flash had blinded him, keeping him from seeing anything beyond the railing.

"Steady, men!" he yelled. "We've been through worse!"

They hadn't and he knew it. His men showed it with their expressions. A few moments ago he'd restored their courage, their faith in him, and now...

Another blast lit up the sky. Twice as strong as the first, it sent the men into a huddle by the mainmast. Their lives meant nothing to them. If they were to die, their only wish would be to find a marked grave somewhere, anywhere. Cast into the ocean namelessly, like something tossed over the side during a voyage, that was a death no sailor desired.

"Tie off the lines and get below," ordered Pizarro.

The ship's mate hastily repeated the command. He helped the crewmen complete their task, sending each to the ladder with a hug. When all had been secured, he signaled his captain and jumped through the opening into the hold.

Pizarro watched the sky burst with electric flame. He yelled at the night storm. "Six weeks longer!"

He glanced at the deck, looking for his coat. No doubt it had washed overboard, a casualty of nature's wrath.

"The ship is yours, spirit," he whispered. "Capsize it if that's your will, but I think you'll see us through this storm. How else will you conceal yourself until you reach the place of your revenge?"

Captain Francisco Pizarro held every hook and line he could grab as he fought his way toward the hold. This night he would spend with his crew. If they were to die, he would die with them.

CHAPTER NINE

Diego's body twitched. He woke, startled by his dream. Pulling his head away from his hands, he checked his glistening forearms. His shirt, completely soaked, clung to his back. He lifted his arms, dragging pages of the books he'd been reading along with them.

"Hey, Mijo," said a voice beyond his door. Two quick raps followed.

Diego spun on his chair, sweeping two of the books onto the floor. The clattering of pages and hard covers made him jump again.

"Hey, hermanito, it's me, Esteban."

Diego's brother poked his head into the bedroom.

"Qué pasa," said Esteban. "You look like vanilla ice cream. What's got you so spooked?"

"Nada," he said. He smiled a bit after hearing his brother's calm voice. "Just doin' some homework."

Esteban came in and shut the door. "It's me, Diego. Tell me what's up. You're scared out of your mind. I can see it."

Diego knocked his desk chair over as he jumped up. He leapt onto his bed, picked up a pillow and flung it across the room. The other one he kept, hugging it close to his chest.

Esteban waited patiently. He'd called Diego out on his lie, and he knew his little brother. He'd spill his guts when he felt ready.

"Remember those dragons last year?"

"The ones at the horse club?"

"Yea."

"You told me they were all dead. You said you and Magnifico killed them all in a battle."

"We did. They're all dead, even their leader, Vipero."

Esteban kept quiet, waited.

"There's someone else, someone worse."

"Órale," said Esteban. "Who?"

"A Dark Lord. He controlled Vipero."

"You said Vipero's dead."

"He is."

"So," said Esteban. "What's the problem?"

Diego slammed his fist against the soft pillow. "I think the Dark Lord is loose. Somehow he got out, escaped the Xibalba."

"What's a Xibalba?"

Diego looked up, locked eyes with his brother. "It's where Satadon lived, and supposedly where he was trapped. But not anymore, he's loose, and we're in trouble."

"Satadon's the Dark Lord?"

"Yea."

"How are we in trouble? What's going to happen?"

"I don't know. I just had a pretty weird dream. Satadon was in it. He said he was there to give me a warning."

"And?" asked Esteban.

"Something about our ancestors, the Mexica, way back in the sixteenth century, and how it's going to affect us here, now, in our time."

"Maybe it was just a dream, Mijo."

Diego shifted his eyes, looked at his brother again, dead serious. "Maybe those weren't real dragons at the horse club last year.

Maybe Magnifico didn't fry half the cars on that street two years ago saving us from those jerks."

"Alright," said Esteban. "I get it."

Diego slumped against his pillow. He wanted to let the tears come, but he didn't want to let his brother see him cry. He was thirteen now, a young man, and capable of handling things.

"So?" asked Esteban. "What are you gonna do?"

"Who knows? I can't do anything but wait."

"What about Magnifico, and Sullivan, the author guy?"

Diego turned his head, placed his cheek on the cool face of the pillow. "I haven't seen either of them for a while."

"Where are they?"

Diego inhaled deeply, then let the air rush away, like a runaway balloon.

"Diego?"

"I don't know. I haven't heard or seen anything. Racquel hasn't seen Estrella either. It's weird."

"Diego? Esteban?" called Alejandra. "Dinner."

"Come on, Mijo," said Esteban. "Let's go eat. You'll feel better after dinner."

Diego just stared straight ahead.

"Come on, perrito. Get up."

Esteban found the pillow Diego had tossed earlier. He fired it at his brother with all his strength, then laughed as it collapsed around his head.

Diego was off his bed in an instant. In seconds he'd tackled Esteban. With one hand pressed against his chest, Diego socked his brother on the arm again and again. Esteban was laughing so hard he couldn't put up a fight.

"Look at you two knuckleheads," said Alvaro, standing at the door to Diego's bedroom. "A fine meal awaits you in the kitchen, and here you are, rolling around the floor like a couple of gatos locos."

Alvaro stepped farther into the bedroom until he loomed over Diego. Wrapping his thick arms around his son's waist, he lifted him off of Esteban as easily as he'd pluck a paperclip from a desk. Diego squirmed and fought, laughing as he lunged at Esteban. Esteban stood in a flash and slapped Diego's head a few times before Alvaro could pull his younger son away. He shifted Diego to his left arm and threw a few punches at Esteban, hitting him in the shoulder and ribs.

"C'mon," he said. "Off to the kitchen before your mother comes down the hall and gives us *all* a beating."

Esteban went through the door first. Alvaro followed, still carrying Diego in his iron grip. He rubbed his son's head on the bedroom door and the hallway on the way to the kitchen.

"Ah," said Alvaro as he passed through the door. Having deposited Diego outside, he walked straight toward the dining room and sat at the head of the table. "There's nothing in the world like the scents coming from la cocina de mi esposa. I'm hungry, Alejandra, what's for dinner?"

"Nothing for you, oso grande, until you show a good example and wash your hands."

"Si, Papa," said Esteban. "If there's enough soap in the bathroom to clean those manos grandes."

Alvaro made a face at his son. "Get in line, both of you. I'll show you how to wash up so your wife will be satisfied."

"Just hurry," said Alejandra, as she set the serving dishes on the table. "If you let my meal get cold, it won't matter how clean you are. There'll be no dinner for any of you."

The three of them washed properly and sat with Alejandra. Alvaro led them in prayers, and the feast began. For ten minutes the only sounds were chewing, slurping, and swallowing.

Alvaro finally sat back and smiled. Dragging a napkin across his mouth, he drained a glass of water before addressing his wife.

"Alejandra, how do you do it?"

"Do what?"

"Outdo yourself every time we sit for dinner."

She smiled. "I like to eat delicious food, that's all. If you enjoy the benefit of my cravings, then it's lucky for all of us."

"Papa's right, Mama," said Diego. "No one can cook like you."

"Si," said Esteban. "Es muy bueno."

"Soon you boys will learn," she said. "I'll teach you how to cook half a dozen excellent meals, so you can impress your wives some-day."

"Why should I have to learn?" asked Esteban. "Catalina is a great cook, almost as good as you."

"Today's woman is destined for more than the home, Esteban," said Alejandra. "You must share the duties of the household, so your wife can pursue her dreams as well.

"Unlike this one," she said, pointing a spoon at her husband, "who doesn't lift a finger around here."

"Cara," said Alvaro, in his best puppy dog voice. "I'm a busy man, with many new contracts. Where would my business be without me to watch over it?"

"You boys should be very proud of your father. He's worked hard to provide for us. As a matter of fact, he's doing so well that I've decided to hire a maid twenty hours a week."

Alvaro looked like he'd been punched in the stomach.

"Don't try that look with me," said Alejandra. "You've been

bragging for weeks about all the money you're making. It's about time you spent some on your wife."

"What will you do with the time?"

"Perhaps I'll spend it serving the community. Or maybe I'll return to school and finish my degree. Diego is thirteen now. I have to think about what I'll do once our sons have left home."

"May I be excused?" asked Diego.

"Wait a minute, Mijo," said Alvaro. "I want to talk to you and Esteban."

"C'mon, Papa."

"It can wait. Your mother and I are interested in what's going on with you."

"They're checking up on us again," said Esteban.

"And if we are?" asked Alejandra.

Diego slumped in his seat, a look of desolate boredom sliding over his face.

"Don't look at us that way, little one."

Before Diego could defend himself, Alejandra held up her hand.

"Tell me about school, Diego," she said.

"We just started, Mama," he said. "What's there to tell?"

Alejandra gently placed her knife and fork on her plate. She pushed the plate forward exactly one inch. "Well, perhaps you can start by telling me why an eighth grade student needs to bring a truckload of history books home at the start of the school year."

"It's just a project."

"Diego," said Alvaro sternly. "Answer your mother properly."

Diego swung his legs under the table. Back and forth they went, a sure sign of frustration. "We have to work up a presentation about a certain period in history. I just thought I'd get a head start."

"That's fine, Mijo, and don't mistake concern for harassment. You know how much your father and I value education. We just don't want to see you exhaust yourself. The school year is long, and with every new level, the classes will get harder."

"Thanks, Mama," said Diego. "Don't worry, I'll be fine."

"Good boy."

Alvaro chimed in before his wife could grill Diego any further. "Has soccer practice begun yet?"

Diego brightened up immediately. "Si, next week is our first practice. Coach Morales recruited a couple of club players from Vista. He fixed it so their families could send their kids to school with us. We're going to kick a..."

"Diego Ramirez!" cautioned Alejandra. "Who taught you to speak in such a way?"

"Sorry, Mama," said Diego, awkwardly. "That's the way we talk on the field."

"Make sure it stays on the field."

"May I be excused?" he asked, clearly restless now.

"When is your first game, Mijo?" asked Alvaro.

"Three weeks, Papa. Will you be there?"

"If I can make it, I will. You know I will."

"Mama?"

"It's hard for me to get away in the afternoon, Mijo, you know that. But if you give me the date and time, I'll try and make arrangements with the senior center."

"May I be excused?" he asked for the third time.

"Okay, Mijo," said Alvaro, before Alejandra could speak up. "Go work on your project."

Diego jumped up before anyone could say another word. He slid his chair in, rinsed his dinnerware and placed it in the dishwasher. Then he ran down the hall to his bedroom.

"What's got into him?" asked Alvaro.

"I caught him at his desk with three or four library books spread out in front of him," said Esteban. "Must be one heck of a project."

"I don't like it," added Alejandra.

"Cara, he's studying," said Alvaro. "Can't we be happy about that?"

"I'm worried, Alvaro," she said. "Actually, I'm scared."

"Don't worry, Mama," said Esteban. "I'll keep a close eye on him."

Alejandra smiled for the first time since they sat down. She loved Esteban so much. He'd grown into such a handsome man, how could any woman resist him? She thanked God for Catalina. She'd make a fine daughter-in-law.

"How are things at the store, Esteban?" asked Alvaro, jarring Alejandra out of her daydream.

"Great. I've got all the best shifts. The manager loves me because I don't cause him any trouble. The owner even came by the other day and talked to me about the management program. One of the long time employees is getting ready to quit, and they need someone to replace him."

"That would be wonderful, Esteban," said Alejandra. "See how far you've gone since you met Catalina? Isn't it wonderful what a good woman can do for a man?"

Alvaro jumped when his wife kicked him in the shin underneath the table. "Yes, son," he said. "Catalina has been great for you. When is she coming for dinner again?"

"I think her parents want to ask you two over to their home."

Alejandra smiled broadly. "Tell them we accept, when they ask, of course." She pointed at her husband. "We might even get a new sports coat for this one."

"If you can find one big enough," said Esteban.

Alejandra smiled. "You'll help me with the dishes?"

"Of course, Mama."

CHAPTER TEN

Diego pressed his palm against the door jamb as he walked into his bedroom. He bent to pick up the clothes hamper he and Esteban had smashed when they hit the floor. Tossing it into his closet, he leaned over again and retrieved the history books he'd knocked off his desk. After smoothing the pages, he folded the covers over, stood, and tossed them onto his desk. Then he stepped into the bathroom.

"I haven't come here to be ignored."

Diego almost jumped through the shower curtain. He turned, dragging his fingers through the air, preparing to draw dragon fire.

"Who's there," he said. "Show yourself."

"I couldn't be sitting in a more obvious place."

"Magnifico?"

"Who else would it be?"

Diego poked his head out of the bathroom, looking around his bedroom excitedly. Finally his eyes settled on his desk, where Magnifico sat, in miniature, grooming his scales.

"Where've *you* been?" he asked sternly.

"Attending to important matters," said the dragon. "We need to talk."

"Okay," said Diego. "What's up? And while you're at it, tell me why you disappeared for so long."

"I'll tell you anything you want to know, but not here."

"Why not here? Let me just close my..."

A three foot long flame shot from Magnifico's nose. "Because if I don't find somewhere where I can expand my size a little, I might have an accident."

Diego smelled the soot in the flame's residue. A second later he grabbed a jacket and slid open the door by the pool.

"C'mon."

Magnifico hopped off the desk and followed Diego out the door. As soon as he could, he allowed his body to grow. In no time he passed the size of Diego's bicycle. He stretched, flapping his wings a few times.

"Diego?"

Diego whipped his head around. He saw his mother entering his bedroom with some dessert.

"Hide!"

"Where?"

"In the pool, now!"

Magnifico flicked his wings and dove headfirst into the water.

"What was that?" asked Alejandra.

"What?" asked Diego.

"Something just ran away. I saw it."

"It was just Jasper from next door. You know he likes to visit me at night."

"That didn't look like Jasper. It didn't look like a dog at all."

"Okay," said Diego. "It was a five hundred pound lizard wearing trunks. He knocked on my door and asked if he could go swimming."

"Don't get smart with me, young man."

Diego smiled up at the plate his mother held in front of her.

"Is that pie for me?"

Alejandra smiled, forgetting about the animal by the pool. "Yes, boysenberry pie, heated, with a little vanilla ice cream."

"Mmmm, thank you, Mama."

"What's the project you're working on?" she asked, turning to look at Diego's library books.

Magnifico floated near the surface of the pool. He could see Diego talking with his mother in his bedroom. He silently cursed his luck. He wouldn't be able to remain submerged much longer.

He felt the spent fire in his belly pushing against his chest. If he just could burp a little smoke or let a few small bursts of flame spit forth from his nostrils. Unfortunately, water presented all kinds of problems.

He could discharge his used fuel while underwater, but unless he did it carefully, he might start a fire on the surface of the pool, or he could fail to expel it completely due to the density of the water. He sat motionless, mentally signaling his guide to wrap up his business with his mother.

"That's a wonderful idea, Diego," said Alejandra, "a historical comparison of the Mexica people, through all generations leading to the present day. May I read it when you're finished?"

"Of course, Mama." Inwardly, Diego scolded himself for revealing so much. Now he'd have to write a report instead of just gathering information.

He scraped the plate with his spoon, then handed it back to Alejandra. "More, please?"

"Oh, no, Mijo," she said. "That's enough for you. Any more sugar and you'd be up half the night texting your friends."

"Okay, Mama, thanks for the pie."

"You're welcome. How is Racquel, by the way?"

Magnifico squeezed his wings around his body. He bent his head over, pressing the tip of his jaw against his chest. Ten times as much fire as he could normally hold swirled around inside his stomach and lungs. He glanced at Diego again, saw his mother standing next to him, gesturing toward his desk. Inhaling to the point of bursting, he clamped down on his insides, refusing to release the smoke and fire.

"She's fine. She's playing soccer this year for the girl's team."

"I'm glad."

"I have to get back to work, Mama. I don't want to get too tired and not be able to finish."

"You're hoping to finish the report tonight?"

"*No*," he said, glancing anxiously toward the pool.

"What's wrong, Mijo? You seem jumpy."

Diego whipped his head back around. "Nothing's wrong. I just want to work a little longer, that's all."

"Are you sure?"

Diego looked up at his mother, crossed his eyes, and smiled like a clown. "Si, Mamacita, yo estoy bien."

"Okay, hijo, enjoy your studies."

As soon as Diego's mother turned the corner and walked into the hallway, Magnifico released every bit of ash and fire broiling his insides. The sooty smoke streamed out in a gargantuan dragon burp, completely filling the pool. Magnifico pressed hard, expelling every bit of breath in his lungs.

Dragon fire followed, erupting from his mouth. A twenty foot blast spewed forth, hit the shallow end, and split into two separate columns. Both streams raced each other toward the deep end, scorching the plaster walls. A line of steaming bubbles trailed the fire, bursting into clouds of ash as the heat overwhelmed them. The roaring flames died out once they reached the pool light, tickling each other lightly before fading into the ripples.

Diego waited as long as he could. He knew his mother walked slowly. She never did anything in a hurry. He slid the door back and stepped through, closing it behind him. He looked back toward the bedroom door one last time.

The water in the pool exploded, rising like a cheering crowd at a sporting event. A huge wave slammed Diego against the sliding glass door. It fell again, slapping everything around it; chairs, towels, the fountain, the diving board, and every door and window facing the pool.

Like a phoenix emerging from its grave, Magnifico shot skyward, swinging his head left and right, spitting fire and gasping for breath. A circle of fire engulfed the pool. Flames shot toward the sky, like gas rushing away from the sun. The temperature of the water rose rapidly, rushing past the boiling point in a flash. Encased in a cloud of hissing steam, huge bubbles burst on the pool's surface in a symphony of muted music. Diego sat in his soaked clothing, staring, knowing he could do nothing.

Finally the churning water calmed. The backyard of the

Ramirez home looked perfectly normal, except for the fact that everything within a dozen feet of the pool's edge dripped water.

Someone raked back the living room door. Whoever wanted out was in a hurry, almost ripping the door from its rail.

"Diego!" whispered Esteban as loud as he could. "You better get lost. Mom's calling the police, and Dad's on his way out h..."

"Diego!" shouted Alvaro. "Que pasa? Are you alright?"

Diego walked around the edge of the house. "I'm okay, Dad."

"What in God's name happened out here?"

"I don't know," said Diego. "I was so scared I hid behind the bushes. I didn't see anything."

"The police are on their way," said Alejandra as she stepped through the door. "Mijo, are you sure you're alright? You're soaked. Come here, I'll get a towel from inside."

"Okay, Mama."

"What are we going to do about all this water?" she asked. "Everything's..."

A deafening sound silenced Alejandra. Everyone but Diego ducked down, thinking a jet had swerved off course, somehow gotten lost, and was now roaring over their neighborhood. Alvaro rushed to his wife's side, covering her with his arms.

"Mira," whispered Alejandra, lifting her eyes.

Magnifico swept past Diego's home in a flash before arcing into the heavens again. He flew by so fast they barely had time to realize it was some type of creature. He was there and gone, swallowed by the night as quickly as he'd appeared.

"Alvaro!" said Alejandra, clearly frightened. "What was it?"

"I don't know, Cara, but it's gone, now." He glanced around the yard. "I think we should all go inside."

Distant sirens caused Alejandra to look up. She expected to

see something horrible floating above their home. Lowering her eyes, she noticed her younger son standing calmly by the shallow end of the pool.

"Diego," she cooed. "Come here."

Only then did she realize that everything around the pool looked normal again. The chairs sat perfectly in place. The accessories, towels, everything had been restored. She looked back at Diego, fear and wonder in her eyes. He looked completely refreshed. His clothes as well, looked as though they'd just come out of the dryer. He stood like a statue, staring into the sky as if waiting for the creature to make a second pass over their home.

"Your father is right," she said. "Everyone in the house."

A few minutes after they'd gathered in the family room, a set of heavy knuckles rapped on the front door. "Police," said an assertive voice. "Open up."

"Coming," said Alvaro.

He walked through the foyer and opened the door. Two police units sat in their driveway, lights on. The rolling multi-colored beams bounced off other homes, lighting up the neighborhood. A fire engine, its siren winding down, stopped in the street just beyond the driveway.

Four capable looking officers stood outside Alvaro's door. The two in the rear rested their hands on the stocks of their pistols.

"Evening, sir," said the officer in charge. "This your home?"

"Yes, officer," said Alvaro. "Thank you for getting here so quickly. Please come in."

The four uniformed officers entered the Ramirez home as they'd been trained. Each took a position where they could guard and inspect potential danger spots.

"I'm Sergeant Rolando," said the lead officer. "We received a call about..."

"I'm terribly sorry, Sergeant," interrupted Alejandra. "Something frightened us, me especially, but apparently it has come and gone."

"It?" asked Rolando.

"I don't know what it was," she said. "None of us do."

"What happened? Can you tell us what scared you so much?"

"I think it might have been a jet," said Alvaro. "At least that's what it sounded like."

"We're a long way from the airport, sir."

"I know. It's hard to explain. Maybe some kids with their loud music."

Sergeant Rolando looked through the room to the far side of the den. He saw Diego staring out the window.

"Pardon me, sir, but is that your son?"

Alvaro turned to look at Diego. "Yes," he said, turning back. "His name is Diego."

"And this one is Esteban?" asked the officer.

"Si, they are both our sons. But what does this have to do with tonight?"

"Nothing. I apologize. I was the sergeant on duty last year when the fire broke out at the horse club."

Alejandra bristled, but kept silent.

"Good to see you again, Sergeant," said Alvaro.

"I thought you'd want to know that your sons are heroes down at the station, at the fire station as well."

Like a steam room releasing warmth, the tension in the room seeped out the front door.

"Thank you, Sergeant," said Alejandra. "We appreciate you mentioning it."

"We'd like it if they dropped by some afternoon. That's when most of the officers are on duty. They'd get a kick out of meeting the two young men who risked their lives to save the horses."

Diego and Esteban beamed. "We will, and soon," said Esteban.

"You're sure everything's okay?" asked the sergeant.

"Yes, I'm sure," said Alejandra.

"We'd like to make a sweep of the property, with your permission of course."

"Go right ahead, Sergeant," said Alvaro. "Can we make you some coffee?"

"No, thank you," said Sergeant Rolando. He turned to his men. "Mike, I'm glad you and Gerardo were able to back us up. Move through the side gates and meet us by the pool. "Paul, you come with me."

Rolando moved through the living room toward the sliding glass door. Officer Gutierrez followed him, hand still on his weapon.

The four policemen expertly searched the yard surrounding Diego's home. Within minutes they'd confirmed that no threat existed on the property.

"Sarge," said Gutierrez. "Look at that."

Rolando shifted his gaze to the pool. The water barely moved, but the murkiness astounded him. It almost seemed like a giant had taken a puff of a cigar and blown smoke into it.

"What do make of that, Pete?"

Officer Mike Peterson crouched down by the water. He dipped his fingers in the pool, then yanked them away, spraying the others.

"Jesus!" he said, shaking his hand quickly. "That feels like a pot of boiling water. Who the heck would keep a pool that hot?"

"Look at the walls," said Rolando.

The others walked a few paces around the sides of the shallow end.

"Looks like burn marks," said Gutierrez. "You can't mistake the streaky pattern and the spread of the flames as they initially impacted the walls."

Sergeant Rolando turned to see Diego standing behind them.

"Can you get your parents for me, son?"

"I think you and your men should leave now."

"I beg your pardon?"

Diego pointed at the pool. "He might just decide to come back. You don't want to be here if he does."

"He?" asked Gerardo Casillas. The officer bent down, hands resting on his knees. "Who might come back?"

"Diego?" asked Alejandra as she stood by the sliding glass door.

"What did you mean?" asked Casillas, gazing directly into Diego's eyes.

In a trancelike state, Diego stared right back. "He'll probably come again sometime tonight."

Alvaro rushed to his wife's side. "What is it, Cara? What's going on?" He shouted at Sergeant Rolando. "Why is that officer questioning my son?"

Casillas never broke eye contact with Diego. "You said he, son. Tell me who you're talking about. Who might come back?"

"Magnifico."

"Should we be afraid of Magnifico?" asked Casillas.

Diego never blinked. "You should be afraid of a lot more than that."

"Are you in trouble, son?"

Diego broke eye contact and looked at the sky. "We're all in trouble."

CHAPTER ELEVEN

"¿Órale?" asked Ricardo, hands on his knees and gasping for air. "What's got into coach? He's gonna kill us all."

"Aye," said Conor, spitting on the grass by their bench. "You'd think we'd angered him somehow."

"He just wants to make sure Irish can keep up with us when we play Vista," said Jose.

Conor kicked his leg back, dragging his cleat over the top of Jose's new shin guard, leaving a dark, grassy stain.

"That's cold, man," said Jose. He tried to catch Conor with a counter strike, but missed him by a mile.

"Yea, you're money," said Ricardo.

"Back on the field in five, boys," said Coach Morales. "Everybody drink some water."

"What's up, coach?" asked Jose. "Who pissed you off this morning?"

"You just made it a two minute break, Navarro. Anyone else want to make a smart remark?"

The players stayed quiet after that. Ricardo walked up behind Jose and slapped him on the back of his head. "Estúpido. Now Coach is gonna be even worse."

Morales turned and looked out across the grass. He saw Diego drifting around midfield, wandering aimlessly, as if he didn't realize his coach had called a break. He'd trained well enough, but Morales could tell his heart wasn't in it.

He worried about Diego. His parents had telephoned him over the weekend. They had no idea what was going on, and they were hesitant to tell him anything specific. They'd asked him to watch over their son, for Diego loved and trusted his coach.

"Let's go, boys," he bellowed. "Back out on the field. Another fifteen minutes of free play and then a half hour of wind sprints."

A collective groan passed through the players like a group burp.

"And if I see anyone going less than full speed, I'll make it an hour of sprints. Now run back out on that field!"

He looked one last time at Diego. "Ramirez," he shouted. "You're off the field, come over to the bench and rest!"

Morales glanced at Conor as he was jogging away. He tossed his head in Diego's direction.

Diego took the long way around, past the south goal. Staring at the ground the whole way, he hadn't noticed the other pair of cleats padding through the grass toward him.

"Diego," said Conor, more a statement than a question.

"Hey, Irish."

"Orlay," said Conor, trying to sound out the greeting the rest of the team used.

"Better stick to English, Irish. Say that the wrong way to a stranger and you might find yourself in a fight."

"Alright then, what's up, Diego? You have Coach pretty worried, and the team, too. We're your friends, can you not talk with us?"

Diego scraped a cleat through the grass, watching the blades flick back into place as his foot slid through them. He let his mind shift until he saw everything in its most primal form. Atoms formed new structures, making up the physical world Diego inhabited.

Conor walked with him for a while, letting his friend sort out his thoughts. They'd almost made it back to the bench, where Coach Morales tried not to notice them. Conor glanced up at the team, especially the two new players Coach had added at the beginning of the year.

"We'll be hard to beat this season," he said, speaking straight ahead. He looked to the side, saw Diego still mentally drifting.

"We'll be even better with my Mom playing goalie."

Diego didn't even wince.

Conor faded back and began running around Diego's left side. He kicked it into high gear, planning to hit him with a cross block. At the last second, Diego shifted his weight and used his friend's momentum to flip him over his waist. Conor crashed to the ground, skidding across the grass like a spent Frisbee.

He rolled over and looked up at his friend. "Well," he said. "At least you're paying attention to something."

He got up and held out his hand. Diego slapped it aside and fist bumped Conor. Conor leaned in for a one-armed embrace, and when Diego complied, Conor took him down easily. Diego lay flat on his back, Conor straddling him sideways with his legs askew.

"Get off me!" screamed Diego. "Joto estúpido, let me up!"

"Do you give me your word you'll talk to me about what's going on?"

"Get off me!"

"Your word," said Conor, "on your honor as a descendant of the Mexica people."

Diego's body went limp. His breathing, violent convulsions only a second ago, calmed quickly. He opened his eyes, seeing the sky in its true form.

"Alright," he said. "Let me up."

"Swear it," said Conor.

"I swear I'll talk to you," said Diego. "On the graves of my father's ancestors, I swear it."

Coach Morales, standing a short distance away, smiled.

Diego, Ricardo, Jose, and all their friends gathered at their tables in the school's quad. The sixth period bell had sounded a few minutes ago, and they had a little while to sit and talk until their parents arrived to take them home.

"Hey, Diego," said Rafael, a guard on the local Pop Warner football team. "I heard the Irish kid beat you down pretty good today. I thought you were tough."

"Shut up, gordo y estúpido," said Ricardo. "You think you're tough? Come out to the soccer field tomorrow afternoon and practice with us. You'll be flopping around like a fish in five minutes."

"It's alright," said Diego, motioning for Ricardo to back off. "You should have been there, Rafael. I took my mind off of him for one second and the next thing I knew I was on the ground. He got me pretty good."

Rafael scoffed. "I'd like to see him try that with me."

"Well," said Ricardo. "Here's your chance. He's coming over here right now."

Everyone turned and saw Conor walking between Racquel and another girl. When Racquel saw Diego she greeted him with a stunning smile.

"Hola," she said.

"Hey everyone," said Conor. He looked over at Lea, who offered her greetings as well.

Lea walked up to her brother and slammed her shoulder into his chest. Rafael's body didn't move an inch.

"Hey Irish," said Rafael. "I hear you like Lea."

Conor smiled. "Aye, she has beautiful eyes."

Lea looked down, blushing.

"You stay away from her," said Rafael in a menacing tone. "I don't want no white boy touching my sister."

Every student in the quad stopped talking and looked over at Rafael.

"I'll leave her alone if she tells me to," said Conor.

"I'm telling you."

"I heard that," said Conor, "and I also hear an echo."

A muffled laugh circled the group.

Rafael moved quickly for a bigger boy. He stood in Conor's face, looking down into his eyes. "You wanna do something?"

"Not with you," said Conor. "I like your sister."

"Punk," said Rafael. He pushed Conor with everything he had. Conor went down hard, but rolled over on his back and stood easily. He stepped into a forward fighting stance, his body low.

"Not here, Rafael," he said. "We have a game this weekend, and I won't be expelled because of you."

"I thought so," said Rafael. "An Irish pussy."

"Shut up, Rafael," said Diego.

"It's okay, Diego," said Conor. He turned to Rafael. "I'll make you a deal. Next week I'll meet you in the gym after school. We can fight on one of the mats. That way we won't get into trouble."

"You'll find a way to snake out of it."

"No, I won't," said Conor calmly. He looked Rafael right in the eye. "I'll be there next Tuesday when we don't have practice. Right after school, okay?"

"You messed up, fat boy," said Ricardo.

"Shut up, Ricky!" shouted Rafael.

Jose walked by the bigger boy, eyes on his shoes and head shaking. "Nice knowing you, homey."

Gll旦巳

"My Mom says it's okay if I eat dinner at your house," said Conor.

"Good," said Diego. "I have some things to show you in those books from the library."

"And you'll remember your promise?"

"That's what the books are for, Irish. We'll look at them a while and then go swimming. That way we can hang out by the slide in the deep end and talk. No one will hear us."

"Aye. That's a grand idea."

Alvaro's truck turned into the school's driveway. Diego looked into the cab and smiled.

"It's my brother, Esteban," he said. "If it was my Dad I'd have to answer a bunch of questions on the way home. Now at least I can wait until dinner."

"What happened?" asked Conor.

"When we get to my house, okay?"

Esteban rolled his father's truck into the circle by the flagpole. Standing on the brake pedal, he leaned over and yanked on the door handle. Diego grabbed it and pulled it wide. He let Conor jump in first and then followed him in. After setting his backpack on the floor, he reached for the handle and slammed the door. Esteban dropped the truck into drive and pulled away from the curb.

"Eh, Mijo," he said after turning onto the street. "How was school today?"

"As good as school ever is, you know."

"Who's the joto?"

"You should know," said Conor.

"Gotta be the Irish kid," said Esteban.

"I'm Conor." He held out his hand, smiling. "Nice to meet you."

Esteban slapped it away, wrapped his arm around Conor's neck and squeezed hard.

"Knock it off," said Diego. He turned his voice toward Conor. "He thinks he's a big stud because he stocks grapes for a living."

"One at a time, no doubt," said Conor.

"We'll see when we get home, muchachos," said Esteban, holding a fist out to Diego. His brother bumped it, then slammed it against the dashboard.

"I hear you play pretty good," said Esteban to Conor.

"Aye, pretty well. Every boy in Europe is born with a soccer ball between his feet."

"South of the border, too," said Esteban. "I played when I was in high school."

"Were you any good?"

Diego laughed under his breath.

"What's that about?" asked Esteban. "I was a hell of a defensive player back then."

"He means when opposing players were getting ready to blow by him, he knew how to tackle them and get yellow cards."

Diego and Conor laughed out loud. Esteban reached over, trying to smack his brother's arm. They pulled up to a stoplight, and before Esteban could stop him, Diego reached over and honked the horn. Then he leaned forward, disappearing completely, making it look like Esteban and Conor were riding in the truck alone and sitting next to each other. At first Conor tried to duck down, too, but when he found he couldn't, he played along by throwing his arm around Esteban's shoulders and leaning on the horn.

"Oh, you clowns are going to get it when we get home," said Esteban, looking from car to car in the intersection. He saw every type of embarrassment. Two elderly ladies sat in the car next to him. They looked at him with utter shock and horror. A very pretty girl in a BMW sat waiting in the opposing left turn lane. She had a smile from ear to ear, which made Esteban die a thousand deaths. A group of boys from the local high school honked their horns behind them, adding to the attention getting frenzy.

At long last the light changed. Esteban stomped on the gas, causing Diego and his friend to bounce hard against the seat back. They laughed even harder, which made Esteban finally crack. He laughed as he zoomed down Bear Valley Parkway toward his home.

"So," said Conor. "This is what you've been studying?"

"Yea," said Diego as he fished a pair of trunks from the floor of his closet. He threw them at Conor. "Here, these ought to fit you."

"I glanced at some of these pictures while the books were still in the library," said Conor. "The stories of the Spanish ships are amazing."

Diego came out of the bathroom with his red trunks on. "You can go in there and change."

Conor held his hand above an artist's drawing of a ship captain's cabin. A man in uniform stood by a thick table, his gaze fixed upon sheets of parchment. His face, lined with many years of salt and wind, closed around his eyes like a protective barricade. But the eyes were no less sharp, and they bore into the maps on the table like a falcon eyeing food from the sky.

"This one I could barely turn away from," said Conor.

"Go change," said Diego. "I want to show you something in the pool."

Conor followed Diego out the sliding glass door. As soon as he jumped into a dive over the water, Conor was right behind him. Both boys hit the surface together, splitting the pool with their turns under the water. Diego came up in the deep end. Conor surfaced by the steps in the shallows.

He wiped the hair out of his eyes and watched Diego stretch his back by inverting both hands and grasping the coping as widely as he could. Conor followed his actions and soon felt his shoulders unwinding as the warm water soothed his muscles.

"What's with the dark streaks on the walls by the pool light?" asked Conor.

"Turn around right where you are," replied Diego. "Look at the walls."

"Jesus and Holy Mary," said Conor. "They're as black as night, and streaked just like those at your end. Why, it looks like…"

"Maybe that's exactly what it is," said Diego.

Conor dove under the water and swam to Diego. His hand grabbed the coping underneath the diving board. He floated up quietly, checking the darkened wall with his fingers.

"It's as smooth as glass," he said after popping his head above water. "Back home we'd call this dragon breath.

"Maybe that's what we call it here, too," said Diego.

"In Ireland it's only legend, Diego, and the stories go back thousands of years."

Diego paused without speaking. He released his arms and turned around. Resting his forearms poolside, he allowed his legs to float aimlessly.

"You said you wanted to know what's been going on."

Conor looked up. "Aye, I did."

"What if I told you that a dragon's been hanging around here for the past couple of years."

"I'd believe you, of course."

"Just like that?"

"You don't question mystical forces, Diego. At least that's what my uncle used to say."

"This is a real dragon, Conor. Sometimes he's so small no one can notice him. Other times he's bigger than half the school."

"Where did he come from?" asked Conor.

"From a contest. I wrote an essay for the school district and won first prize. An author came to the library here at school and gave me a dragon statue. I swear, from the first moment I touched it I knew it was alive."

"You're lucky, Diego."

"Yea, lucky."

"Every kid in Ireland would give the rest of their lives if they could have a dragon for a week. You might be friends with this fellow for a long time."

"Yea, I think you're right."

"So," said Conor, "he's the one that blackened the walls of your pool?"

"Yea, he popped into my room the other night. Said he had to talk to me. My Mom walked in on us, so he flew into the pool and stayed underwater until she left."

"I wonder why he went off on your pool."

"He's a bit unusual, but I can't see him doing this unless he had a reason."

"Was he angry?"

"He's always pissed off about something," said Diego.

Conor look at his friend with concern creasing his forehead.

"It's not like that. He's a grouch, but he's a good guy. I'm pretty sure he wants what's best for our world."

Diego let himself disappear beneath the water. He exhaled and dropped slowly to the bottom of the pool. He stayed there for a minute before pushing himself back up. When he surfaced, Conor was in the same place, waiting for him to finish his story.

"Trust me," said Diego. "I've seen the bad ones. It's easy to tell the difference. Magnifico's never tried to kill me, well, not really. There were a few last year that wanted to waste me."

"Mother of God," said Conor. "This is all true? It's not some joke that'll make me look like a fool tomorrow at school?"

"You can't tell anyone!" said Diego forcefully. "No one knows except Esteban, me, Racquel, and now you."

"Everything you've said has been about the last two years," said Conor. "What's happening now? Why did your dragon..."

"Magnifico," said Diego.

"A grand name," said Conor, smiling. "Why did Magnifico come to your home the other night looking for you?"

"I don't know," said Diego. "But I think it has something to do with those books in my bedroom."

"It's the picture I pointed out, isn't it. The one with the ship captain looking at the maps?"

"Yea," said Diego. "I was there, in that cabin but he wasn't there. Another man commanded the ship."

"What?" asked Conor. "That's history from over four hundred years ago. How could you have been there?"

"You don't believe me?" asked Diego, suddenly upset with his friend.

"Let's say I do. What does a ship captain in the early sixteenth century have to do with you?"

"I'm not sure, but I know I was on that ship. It happened in class the day I asked you to get all those books for me. I started daydreaming about this other captain, in that exact cabin, and he was looking over those same maps. Only he wasn't the only one there."

Conor stared at Diego.

"A spirit was there with him, something from the ancient stories of the first suns. It's hard to explain, but I know it. He's dangerous as hell and very powerful."

"What makes you think it was that ship, and why was there a different captain in your vision?"

"Because I saw it in Racquel's book in history class. As soon as I woke up I saw the page flip over in her book. The different captain was there, in the picture, but the spirit wasn't. That's how I knew something weird was happening, and that's why I asked you to get the books from the library."

"What does it all mean?"

"Who knows?" said Diego. "But something big is going to happen, I'm sure of it, and whatever it is, it has to do with my ancestors."

"Your grandparents?" asked Conor.

"My ancient ancestors, the Mexica, remember? The ones you made me swear to at practice?"

"Oh, aye," said Conor. "Well, we know the history, right? The Spanish came to the new lands and conquered the Aztecs. Whether by war or disease, they pretty much wiped them out."

"Diego?" shouted Alejandra from the living room door. "Are you out here in the pool? Is that cute Irish boy with you?"

"Yea, Mom," said Diego. "We're here by the slide."

"Hello, Mrs. Ramirez," said Conor.

The two boys heard Alejandra's footsteps as she rounded the

shallow end. She appeared from behind a wall of ferns that stood next to Diego's room.

"Hello, Conor," she said, smiling. "I'm so glad you can join us for dinner. It's wonderful to have such an appetite at my table."

"With your cooking it's hard not to be hungry," said Conor.

"Your friend is a sweet talker, Diego," she said, winking. "You boys have fun. Be ready for a feast tonight."

She turned and walked back toward the house, but stopped after a few steps. Diego, do you have homework?"

"Si, Mama."

"Try and complete your assignments before dinner."

"Okay, Mama."

"Conor, do you have work to do for school as well?"

"Mom!" said Diego. "He's not your kid!"

"We all share parenting responsibilities where our children's well being is concerned."

"Aye, Mrs. Ramirez, I have my backpack with me. We'll do our assignments together, won't we, Diego?"

"That's fine, good boys." She turned again and disappeared into the house.

"Quick thinking," said Diego.

CHAPTER TWELVE

Racquel dropped her backpack and climbed onto her bed. She turned on her cell phone and looked for messages. Disappointed at not seeing anything from Diego, she quickly pulled up his contact screen. She dashed off a text, asking him to call her as soon as he could.

She draped her jacket over a chair and walked into the bathroom. Allowing the hot water to warm, she looked into the mirror, checking her skin. She saw something on her cheek and grimaced.

"Come, now, you're the only one who'll ever notice that."

Instead of jumping in fright, Racquel merely shifted her eyes in the mirror and looked behind her. Estrella stood in the shower, washing her scales under the dribbling stream.

"I expected to see you sooner than this," said Racquel.

"I'd wished to be here earlier as well."

"What kept you? I was worried."

"A gathering of dragons and conduits," said Estrella. "The fifth sun has entered our galaxy."

"That's wonderful."

"Oh, Racquel, if you could only experience Celestina's beauty, her radiance and warmth, her love for all beings."

"Will I, someday?"

"Of course, as will every creature in the galaxy."

Racquel walked across her bedroom and quietly closed the

door. Returning to the bathroom, she leaned against the sink and faced Estrella.

"What is it you're not telling me?"

"As wise as you've ever been, my dear," said the dragon, as she craned her neck and pointed her snout into the dripping water.

"Why hasn't the fifth sun appeared?"

"She cannot."

"What prevents her?"

"Satadon."

Racquel recoiled in horror. "It can't be. He never escaped the Rift."

"Apparently he has, and he wields unspeakable powers."

"How?" asked Racquel. "How did he escape?"

"We don't know," replied Estrella. "The Rift is empty. No life force exists there. That much we do know."

"What about Sol?"

"His power is not limitless, Racquel. Even the unity of Sol and Celestina cannot solve the riddle. Satadon has tapped a source none of us can identify."

"And Magnifico?"

"He tried to contact his guide a few nights ago. Diego's mother nearly caught him. I dare say if she'd kept him under water for another few seconds, Diego's neighborhood might not exist."

"I'll see him tomorrow at school. I'll tell him Magnifico wants to meet with him."

"No, Racquel," said Estrella. "It must be tonight."

"It's good to finally meet you, Conor," said Alvaro, holding out a beefy hand. "We've seen enough of los dos maniquis, Jose y Ricardo, eh, Alejandra?"

"Those boys are treasures," said Diego's mother. "I don't want to hear another word about them."

Diego leaned over to Conor. "Someday he'll be talking about you like that."

"¿Que?" What was that?"

"It's wonderful to be here again, Mr. Ramirez," said Conor, "and I'm glad to finally meet you."

"You're always welcome at our table, Conor."

"Thank you. I might have to name a permanent chair for myself."

Conor sat in Esteban's place. He joined the family as they gave thanks for the food on their table, and watched as Alvaro took the first portion from each serving dish.

"It all smells delicious," he said. "What is it, Mrs. Ramirez?"

"Flank steak," she answered, "marinated with a fine Mexican sauce. The vegetables were lightly broiled with sea salt. You'll have to tell me if you like them."

"Fancy descriptions are for women," said Alvaro, passing the first dish to Conor. "Eat hearty, son, and enjoy the wonder of my wife's cooking."

"Take all you wish, Conor," said Alejandra. "There's more of everything in the oven."

"Aye, I will, and thank you."

Conor and Diego ate their fill, with Conor minding his table manners a lot more than Diego. More than once Alejandra had to shoot an angry reminder at her son for eating like un cerdo.

"You boys have a big game coming up, yes?" asked Alvaro.

"Yea," said Diego. "Against Vista."

Alvaro chuckled. "They're going to be pretty mad at your coach for stealing their players."

"They wanted to come to Escondido," said Conor. "They knew we had a better chance at winning the league title this year."

"Yea," said Diego. "They're eighth graders. This is their last year at this level. Next year they'll be going up against high school players. They have to look good now so the coaches will pick them as substitutes when they're freshman."

"I don't think you boys will have that problem," said Alvaro.

"Conor won't," said Diego. "That's for sure."

Alejandra smiled. "All the boys say you're a very talented player."

Conor blushed. "I'm only as good as the team around me, Mrs. Ramirez. Diego and his friends make me as good as I can be."

"You see?" she asked of her husband. "This is what I told you. Very humble, this one."

"And he eats like un caballo."

"Alvaro, what a horrible thing to say to a young boy. Apologize this instant."

"It's okay, Mrs. Ramirez," said Conor. "My family jokes like that all the time. I'm used to it."

Alejandra shot a wicked glance at her husband, then smiled coyly.

"Well, we're going to try our hardest to make that game, aren't we, Alvaro?"

Diego's father stuffed the last bite of steak into his mouth. He looked up when he heard his name called, half smiled, and nodded. Two lines of sauce snaked down his chin.

"Awww, gross, Papa," said Diego. He reached over, trying to cover Conor's eyes. Of course, Conor had to duck his head and sneak a look. He laughed lightly, not wanting to seem too delighted at Alvaro's expense.

Alejandra shook her head. "I guess we can take that for a yes, boys."

Alvaro burped a little. "Yes, we'll try," he said.

"Conor," asked Alejandra. "Have you had enough to eat?"

"Wait for dessert," whispered Diego.

Conor smiled, then blushed as he looked at Alejandra. "Maybe I should save room for dessert?"

"Eat whatever you like," said Alvaro. "Don't let this one tell you what to do."

"Great food, Mrs. Ramirez," said Conor. "A lot of kids in Ireland don't have the chance to eat meals like this."

"Come here whenever you want," said Alvaro. "In fact, why don't you ask your parents if they'd like to come for dinner some night?"

"Aye, that'd be grand. They'd like that."

"Have they made many friends since you moved here?" asked Alejandra.

"There's plenty at church they've gotten to know, but not too many in the community. They're friendly folk, too, you'd like them."

"I'm sure we would," she answered. "If you give me your number, I'd be happy to call them."

"Can we be excused?" asked Diego.

"Excuse me?" said Alejandra.

"May we be excused?" asked Diego and Conor together.

"Of course, boys," said Alvaro.

The two of them pushed their chairs in, gathered their plates and silverware and walked into the kitchen. Conor returned for their glasses as Diego rinsed and placed everything in the dishwasher.

"We'll be in my room, Mama," said Diego as they ran down the hall.

"How was school today, girls?" asked Mariana.

"Bueno," said Claudia.

"Okay," said Valeria.

"Nothing? Nothing happened worth mentioning? Racquel?"

"We practiced a new song today in choral."

"Which one?"

"Ave Maria."

"Such a beautiful song. Who will sing the lead, you?"

"I don't know, Mama. We can audition for the lead, but there are many girls with good singing voices."

"But none can sing like you, hija," said Arturo. "You have the voice of an angel."

Racquel's sisters mimicked hoarking their food onto the table.

"Both of you could sing lead in the church choir, if you weren't so intent on talking about boys all the time."

"Boys are interesting, Papa," said Valeria.

"Not the ones you hang out with," said Claudia.

"At least I don't date my sister's leftovers."

"You mean the ones that leave you for someone better?"

"Enough," said Arturo. "Must it be the same thing every night? If you spent half the time on your studies as you do bickering and seeing boys, you'd both have scholarships by now. You could save your mother and me a lot of money."

"You *could* act a little more like your sister," said Mariana. "Perfect grades ever since she started the first grade. All you have to do is apply yourself."

"Like little miss perfect?" asked Claudia. "She goes to school, comes home, studies, and practices singing and writing on weekends."

"And now she's made the soccer team," added Arturo proudly.

Racquel sat quietly as her parents exchanged words with her sisters. She hadn't heard anything, really, because all she could think about was Estrella's last comments.

Somehow she would have to leave the house as soon as she could. She wouldn't be able to excuse herself without finishing her dessert, and she couldn't very well wolf down her food and then ask to go.

"Racquel," said her mother. "Have you lost your hearing?"

"She's too busy thinking about Diego," said Valeria.

"Oh, Diego, mi amor," said Claudia. "Te amo muy mucho."

Racquel looked to her mother for support, but Mariana just smiled. She'd been a young girl once herself, and she knew all about crushes.

"He's grown into a very handsome young man," she said. "Not quite the head turner his brother is, but a very good looking boy all the same."

"*Oh, Diego,*" sang Racquel's sisters.

Racquel saw her way out. "May I please be excused?"

"Si, Chiquita bonita," said Arturo. "And you two," he said, giving Valeria and Claudia the look they knew very well, "will give me a break in the kitchen tonight. I want everything spotless in an hour."

"Papa!" they both cried together.

"I have homework," said Claudia.

"I need to call some friends about this weekend."

Arturo held his hand up. "You can play games when you're done cleaning up. And Claudia, I want to see your school work, finished, before you go to bed."

"Papa!"

"Diego," said Racquel.

"What is it?"

"We have to meet, tonight, now."

"What?"

"Estrella came to see me. Something's up. Magnifico is really upset. He told her he tried to visit you the other night."

"It didn't work out," said Diego, beginning to get upset himself. "He nearly fried every piece of furniture on our deck. He almost made a guppy pond out of our pool, and I had to explain it all to my parents and the police."

"All right," said Racquel. "I'm sorry, but we still have to meet with them tonight."

"Where?"

"The horse club," she said. "I'll get one of my sisters to drive me up there."

"You don't even get along with them."

"I'll do her homework for her. It won't be the first time."

"There's something else."

"What?" she asked, the strain showing in her voice.

"I've got Conor here with me."

"You'll have to bring him along."

"I can't..."

"We don't have time," said Racquel. "Estrella told me that Magnifico, Nathan, and Jenna are already there. She probably is, too, by now."

"Who's Jenna?"

She's my, oh just hurry over there, Diego. I'll introduce you when I arrive."

"Okay," said Diego. "We'll leave now."

"I'll see you in about twenty minutes."

Racquel ended the call and stuffed her cell phone in her back pocket. She ran down the hall and into the kitchen.

"What do *you* want?" asked Claudia.

"I need a ride to Diego's house."

"Get outta here."

"I mean it. I need a ride right now. I'll do your homework for you."

"All of it?"

"Every page. Now get your keys."

"What about Mama and Papa?"

"Never mind them. I know what to say. Let's get the kitchen cleaned up."

Five minutes later Claudia slipped into her shoes. She tied a light coat around her waist and grabbed her brush. After tugging it through her hair a few times, she tossed it on the dresser and grabbed her keys.

"Let's go."

"We've got ten minutes to do our assignments," said Diego.

"Where're we going after that?" asked Conor.

"To see something you won't believe."

CHAPTER THIRTEEN

"Mama?"

"What is it, Diego?"

"I'm going to take Conor down to the market for a little while. We'll come home with Esteban when he gets off work."

"What about your homework?"

"All finished."

Alejandra walked into the foyer. She looked at her son and his friend.

"You finished your school work that fast?"

"Si, Mama," said Diego.

"Conor?" she asked. "Is this true?"

"Mama!"

"Yes, Mrs. Ramirez. We finished just now. If it'll make you feel better, I'll get my notebook and show you."

"That's okay," she said, looking at the boys sideways. "I just want to make sure my son isn't trying to pull a fast one on me. I'll expect both of you home with Esteban."

Diego turned to go.

"Conor," said Alejandra. "Why don't you give me your parents' number now? I can tell them when you'll be home and invite them for dinner at the same time."

Conor followed her into the kitchen and gave her his number. He and Diego walked out the door afterward, shutting it gently after them. When they got halfway up the driveway Diego took off running. Conor fell in behind him, and after a few hundred yards they rounded the corner by the entrance to the horse club.

"I thought you told your mother we were going to the market," said Conor.

"Shh," replied Diego. "Stay quiet, and don't speak to anyone until I say it's cool."

Conor didn't answer. He knew better. His uncle's words rang inside his head. *Mystical forces are at work here, boy.*

"Hold," called a low rumbling voice. Neither Diego nor Conor could see the owner of the command, but they obeyed.

"That one does not belong." A menacing snarl accompanied the remark.

Conor held his ground. Diego motioned for him to do just that.

"He's with me," said Diego. "He's my guest, and I'm the guide."

"Send him away then, guide, or I'll see to his departure."

"You'll do nothing but greet him, formally or informally. It's your choice, but he stays or we both go."

"Stubborn boy!" A thunderous growl poured over the two of them. Their hair and clothing wavered as the hot breath rumbled by. A moment later two huge dragons materialized in the ring. Sullivan and Jenna appeared just afterward.

Magnifico took three steps forward and thrust his flaming jaws over the fence. His fangs stopped inches short of Conor's nose.

"How dare you interfere..."

His comment tumbled to the ground like ashes falling from a cigar. He stepped back far enough to bow low before Diego's friend.

"Greetings, Champion," he said. "We are honored."

Diego looked over at Conor, then back to Magnifico.

"I should bow before you, leader of the sun dragons," said Conor. He knelt, holding his right arm out in front of him. "My lord."

He raised his eyes to meet Estrella's. "My lady."

"Conor Jameson," said Estrella. "The elders on the sun are telling many stories about you, young man."

"The honor is to serve," said Conor, giving the formal greeting Purugama had taught him. "Forgive me. Racquel called Diego and said we had to leave immediately. I'll gladly wait by the gate until you conclude your business."

"Nonsense, Conor," said Estrella. "You might prove to be as important as any of us. Perhaps your counsel will be requested."

"Greetings, Conor," said Sullivan, holding out his hand. "I've heard much about you and your big friends. I hope to meet all of them someday."

"I am honored, young man," said Jenna. "And this must be Diego, Magnifico's guide?"

"Yes," said Sullivan. "Diego, Conor, this is Jenna, Racquel's conduit."

Conor greeted her formally. He stared at her, mesmerized by something he couldn't pinpoint. He felt he knew her, but couldn't remember exactly.

"Diego," said Sullivan. "Are you going to do anything besides stare at your friend?"

"Racquel, dear," said Estrella, turning to welcome her guide.

"Guide," said Magnifico, bowing slightly.

Racquel hugged Diego, whispering lightly. "What's wrong? You look like you've just seen a ghost."

Conor greeted her, giving her a light hug before releasing her to the others.

"Now," said Magnifico, "for the reason we're all gathered again at this ridiculous horse club."

Estrella sat with her tail wrapped around her legs. Racquel walked up the golden scales. When she saw Conor staring, she motioned for him to sit beside her. After glancing at Estrella for approval, he ran up the tail and seated himself.

The dragon was ten times Purugama's size, and she was the smaller of the two. Diego's dragon looked twice as big as Racquel's. He couldn't imagine riding such a huge animal.

"Satadon has escaped the Rift," said Magnifico. "Sol told me this only a week ago. We don't know where he is, but we do know the fifth sun is trapped within Sol's spiritual path while he roams free. Unless Celestina can break away and form her own association with the planets and stars in our galaxy, the prophecy cannot unfold."

"I know where Satadon is," said Diego, having composed himself.

"You?" laughed Magnifico. "You claim knowledge the sun can't determine?"

"I'm the guide, in case you've forgotten."

"Tell us more," said Magnifico, settling down next to Estrella.

"Oh, stop it," she hissed, fire shooting from her mouth. "How many times must your guide prove himself?"

"Tell us your story, Diego," said Sullivan.

"Satadon appeared before me in a vision, or a dream, I don't know which." He related the events in the classroom with Racquel's book, about the differences in both the vision and his dream.

"The spirit was Satadon," he said. "I'm sure of it."

He spoke of the night Magnifico came to his home, how earlier in the evening he'd fallen asleep while studying the library books. He talked about his bizarre dream, about the boy who'd bought Magnifico as a statue, and the chase, and then all the people in the temple. He gave detailed descriptions about the nobles, and the different styles of clothing people wore.

"Ancient Mexica culture," said Jenna. "I studied it during the time."

"Yes," said Estrella. "I agree."

"That's what we're covering in history class right now," said Racquel.

"I chased the boy into the temple and took back the statue," said Diego. "Before I knew it I'd been caught and taken captive by a group of strong men, guards or something.

"They brought me before another group of men. The garments of these four were much brighter than anything worn by others in the temple. Gold bands decorated their arms and waists. One of them stepped forward and spoke, demanding to know what had occurred.

"After telling our stories, everyone in the temple just blinked out of existence. At first it was only a few, some of the soldiers holding me, one of the nobles, but then everyone vanished, even the crowds in the stands.

"Soon only two of us remained. Then the boy began to change. He became a spirit. I knew it had to be Satadon."

"How could you be certain?" asked Magnifico. "There are many who serve the darkness. Any number of them could have entered your dreams."

"He admitted it," said Diego. "He told me, and he told me something else, too."

"What, Diego?" asked Sullivan. "Tell us."

"He said he was the guide to the ancients."

CHAPTER FOURTEEN

"It isn't possible," said Sullivan. "The ancients have been asleep since before the first sun."

"I won't believe it," said Estrella. "He's using Diego to trick us. It's a ruse, nothing more."

"It is said that only the ancients can travel through time," said Jenna, standing next to Sullivan and holding his arm. "If Satadon truly has found a way to the past, an alliance with them must be considered a possibility."

"But why?" asked Sullivan. "Our teachings told us they'd always been neutral. They would never choose sides and favor one over another."

"Unless something happened that angered them," said Diego, looking at Magnifico.

"Watch your tongue, boy."

"Maybe I should have been watching yours. If you'd been truthful with all of us from the beginning we wouldn't be talking about this."

Magnifico's tail rose up and slammed against the packed dirt. The force of the impact splintered the fence line for twenty feet on either side and dug a trench in the ground a foot deep.

"Do you claim knowledge beyond mine, Guide?" Fire shot sideways from Magnifico's mouth. "A thirteen year old boy, and one easily led astray by the words of a demon spirit?"

"I want to know why you took the Sol Dragones into battle against Vipero," said Diego.

"The prophecy!" shouted Magnifico. His rumbling voice shook the grounds. The horses whinnied, stirring nervously in their stables. "If we hadn't won the battle he'd have taken Sol for his own, destroyed your planet, and..."

"That's it, isn't it?" asked Diego. "He would have taken something that belonged to you?"

"You test me, boy."

"Then strike me down if you can't take the truth! You wanted to keep your place as ruler of the Sol Dragones. That's why you sacrificed so many of your kind in battle. Think of all the dragons that willingly gave their lives for you. Not for Sol, not for the prophecy, but for you."

Magnifico seethed but kept silent.

"You used them, and you used us, even your own mate as pawns in your personal war with Vipero."

Magnifico looked toward the stars.

"Don't shy away from it," said Diego. "Tell us why!"

"Because," said Magnifico without turning. "Vipero was my brother." He walked away, through the broken fence, until he reached the trees that bordered the bridle trail. Once there, he coiled his body and lay down, burying his head in his tail. "I'm sorry," he said, his voice muffled. "I thought I could save him, turn him back to the light. I wanted to share Sol with him."

"It's true, Diego," said Estrella. "Vipero and Magnifico were sired by the greatest dragon the suns have ever known. Until Satadon corrupted Vipero's mind, they were as close as two dragons could be.

"Imagine your own brother turning against you. Imagine being forced to fight him to the death. Imagine winning the battle, only to see your brother die. Could you live with that pain so easily?"

"But Satadon told me..."

"Satadon killed his own kind out of a drive for lust and power. He would do anything to achieve his goals, even turn you against your own dragon."

"If Magnifico and his guide are at war with each other," added Jenna, "then half his work is done. He will lie to anyone to get what he wants, just as he lied to you."

Diego stood with his hands in his pockets. He looked up at Racquel and Conor, saw their expressions and looked away. He sought comfort in Sullivan's eyes, but found nothing but embarrassment and disdain. Only Jenna gave him a reassuring grin with a nod towards Magnifico.

Hands still firmly planted in his jeans, he walked over to his dragon and sat down. Magnifico kept his eyes closed, but shot a gust of thick smoke all over Diego. When it cleared, the front half of Diego's body looked like someone had tossed a shovel full of chimney soot at him.

"Sorry," he said, wiping his face and neck. "And I'm sorry about Vipero. I guess that's why you didn't want to tell me about him before the battle. It must have been tough on you."

Magnifico raised his head high and blew the remaining ash from his nose. A pillar of fire twenty feet high followed it.

"How could you possibly know?" he said, getting to his feet. "Come, there are riddles yet to be solved."

Diego walked next to his dragon as they reentered the ring. Conor looked on, eyes wide as he watched his friend casually strolling next to Magnifico. He felt a kinship with Diego, but his bond with Purugama seemed like nothing compared to what he saw before him. A dragon! Something from the early stories of his land.

"Racquel," he whispered. "Will there be a time when I can speak to these creatures?"

"You mean tonight?"

"No. Sometime in the future, that's..."

"Wait," she said, holding her fingers to her lips.

"I must talk with Sol," said Magnifico. "Estrella, I need your counsel."

He turned to Sullivan. "Nathan, will you and Jenna work with the guides and learn what you can about their history?"

"Of course." He looked at Jenna, who nodded her agreement.

"What can we do?" asked Conor.

"Nothing, Champion. This is our fight. We will not call upon you and your kind to stand with us."

"We can help."

"You will not interfere," said Magnifico. "I haven't time to give you a lesson in the instability of inter-dimensional warfare."

"Ask your mentor for his counsel," said Estrella. "He will explain it to you."

"We'll meet here again in a week," said Magnifico. "I want to know where Satadon is, and how we plan to counteract his latest strategy."

"Racquel," said Jenna. "Come with me. I will send you home."

"C'mon," said Diego, slapping Conor on the shoulder. "We've got to hustle down to the store. We're going to have to take the street route in case Esteban's already gotten off work."

The two boys waved their goodbyes and ran through the gates of the horse club. Magnifico watched them go, giving them plenty of time to turn the corner.

"We've got trouble, Nathan."

"If Satadon has the ancients as his allies," said Sullivan, "we're finished."

"Nonsense," said Estrella. "Let us seek proof before we yield. Satadon is evil, and every sinful trait of his being works against him. He tried to turn Diego against you, my lord, and he failed."

"Foolish child," groused Magnifico.

"Will you turn against him out of your own stubbornness? Now who is being foolish?"

"I'm concerned, that's all."

"As are we all," said Estrella. "Let's wait until we have more information, more facts, and then we can plan our defense."

"She's right," said Sullivan.

"Yes," said Magnifico. "Of course she is."

"What is it?" asked Jenna. "Tell us, lord of the sun dragons. What is it that troubles you so?"

"I fear for Diego," said Magnifico, "and for his people."

CHAPTER FIFTEEN

The bell ending sixth period rang out like a call to arms. Conor and Diego left their classrooms and headed toward the quad. As they walked into the sunshine, Jose and Ricardo joined them from the opposite building.

"How you feeling, Irish?" asked Ricardo.

"Okay, I guess."

"You ready for this?" asked Jose.

"Oh, aye, but it doesn't matter, really."

"What do you mean?"

"It's going to happen, one way or another, right? Yolo."

Jose shrugged his shoulders. "Yea, yolo."

"Gotta tell you, though," said Ricardo. "Rafael's pretty pissed off. We've been teasing him all weekend."

"Should I thank you?" asked Conor.

"Just watch yourself," said Diego. "He's been in a lot of fights."

Conor smiled as they approached the gym. "Well, I guess we'll give everyone a good show, then, eh?"

"Just make sure you're awake for the ending," said Ricardo.

The four of them passed through the doors of the gymnasium. Conor looked all around as cheers and cat calls assaulted his ears. He saw Lea and Racquel and a bunch of their friends.

Then he saw Rafael, standing with most of his teammates. They'd won the unlimited division Pop Warner title for two straight years. They played strong, solid football, and they had a great coach who kept them in top physical condition.

Conor walked through the throng of students cheering wildly for both boys. His three friends stayed close behind him, watching for anyone hoping to make a name for himself by getting in a lick or two before the fight started.

They burst through the lines and stood across from the football team. Rafael looked ready to run across the mat without waiting, but the wrestling coach took control immediately.

"Boys, take your shoes and belts off, and empty your pockets. I want to see everything on the ground in front of you."

The tradition of settling differences as an organized sport had changed things dramatically at Diego's school. If a dispute occurred on campus, security took control before things went to the next level. They separated the students, ordering them to report to Coach Carlyle before their next class. A wrestling match was scheduled, the students reported at the appropriate time, and in most cases, a dangerous situation was diffused before anything really bad could happen.

After a semester with adults managing the discipline, a peculiar thing began to occur. The students took matters into their own hands, keeping opponents apart until a match could be arranged. The fact that most matches turned into all-out brawls didn't bother the school so much. Better that they get their aggressions out in a controlled environment than out on the street.

"He looks angry," said Conor.

"I told you," said Ricardo. "We really chirped him."

"And bigger, too," said Conor.

"He's hench, for sure," said Jose.

"Use his size against him," said Diego. "You can't stand and throw with him, he's too strong."

Coach Carlyle called the boys to the center of the mat. The noise in the gym rattled off the aluminum lights dangling from the ceiling, ricocheting back down to the students.

"Shake hands, boys," said Carlyle.

Conor stuck out his hand and smiled. Rafael slapped it away, then spit on the mat in front of him. Jeers went around the circle of students like a wave around a stadium.

"Put these on, both of you."

Conor and Rafael pushed their hands into some twelve ounce boxing gloves. Carlyle closed the Velcro straps and wound heavy tape around each boy's wrists.

"If I say stop, you stop," said Carlyle. "Is that clear?"

The boys looked over and nodded. Even in their warrior moods, they knew Coach Carlyle could pick both of them up in one beefy arm and hold them down on the mat until help arrived.

"If someone gets knocked out, it's over. If someone taps out, it's over. Anything happens after that and you belong to me until the principal gets here. Clear?"

Conor and Rafael stared at each other.

"Clear?" he asked again.

"Yea, coach," said Rafael.

"Aye," said Conor.

"Then get to it!"

Neither boy heard anything after that. The gym exploded with cheers and howls. As hundreds of voices sang out, Conor and Rafael circled the mat, sizing each other up.

The crowd measured fifteen students thick. Word had gotten out within a day of Conor's verbal altercation with Rafael. No one knew if the Irish kid could handle himself, but they all knew Rafael's reputation.

As Conor expected, Rafael charged first, coming straight ahead in a bull rush. With arms stretched wide, he wanted to tackle Conor and make a quick end of it.

Conor waited until the last second and dipped low to his right. He stuck out his leg and swept it underneath Rafael's charge. Rafael went down awkwardly, rolling into a wall of students. A roar went up as he vaulted to his feet again, facing Conor with rage in his eyes.

Conor watched Rafael's legs for another advance. He knew he wouldn't be able to sidestep him all day. He had to stay clear of him, though, if Rafael got his hands on him it would be over quickly.

Rafael came forward again, this time with measured, determined steps. Each time Conor stepped to either side, Rafael would mirror the move with one of his own. He wouldn't make the same mistake again.

When he got close enough he lashed out, flinging his arms at Conor. Conor stepped forward this time, almost walking right into Rafael's chest. He knocked Rafael's arms away with his left arm and pushed his right arm underneath Rafael's neck. He swept his shoe toward Rafael's feet, upending him. The bigger boy floated in the air for a second before crashing down on the mat, flat on his back.

The crowd roared again, but their cheers died quickly as Rafael rolled toward Conor and grabbed his ankles. He jerked his hands and Conor went down like a scarecrow in a tornado.

Rafael was up and on top of him in a second. He held Conor's neck and began pounding away with his free hand. Conor managed to deflect most of the blows, but some found their mark.

Bruises mushroomed on Conor's face before he could hike a leg up and around Rafael's chest. He hurled him off and rolled away, standing quickly. Ripping his shirt off, he wiped his face and checked how much blood had stained the cloth. Then he threw it backwards and spit bloody saliva in Rafael's direction. He waved his hands toward himself, taunting the bigger boy.

"C'mon, oso, is that all you got? They told me you were tough."

Rafael cursed Conor, running straight at him again without seeing the obvious, a very angry Irish teenager. And this time Conor wasn't in the mood to sideswipe the charge.

When Rafael got close enough, Conor jumped straight up. His feet flashed in a blur. Rafael's head snapped back and he went down hard. Conor danced around behind him, yelling at him to get up.

Rafael rose slowly. He wiped his sleeve across his mouth, feeling the huge cut in his lip. He sucked in a mouthful of blood, spitting it on the floor at his feet.

Conor could see it in his eyes. In Rafael's mind, the fight had gone on long enough. He'd let the Irish kid have his fun, and now he was going to end it.

Rafael walked straight at Conor, hands up, ready to ward off blows, whether they came from hands or feet. He would wade in and take whatever Conor gave him until he got his hands on him.

Conor snapped off two kicks, one to the stomach and another to the head. The first landed squarely, causing Rafael to slow a bit. Rafael blocked the second, and it glanced off his cheek leaving an opening. He wrapped an arm around Conor's neck, swung his other arm underneath his flailing leg, and lifted him high off the ground.

Conor felt the mat slap his back and the air leave his lungs at the same time. A second later Rafael smashed an elbow against his temple and knocked him cold. He raised his fist to deliver another blow, but Coach Carlyle grabbed his forearm in an iron grip.

"Fight's over, son. He's out."

Rafael stood, glaring down at Conor. He saw his eyes flutter and then open, and when felt certain Conor could see him, he lowered a glove and held it over his head.

"C'mon, Irish. Get up."

Conor grabbed the leather glove. A second later he was up with an arm around Rafael's shoulder.

"You fight good for a soccer player."

Conor smiled, his cheek swelling.

"We gotta get you fixed up," said Rafael, "if you're planning on seeing my sister."

"You hit hard," said Conor.

"Just wait 'til Coach Morales sees you at practice tomorrow," said Jose. "This is gonna feel like raindrops."

"You wanna be next?" asked Rafael. "Here," he said, handing Conor over to Jose and Ricardo. "Take him."

"Good fight, oso," said Diego, fist bumping Rafael.

Coach Carlyle walked both boys over to a bench in the corner of the gym. He opened an old Marine Corps ammo box he kept in his office and started removing first aid supplies. He retrieved a pair of scissors and began cutting away the tape holding the gloves on.

"Jesus, kid," he said to Conor. "Did you have to block so many punches with your face?"

Conor smiled. "I just wanted to make him look good."

"Yea?" said Rafael, "you made me look great."

Carlyle patched Conor up quickly. He gave him a handful of gauze and bandages, instructing him about when and how often to change the dressings. "It'll look way better tomorrow morning after the swelling goes down.

"Alright, Rafael, you're next."

"I'm good, Coach."

"And I just joined a convent."

Laughter bounced around the gym, releasing much of the tension leftover from the fight.

"You're going to need at least four stitches on that lip."

"I don't have time to go to the hospital. I have to study."

"It's either me or a professional, take your pick. That lip is split wide open. Walking straight into a flying front kick isn't the smartest thing you ever did, son."

Rafael touched his lower lip. It felt fat, numb, and definitely split into two pieces. "Pretty good, Irish," he said. "You'll have to teach me that someday."

"Class begins the day after soccer season ends," said Conor. He looked up at Rafael's teammates. "Anyone's welcome."

"Okay, Coach," said Rafael. "I'll go to the hospital, but only if you take me."

"I'll get my car." Carlyle pulled his whistle around his neck and shot a blast that made everyone cover their ears. "I want this gym cleared in five minutes. This boy needs medical attention. I can't leave until everyone's gone and the gym is locked, so scram!"

Lea walked up to her brother. "¿Estás bien, hermano?"

"Yea," said Rafael. "I'm fine. Talk to your new boyfriend. He's the one that needs the help."

"Conor?" she said, tipping his chin up so she could see his face. She winced as she looked at the bruises. "You don't have to fight for me."

"I wasn't. But you can pretend I was, if it will make you like me more."

She smiled and cradled his cheek in her hand, then left with the rest of the students filing out of the gym.

"Okay, Rafael," said Carlyle. "Let's go." He turned to Conor. "You'll be all right?"

"Aye," said Conor. "I've got my friends with me."

Diego and Jose picked him up by his armpits. Ricardo grabbed his backpack.

"Hey, Irish," said Rafael.

Conor looked over.

"See you tomorrow?"

"Aye," he said, smiling.

CHAPTER SIXTEEN

"Jesus, Conor," said Coach Morales. "What truck ran you over?"

Conor smiled and started jogging onto the field.

"Whoa," said the coach. "Come here, son." Morales checked out his face and right arm. "Take your shin guards off."

Conor took off his cleats and pulled the shin guards over his socks.

"That's it," said Morales. "No practice for you today."

"Coach!" said Conor quickly. "It looks worse than it is. I can practice, promise."

"You've got too many bruises, Conor. For God's sake, they're bleeding into each other. You get blood pumping into those too fast and you might be out for the season. I won't risk that for one practice. Besides, we'll need you this Saturday against Vista."

"Can I stay out here?" asked Conor. "I just want to be with the team, okay?"

"Okay, Conor. But if I see you so much as throwing a ball in, I'm pulling you from the Vista match. Your health is more important than a soccer game."

The rest of the team ran drills and plays for over an hour, taking breaks whenever Morales called for them. Conor was always there, tossing towels and passing out water bottles, even helping Diego give encouragement to the other players.

"Don't let Ricardo box you in on the sidelines like that, Marco.

Think about what you'd do if he were coming at you with the ball. Break away quicker, make him guess instead of allowing him to dictate the action."

"If he was defending me," said Ricardo, "I wouldn't have to do anything but run straight through him."

"You wish, Bobo," said Marco, one of the younger players on the varsity squad.

"An In n' Out burger says he goes right around you in three tries," said Conor.

"You better sit down, Irish," said Ricardo. "I think you're losing it after the beat down Rafael laid on you."

"Right after practice," said Diego. "Today, in three tries."

"C'mon, Ricardo," said Jose. "The kid's nothing."

"And I get to coach him," said Diego.

"You can be his girlfriend, for all it'll do for him," said Ricardo. "Okay, after practice."

Marco looked over at Conor, who looked at Diego, who looked back at Marco and nodded.

"Back on the field, boys," yelled Coach Morales. "Let's run the special plays we diagramed for this weekend."

After practice the coach held a quick meeting on the field.

"We've got two more days to get ready for Vista. Those guys have been playing together since they were in diapers, so don't get any ideas about how you're going to trash talk them out of their rhythm. They have a great coach, they're disciplined, and every one of them can score.

"Oh, and one more thing. Their goalie has a wingspan like a 747. If you're going to go for the sidebars, make sure he's not positioned where he should be, in the middle of the goal. He's too fast and too sharp to blow one by him, unless it's a rebound and he's got no chance to recover."

"Why don't we just forfeit, coach?" asked Diego.

Morales snapped his head around, glared at him.

Diego stared right back. "We're damn good, you know."

"That's exactly the kind of attitude that's going to make you lose this match. If you boys go in there too confident, they're going to make you look like idiots. Is that what you want?"

"Easy, Coach," said Jose. "Nobody said that. We've been working our asses off, that's all, and all we've heard is about how great every other team is. We're good too, right?"

"You guys are *great*," said Morales, "and that's the last time I'll ever say that. Our team has unlimited potential this year, and I don't want you bobos blowing it by being overconfident. We're going into every game completely prepared and totally humble."

The boys started to get up and grab their gear.

"I didn't dismiss you guys."

They all looked around, whether seated or standing.

"You all worked hard over the summer, and it shows. I'm impressed by the way you guys trained. I'm proud of all of you."

Diego looked around at his team members. They all checked each other, wondering who might speak first.

"Now get the heck outta here!" Morales stood and stretched his back. He watched as about half the team ran toward the locker room. About five boys remained on the field, looking like they were lining up for drills.

"What's going on?" asked the coach. "I said you could leave."

"Nada, coach," said Jose. "We're gonna show Marco how to look stupid trying to get past Ricardo."

Marco smiled, lowering his eyes.

"We got your back, buddy," said Diego, slapping Marco's shoulder as he jogged by him. "C'mon."

Coach Morales saw Conor walking toward Marco as well. "Uh uh, Conor, you heard what I said earlier."

"I'm not going to do anything but help him, okay coach?"

Ricardo stood about fifteen yards downfield. He paced back and forth like a jaguar in a cage. His honor was at stake, and he wasn't about to let a seventh grader get the best of him with a soccer ball.

Diego, Conor, and Marco huddled together, hands on knees, talking quietly. After a minute, Marco broke away from his teammates and ran toward the sideline.

"Remember," said Diego. "That's an In n' Out number one combo for both of us if he passes you in three tries."

"And burgers for Jose and me if he doesn't," replied Ricardo. "I'm hungry already."

Diego tossed a ball in. Marco let it bounce twice before picking it up in stride with his right foot. He kicked it forward, dribbling it toward Ricardo, who suddenly ran full speed and executed a perfect tackle.

Ricardo kicked the ball up to his knees, bounced it a few times, then headed it back to Conor. "That's one," he said.

Diego waved Marco over. "That's okay," he said quietly. "There's no way he's going to try that twice, so don't look for it."

Marco glanced over at Ricardo, then back to Diego. He brushed a few blades of grass from his jersey.

"He's going to shadow you this time, make you fight for the ball, and the whole time he'll drive you closer and closer to the sideline."

Marco looked over to Conor, who had the ball slung between his arm and hip.

"Don't let him force your hand," said Diego. "When he gets close, move the ball where you want and make him react. He still might take it away from you, but he'll have to work to do it."

Diego looked at Marco, lowering his head so he could see into the younger boy's eyes.

"Got it?"

"Yea."

"Don't worry," said Diego. "It's just fun, and it'll help you learn."

Diego smacked Marco on top of his head. Marco turned and ran toward Conor, who tossed the ball toward the center of the field. Marco took it cleanly on a bounce and ran hard toward Ricardo. He dribbled the ball furiously as he charged his teammate.

He'd heard Diego's words, and as he hustled down the field, he saw a flicker of panic in Ricardo's eyes.

Ricardo ran up to challenge him, but Marco had incredibly quick feet. He watched his younger teammate guide the action toward the center of the field for a moment and then cut to the outside at an impossible angle for him to intercept him. He ran like the wind, but Marco had him cold, so Ricardo did the only thing he could, he dove headfirst and grabbed the ball like a goalie.

Marco went flying, head over heels, landing on his butt and skidding a few feet. If he hadn't been laughing so hard, he might have called 'foul' on Ricardo for touching the ball illegally.

Conor and Diego didn't care. They were laughing too, but they screamed and tossed imaginary yellow cards into the air. Even the coach got into the action, whistling Ricardo repeatedly as the poor kid lay on the ground holding his belly.

"That's two burgers for using your hands," said Diego.

"No way!"

CHAPTER SEVENTEEN

"¡La tierra! ¡Alli, la tierra!"

Captain Pizarro emerged from his cabin, telescope in hand. A soft breeze tickled his chin as it drifted through his beard. The lace border at the top of his shirt fluttered against the underbelly of his neck. He brushed it away twice, then dismissed it as another irritation of his superior rank. He braced himself against the railing, extending the glass and looking toward land.

"Furl all sails," he ordered.

"Furl sails!" shouted the mate.

The crew jumped into action. After several months at sea, their excitement about the prospect of stepping onto dry land couldn't be contained. The sails disappeared up the masts, as if a giant had grasped the yardarms and rolled them up in his hands. Sailors and soldiers flew about the deck, preparing to dock the ship close to shore.

"Rowers to their stations," said Pizarro.

"Lower all boats! Rowers to their benches!"

"Fifteen degrees port, helm."

"Fifteen degrees port!"

The huge wheel spun slowly. With the sails up, and the ship barely moving, two soldiers had to help the helmsman steer.

Dozens of rowboats splashed down beside the ships. Sailors jumped aboard, grabbing oars and waiting for their comrades to join them. Others fastened thick ropes around the foremast and forecastle, tossing the lengthy twines beyond the bowsprit to the boats waiting below. With a master yelling cadence on each row-boat, the oarsmen quickly matched each other's pattern. They propelled the ship forward, the men groaning with each grueling pull.

Pizarro peered through his scope, eyeing the coastline like a cormorant seeking a freshly laid nest.

"There," he said, handing the telescope to his mate. "Your anchor point."

The mate looked through the scope, sighting along his captain's outstretched finger. "The inlet?" asked the mate. "The one shadowed by the large rock formation just beyond it?"

"The very one," said Pizarro. "Buen hombre." He clapped his mate on the shoulder. "With the gold we bring back for the crown, I'll be able to give you your own vessel."

"Aye, sir," said the mate, straightening his posture. "Muchas gracias, Capitán."

"Call me when we've dropped anchor."

Pizarro cheered his crew before turning to reenter his cabin. Their praise peppered his shoulders as the door closed behind him.

He shrugged off his scabbard, setting the sword delicately against a corner locker. Rolling his maps up one by one, he inserted them into their containers.

He looked around slowly, scanning the cabin for his extra passenger. He sensed nothing, but that hadn't saved him in the past. The spirit spoke without substance, moved about the cabin without disturbing a mote of dust. It even slithered along his shoulders once or twice, either to reassure or terrify him.

He felt nothing and decided to trust his instincts. For the first time in over six months he let his breath completely leave his body.

He neither cared where the spirit had gone nor how long it might be away. The darkness surrounding his soul during the journey had finally departed. He would enjoy a few moments in the light.

He turned and knelt in front of the cross he'd placed over his berth. Bowing his head, he prayed for his queen, for the crown of España, and for the safety of his crew and family. Holding his hands together before his chest, he reaffirmed his belief in his mission.

The queen had charged him with finding new civilizations and trading for or confiscating their gold. The spirit had given him a new course to follow, but that mattered little. He would perform his duty and return to Spain. Once there, he would ask the crown to discharge him from military service.

He felt his kneecaps grating against the hard wood of the ship. He resisted the urge to move as he daydreamed about his wife and his home in Zaragoza. With the help of the Holy Trinity, this final voyage would bless him with enough gold to buy freedom for his family for generations to come.

He would deal with the native peoples fairly and with respect, but also with a firm hand. If they would not trade for what Spain desired, they would feel the sharp edge of their swords, the sting of their muskets. If they stood aside and let the soldiers take what they wanted, they would not be harmed.

"Capitán?" Three harsh raps sounded on the door.

"Yes," said Pizarro. "What is it?"

"The anchor is down."

"Prepare to disembark."

Nobles and soldiers ran wildly about Tenochtitlan, the great capital of the Mexica empire. Word had come that floating vessels had appeared beyond the forests that guarded their city against the endless sea. The God of the temple had spoken, telling them about the men emerging from the ships.

"Huitzilopochtli speaks," said the high priest, one of the few permitted to enter the great temple. "We must attack and destroy them, those are his words!"

The four nobles standing anxiously in front of him trembled at the thought of their God awakening after the long years of silence. "We will prepare," said one of them. "We will welcome them into our city, treat them as honored guests, feed them, and then take them prisoner."

Agitated, the priest stepped forward, challenging the noble. "Do you question the words of our God? If we take them prisoner and they escape, they will destroy us."

After patiently listening to the words exchanged by the high priest and his nobles, a strikingly handsome man stepped through a doorway and approached them. Brilliantly colored cloth encased his midsection, draped around his shoulders into a flowing cape, and fell from an elaborate headdress. He wore gold arm and leg bands, and a necklace bearing enough jewels to support a Spanish family for a year.

"Great one," said the high priest. "Huitzilopochtli has spoken. We will be overrun if we don't destroy the strangers."

"We know nothing about them," said the noble. "They could have superior weapons, or they might be coming in peace."

Moctezhuma gazed at the sky. "Have the stars traveled from the land to the ocean? Has anyone seen the ghost woman, or heard her cries during the night?"

"Our God commands us!" shouted the high priest. Immediately bowing, he shuddered at his stupidity. He dared not raise his eyes.

Dismissing his protests, Moctezhuma motioned toward the doorway with his hand. "Have the captain of the guard prepare his men. Do not move against them until the nobles give the signal. We must reassure the strangers that they are in no danger. You will instruct our soldiers not to kill any of them unless forced to do so. Do you understand?"

The high priest rose, glaring at the noble, whose position did not allow him to give orders to the guardians of the temple. Nevertheless, he obeyed.

"It will be done," he said.

"Huitzilopochtli was wise to select such a patient and devoted servant," said Moctezhuma. "The jungle will delay them. We have many days until they arrive. Let us make good use of the time."

Like the unfurling legs of a spider, the group of rowboats fanned out toward land. Controlled by eight strong soldiers, each boat turned and slithered toward shore.

Francisco Pizarro stood in the lead boat, one leg balanced on a plank, the other tipped slightly over the front rail. He looked majestic in full uniform, the chains and charms of his native country shining brightly in the midday sun. He squinted, looking ahead for any sign of humanity.

"There," he said, pointing his hand to the left. "Follow my arm as we get closer to shore."

The men rowing Pizarro's boat stared at the lead oarsman. He alone would maintain eye contact with their captain. They would pull until their shoulders felt ready to explode, and then keep pulling. They owed their captain their lives, for he'd seen them through three violent storms and guided them back toward the wind on many occasions.

The other rowboats took their cues from Pizarro's. They held a tight formation, everyone watching everyone else, keeping themselves safe from harm, whether from land or sea.

After twenty minutes, the lead boat pressed into the soft, blonde colored sand. Pizarro stepped over the rail onto dry land. He turned and took the flag of Spain from one of his men. As he stalked up the shoreline, the soldiers in his boat disembarked and rushed to his side. The loosed their swords, making certain the scabbards hadn't fouled during the passage.

The other boats hissed as they pushed into the shoreline, and soon Pizarro had nearly fifty men standing around the flag, ready to advance through the forest and find any native inhabitants.

"Climb that outcropping." he said to one of the nimblest of his men, "Find the way to a city."

"Aye, sir," said the soldier before turning and jogging toward his objective. He'd gotten less than fifty feet when the bushes parted, giving Pizarro and his men their first looks at Mexica warriors.

"Impressive," said Pizarro.

"And striking," added an officer of the guard.

"But hardly formidable," said Pizarro. "They have no armor, and their shields are not made of metal."

"Their spear tips certainly look deadly," said the officer. "Look at the man on the right."

"They obviously weren't sent here to detain us, or do battle. They are only six in number."

"The forest might hold more, so keep your guard up."

"My guard is never down, sergeant," said Pizarro.

Without fear, the warriors walked toward the strangers. Their eyes expressed no hostility. Curiosity seemed to outweigh other feelings.

"What do we do now?" asked a soldier.

The man in the lead held his spear aloft. Pizarro's men tensed, many reaching for their swords.

"Hold," commanded Pizarro. "Release your weapons."

His men complied. Pizarro looked at the Mexica warrior, asking for guidance with his eyes.

"Come," said the man his own tongue.

"The men from boats five and six will remain here," said Pizarro. "If you see any sign of aggression, have two men take each boat out of arrow's range and wait for us."

Pizarro gave a signal to the Mexica, motioning to him that they would follow. Then he turned back to his men.

"If we're not back within a week, return to the ship and launch all boats. Tow the galleons as close to shore as you can and offload the horses and all our battle gear. Head inland through the jungle and find the city. Demand our release, and if they do not comply, attack without mercy."

"Si, Capitán," said the ranking soldier, saluting.

⊓⎍⊐

"They come," said Huitzilopochtli.

The high priest touched his forehead to the ground. He felt the cool sand and crumbled shells pressing against the skin below his hair. His legs and feet throbbed from kneeling for so long, but it comforted him to stare at nothing. He'd lifted his eyes once, only to see the stone deities staring back at him. Certain he'd seen one of them move, he pressed his head into the sand and stayed there, afraid to look up.

"You must watch the nobles closely," said Huitzilopochtli. "They may try to bargain with the strangers to gain power among our people. If they are successful you will lose influence."

"They created the plan themselves," said the priest. "Moctezhuma would not allow me to set your wishes in motion. I don't know where to place my trust."

"Do you question the strength of the walls around you? What would happen if they suddenly crumbled, much like your faith in me?"

"Oh, Huitzilopochtli, my God," said the priest. "I will forever be your servant. My devotion to you is as strong as the jungles guarding this city."

"Let it always be so. Do not anger me again or I'll cause the ground to tremble, my temple to collapse."

The priest's forehead pressed harder into the sand. If he could have pushed his way into another world he would have. His body shook as he prayed silently.

"Watch the nobles," said Huitzilopochtli. "If they do anything but follow their original plan, have your soldiers kill them and then the strangers as well."

"As you command," said the dazed priest. As best he could on his aching limbs, he rose without looking and backed out of the temple.

Pizarro marveled at how quickly the Mexica moved through the thick forest. After four exhausting days, he and his men dripped sweat as they struggled to keep up. Many times the native warriors had to halt their progress to allow the strangers to catch up and reassemble.

"How much longer?" he asked of his guide.

The lead Mexica stared at Pizarro, unmoving and mute.

"They can't understand us," said Pizarro's soldier.

The warrior slapped his spear against his body, then pointed it toward the forest. He and his party disappeared into the brush. With a single look behind him, the warrior motioned for Pizarro to follow.

Never having seen so many different trees clinging to each other, the soldiers felt the woods must be haunted. The winding branches became heavier with every step. After they pressed one aside another would slap against a leg, arm, or their entire body. It became a battle of wills, and the jungle was winning.

"How will we find our way back to the ship?" asked the sergeant, gazing about at trees of every description. "We'll never see a trail or be able to keep a target ahead of us."

"Faith, Cardona," said Pizarro. "Our Lord has led us this far. He will not leave us to stumble through this forsaken jungle forever."

Pizarro turned his eyes forward again, nearly walking into the back of a Mexica warrior. All of them had stopped at the edge of a stand of roots that were so thick, Pizarro wondered if they'd gotten off track.

"Come," said the warrior, jabbing his spear forward.

They stepped through as if the roots weren't there. Pizarro matched their footfalls, and as he did, he saw light emerging from a few cracks here and there. The farther they moved through the vines, the less dense they became.

As if accessing a doorway, the Mexica stepped through a final brace of branches, out of darkness and into the light.

Pizarro followed. One by one, his men, sweating and filthy, emerged from the forest. Without a word, they lined up abreast of one another, every one of them staring, eyes wide with wonder.

Rimmed by mountains and within the center of a vast lake lay an expansive city. The architecture and detail stunned Pizarro and his men. A precise system of canals meandered through the structures, working their way toward the center, where a group of large, impressive buildings nested within an area completely free of any foliage. It seemed as though everything had been raised from within the lake by some feat of engineering unknown to the Spaniards.

A lengthy pathway led from the edge of the forest toward the entrance to the city. Pizarro followed its track, looking onward as it fed into a grid of roads and aqueducts.

"I don't believe it," said Sergeant Cardona. "There must be a hundred thousand people living here."

"Twice that many, I'd say," said Pizarro.

"Tenochtitlan," said the lead warrior proudly.

Pizarro stepped forward, stood next to the man, mouth agape. "Who built this?" he asked. "How long has it been here?"

"Tenochtitlan," repeated the warrior. "Mexica Tenochtitlan."

"This must be their city," said Cardona. "They built it. Look at the warrior's face, it shows in his expression."

"Come," said the Mexica. "Come."

"Watch yourselves," said Pizarro, "and each other."

The soldiers held a tight pattern, even while looking upon the marvel of the Mexica empire. As they moved through the city, people of every description gazed at them. Markets selling a spectacular assortment of goods thrived, bizarre animals moved freely about, and children laughed, touching their shields and armor before racing away.

They passed huge stalls where the aroma of delicious foods assaulted the soldiers' stomachs. They'd eaten sparingly in the morning because of their abrupt arrival. Starved after the lengthy hike, they felt ready to rush forward and eat everything in sight.

The lead warrior watched the soldiers closely. He motioned for

Pizarro to look upon a high wall. Then he imitated himself eating. He pointed again toward the higher elevation.

"Just a little farther, men," said Pizarro. "I think our hosts have prepared a meal for us."

A light cheer rose up amidst the soldiers. They quickly fell into step behind Pizarro, who followed the warriors up the stairs.

Six levels further up, a magnificent courtyard opened before them. It appeared to be a theater, or some type of entertainment area. The tables set around the arena contained more food than the soldiers could eat.

Cardona nearly jumped out of his shoes trying to get at the meal. The rest of the soldiers stood ready to follow his lead.

"Hold," said Pizarro. "It looks like we'll eat soon enough. We won't offend our hosts by diving in before we're invited."

As if awaiting a signal, four nobles suddenly emerged from a dark hallway. Magnificent in their gowns and jewelry, they walked single file toward Captain Pizarro. When they reached him, they fanned out, standing in perfect sequence with each other. Moctezhuma appeared, then walked forward to stand amongst them.

The noble who'd spoken to Diego in his dream tried to make the captain understand they'd been sent to welcome them to their city. He waved his arm in the direction of the food, then at Pizarro's men.

"I have come on behalf of..." began Pizarro.

Moctezhuma held up two fingers, waving them by his ear. Then he also pointed to the tables, motioning urgently for Pizarro's soldiers to eat their fill.

Pizarro smiled at Moctezhuma, no doubt the leader of the Mexica people, and then nodded toward his men. He pointed to the beautifully dressed man and then at the tables filled with food.

Moctezhuma understood, but again he signaled for Pizarro's men to eat. He smiled at the captain, waving his hands toward the tables.

Pizarro turned to his men. "Eat as much as you want, gentlemen, but don't be lazy about it. I want to conclude our introductions and get back to the ship as soon as we can."

The men descended on the tables like locusts.

Moctezhuma and the nobles couldn't hide their disgust as they watched a horrible display of uncivilized behavior. Pizarro's men didn't bother with plates and cups. They ate right from the tables, grabbing whatever they could and stuffing it into their mouths.

The soldiers began to joke and yell amongst each other. Scraps flew from their mouths as they ate and talked at the same time. Some even used their swords to cut meat away from bones when the pickings became slim.

Pizarro stayed with his hosts, and only when one of them brought him a plate did he relax and enjoy the food. He ate cautiously, minding what he saw in the expressions of the nobles. Even though he saw the disdain in their eyes, he refused to criticize his men. They'd been on a long and treacherous voyage and deserved a break from orderly behavior.

As the soldiers tore through the food, they paid little attention to anything outside the courtyard. Hunger had overcome every other consideration. Those few moments were all Moctezhuma needed.

From eight different entrances, two hundred Mexica warriors flooded the arena. They surrounded the conquistadors, giving them no room with which to draw swords or defend themselves. Spear points, laced with deadly poison, dangled inches away from every soldier's neck.

"What?" asked Pizarro. "What is this?" A man used to having his orders followed, he dropped his plate and demanded an explanation.

Three spear tips appeared from nowhere. Each closed in on Pizarro, causing him to back into a wall of Mexica warriors.

Moctezhuma removed his weapons as speedily as if he'd spent years in Pizarro's uniform. After handing them to one of the warriors, he motioned for the rest of the conquistadors to disarm.

The veins in Pizarro's neck bulged as he sorted through his options. He found few to his liking. He had walked into a trap, and worse, he'd brought his best men with him.

"Drop your weapons," he ordered. "Everything, down to the smallest knives in your vests. Don't give these bastards a reason to stick you with one of these lances."

His men complied. As they did so, a dozen warriors moved through their ranks, collecting the weapons.

Cardona looked at Pizarro, pleading silently to let him fight. His captain shook his head as he watched their weapons disappear down a hallway.

A soldier named Acalan directed Pizarro and his men to a different entrance. At first they wouldn't budge, but when their captain ordered them to comply, they walked single file toward the passageway.

Pizarro sent his men along, one by one. He patted each one on the back, assuring them they'd be safe and well cared for. He had no idea what to expect, but he would keep a good attitude for his crew.

After the last had passed him by, he fell in line just ahead of the largest of the Mexica warriors. He wasn't especially tall, but

Pizarro could tell he was incredibly strong. Without their weapons, his men would have no chance against these sturdy, well trained men.

Followed by Moctezhuma, the nobles led the assembly down through a maze of levels and hallways that finally ended in an unlit, underground cell structure.

"We've done nothing to deserve this treatment," protested Pizarro. "At least provide us with proper guest quarters. You have our weapons. Certainly you don't believe we'll revolt with bare hands?"

The warriors quietly guided Pizarro's men into rows of rock walled rooms, each capable of holding four or five occupants. There were no doors on the cells, but six of the small rooms fed into a skinny hallway guarded by a disciplined group of Mexica guards. If the conquistadors hoped to escape, they would have to run single file into a group of men holding poison tipped spears.

Pizarro entered his cell along with three other soldiers, still objecting to their treatment.

"We have twenty times this number back on our ships. They have orders to attack your city if we don't return. You are sealing your own fate by keeping us here."

Acalan stared at Pizarro with neither love nor hate in his eyes. He didn't understand the man's words, but as a seasoned warrior, he understood a hostile threat in any language. He tried to make Pizarro comprehend the penalty of any attempt at escape.

"You're all savages," screamed Pizarro, "a backward race of creatures unworthy of the crown's mercy!"

Chapter Eighteen

Magnifico and Estrella descended through the roaring flames of the sun. They acknowledged a member of the Sol Dragones here and there, greeting them warmly as they passed. As they landed, they saw a half dozen of the largest dragons in Magnifico's army, with Misterioso standing first among them. Some of his guard sat grooming their scales, but even so, Magnifico could tell they'd be ready to fight to the death in an instant.

They'd been given the ultimate honor, defending the entrance to Sol's inner chamber. No one other than Magnifico could enter, unless another dragon accompanied him, of course. On this day Estrella walked beside him. With his black scales glistening, and hers aflame in golden splendor, the pair gained everyone's immediate attention.

"Greetings, Misterioso," said Magnifico.

"My lord," said Estrella.

"May the sun warm your souls for all time," said Misterioso.

Magnifico turned and nodded to the others. Their expressions gave him comfort. They would die protecting the chamber, even if it were only Sol within. With Celestina accompanying him, their resolve burned hotter than the sun's fire.

Misterioso changed colors a dozen times before vanishing completely. He padded by Magnifico silently, seeing if he could sneak around his backside.

"If I hadn't known a second ago you stood before me," said Magnifico, "I couldn't tell where you are now. I applaud you, Misterioso, your efforts at secrecy should be commended."

Misterioso's body flashed brightly, becoming white hot like the sun. A moment later it cooled, shifting to its normal coloring.

"Have you chosen another mate, dragon?" asked Estrella. "There are many worthy females who would be honored to share time with you. We need more dragons with your remarkable abilities."

"Quiet, woman," said Magnifico. "We're here to discuss matters of importance."

"Hush," said Estrella. "What could be more important than rebuilding our armies, or have you forgotten the cost of the Rift battle?"

"I've forgotten nothing," growled Magnifico. He turned away, addressing Misterioso again. "Let us fly together later. I want to see how well you've trained your guardians."

"As you wish, my lord."

"Come, Estrella."

"So, in the sixteenth century, the Spanish conquistadors came to what is now Mexico and destroyed the Aztec civilization?" asked Sullivan.

"Yes," said Jenna. "That's how I remember it."

"That's what our history books show," said Racquel.

"Their destruction came about by disease as much as by force of arms," said Jenna. "Is that not correct?"

"Again," said Diego. "That's what our books say. I've been reading a lot about it lately."

"Is there anything that stands out about the period in history, something we could use that Satadon hasn't thought of?" asked Sullivan.

"I doubt the Lord of the Dark Rift would let anything pass by him unnoticed," said Jenna.

"There must be something."

"Nothing that I've seen," said Diego. "But then again, I'm searching through middle school library books."

"Did he say anything in your dream, Diego?" asked Racquel, "something about the ancients or the Dark Rift?"

"No, but the dream's getting hazier. I'm having trouble remembering it."

"There must be something in Mexica culture that can help us," said Jenna, "perhaps their traditions or their deities."

"What about math?" asked Racquel. "The Mayans and the Aztecs were the first in the Americas to understand how to work with mathematics."

"Yes," said Jenna, "in the areas of engineering, astronomy, agriculture, and many other applications. That could be the key, or maybe a combination of math and their Gods."

Diego had his laptop up and running a second later. "It'll take a few minutes for me to login to the library's Wifi. There are tons of professional articles that might help us."

"Is there a restroom?" asked Sullivan.

"Over by the entrance," said Racquel, "to the left of the information booth."

"Greetings, my children. May the light of love warm your spirits always."

Magnifico and Estrella bowed low in the presence of Sol. Their scales peeled away from their bodies so they could accept the purity of his being. They stayed in a position of submission, waiting for the fifth sun to greet them.

"Rise, dragons," said Celestina. "Never bow before me, for it was you who freed me from the Dark Road."

"We can do nothing else, mother," said Estrella. "Your greatness demands our utmost respect."

"I demand nothing from you or from any creature hoping to gain warmth from my existence. I live to serve you, Estrella, and you, master dragon."

"I await the day when your kindness spreads throughout the galaxy like a blanket of newly formed stars," said Magnifico.

"Tell us your story, dragons," said Sol. "What have you learned?"

"Satadon has gained powerful allies," said Magnifico. "The ancients have appointed him their guide."

"It cannot be," said Celestina. "Throughout the long eons, the ancients have never chosen sides. Nothing has proven important enough to wake them, not even the battle for the Rift."

"Sol?" asked Magnifico. "What might have happened if Vipero had defeated us? Would he have gained the power to destroy earth, upset the alignment of the galaxy, and taken control of your spiritual power?"

"Vipero himself could do nothing," replied Sol. "Even Satadon's powers would have faltered if he'd attempted such a transformation."

"Then how..." began Estrella. "No!"

"Yes, my daughter," said Celestina. "Only the ancients could summon the forces necessary for that type of planetary alteration."

"But why?" asked Estrella. "Why would they wish for such an outcome?"

"That is something we may never know," said Magnifico. "But we better prepare for the worst. If the ancients have joined with Satadon, we must plan for anything."

"Their powers are unknown even to us," said Sol. "They've hidden themselves for so long, even we cannot understand them any longer."

"The Mexica developed their own set of symbols," said Diego. The hand, heart, and arrow were used in agricultural measurements."

"What does it mean?" asked Sullivan.

"Shh, my love," said Jenna. "Let him finish."

"I'm trying to find measurement systems relative to space."

"Or time," added Racquel. "Remember, Satadon appeared in your dream during Mexica rule, in the sixteenth century. We've got to find out if they ever discovered anything about time displacement."

"Not possible," said Sullivan. "Humans have never come close to understanding time travel."

"Diego and Racquel looked around at Sullivan. "No one we know about, right?" they said together.

"They were a brilliant people," said Jenna. "Modern anthropology and paleontology hasn't scratched the surface of their accomplishments and knowledge. The symbols alone have confounded researchers for the last five decades."

"Exactly the reason to dismiss it," said Sullivan. "What are we going to find that's eluded professionals for fifty years?"

"You don't mind if we try, do you?" asked Diego, without looking around.

"Of course we don't," said Jenna.

"As long as we pursue other avenues as well," said Sullivan. "Remember, we still don't know where Satadon is, nor do we know what his plans are."

"I know where he is," said Diego.

"Me too," added Racquel.

"The question is," said Diego, "how do we get there?"

"I sense no sign of Satadon in our galaxy," said Sol.

"Has he left?" asked Estrella. "Perhaps he's used the Dark Rift to escape to another universe."

"Anything is possible, now that the ancients have joined him."

"But where would he go?" asked Magnifico, "and for what purpose?"

"May we consider another possibility?" asked Celestina.

"Speak, mother," said Estrella. "Share your wisdom with us."

"Where might not be the question," she said. "We are thinking one dimensionally. Maybe the question should be when."

"Of course," said Magnifico. "The battle in the Rift is over. He can do nothing to alter its course. But if he were to go back in time..."

"I don't see the logic," said Estrella. "Drifting back in time would place him before the Rift Lords he killed. They are wise and shrewd. They would discover his plan through his memory of the future, and they would destroy him."

"How can we know he'd stay within the confines of the Rift even if he traveled back in time?" asked Sol. "The ancients have the power to upset galactic alignments. Certainly they could disrupt the ebb and flow of time to suit their guide."

"Then I ask you again," said Magnifico. "Where would he go, and why?"

"He's here," said Diego, pointing to a heading in an article, "in the land of the Mexica, five hundred years ago."

"I agree," said Racquel. "It's the only thing that makes sense."

"Would you explain it to us?" asked Sullivan.

Diego looked at Racquel and shrugged his shoulders. "I don't know why," he said. "I just feel it. He was there in my dream. So was Magnifico, at least in statue form."

"What did he say?" asked Racquel. "Do you remember anything specific, something that might convince us?"

"He told me we would all die, that we wouldn't know the place, or the time, but because he was guide to the ancients, our people would die."

"The Aztecs," said Sullivan. "They're the key. Satadon must be planning something in the past that will affect us here in the present."

Diego began clicking through screens of history books describing the conquest of the Americas by Spain. Every so often a picture would appear in the corner of the screen, surrounded by a caption and the accompanying text. After about twenty pages, he suddenly stopped, eyes locked on one particular illustration.

"What is it, Diego?" asked Racquel. "What's wrong?"

"Open your textbook to the page with Captain Cortés's picture."

She dropped her book on the table in front of them. Grabbing a colored page marker, she pulled a group of pages over, revealing the picture.

Diego shook his head. "Cortés isn't sailing to the Americas."

"What do you mean?" asked Sullivan.

"I knew it that day in class, but I was so intent on the spirit I saw in the wall, I..."

"Tell us, Diego," said Racquel.

"Satadon ordered Cortés to turn back to Cuba, to *not conquer* the Aztecs. Cortés refused, but Satadon threatened him, he almost killed him in fact. Then Cortés swore on his mother's and father's lives he would sail back to Cuba and follow his governor's orders.

"This man, Captain Francisco Pizarro," he said, pointing to the picture on his laptop screen, "he's the one Satadon is bringing to destroy the Mexica people."

"How can you be so sure?" asked Sullivan.

"The last thing I heard Satadon say before the cabin doors closed was that he'd found a different captain to carry out his plans."

"My God," said Jenna. "He's going to change history."

CHAPTER NINETEEN

"You men!" screamed Pizarro, leaning out of his cell. "Let us out, or call your leaders back. I must speak with them."

The warriors guarding the conquistadors stared at the captain in confusion. They didn't understand a word the man said, and his gestures made no sense.

"Go and bring your leader," said Pizarro, waving his arms wildly in the direction of the exit. He took three steps out of his cell and pointed forcefully up the stairs. "Now!"

The warrior in charge advanced, threatening Pizarro with his spear. He lunged forward.

The spear tip froze an inch from his throat. The guard slowed and stopped moving. Pizarro's men stopped talking, moving, and breathing.

A foul smelling stench filled an icy wave that rippled slowly over the bricks and figurines, smothering the prison in a demonic spell.

"Show yourself, spirit," said Pizarro, more confident than he felt.

"You've seen me," said a voice too low to make out. "After all, it was you who brought me here."

The chill swept over Pizarro's body, locking his limbs in place.

"You will destroy the people in this city," ordered Satadon.

"That is not my queen's wish," said Pizarro, through lips left unharmed by the spell.

"Then I will command them to annihilate you. There will be nothing left, no ships, no weapons, no men. Everything will be burned and cast into the sea."

Pizarro watched with helpless eyes as the horrible spell raced up and out of the prison. With an almost lifelike hunger, it spread over every wall and floor. Just before turning a corner in the steep stairwell, it shifted from dense and cold to clear and mild, like warm water streaming across a ship's deck.

"My latest creation," said Satadon. It will swarm this city and infect every inhabitant. The transformation will be so subtle, none of them will know how they've changed, or how they will help me with my plans."

"If you want to kill them, do so with your spell," said Pizarro. "You don't need us. Let me gather the gold we seek and leave this cursed place. Do what you will with the natives. They're savages. I care nothing for their safety."

"You will serve me, Captain. Your part in this scheme was set millions of years ago. It has already occurred, and will repeat itself many times."

"What do you want from us?"

"I want you to fulfill your destiny, nothing more," said Satadon. "You will wipe the Mexica civilization off the face of the earth. My spell will ensure the additional outcome I seek."

Pizarro stared at the shifting cloud before him. Trying to move his limbs was impossible, and what would he do if he could? He had no weapon, and even if he did, what form of arms could one use against a spirit?

"Agreed," he said. "Let me return to my ships. I'll gather my men and lay waste to the city. We will kill every man, woman, and child within a mile of its borders."

"Do you take me for a fool, Captain?" asked Satadon. "I can't spare the energy to chase you down and sink your boats after you try to make your escape."

"Damn you, spirit. May the God of my father crush you and all your kind. You filled my mind with your lofty promises. I blame myself for believing your lies."

"You will command your troops to prepare for battle, captain. Send your sergeant back to your ships alone. Tell him if he doesn't return with your army, the warriors will kill everyone in this prison. The Mexica are proud and brave, but even if they weren't, they would fight to protect their home."

"How can you be so sure?" asked Pizarro.

"They cannot refuse a request from their God."

"But their God is..."

"Yes," said Satadon, laughing in a hissing whisper. "Huitzilo-pochtli."

CHAPTER TWENTY

The crowd around the soccer field cheered wildly. They'd come to watch the only undefeated teams in the Avocado League play their first match against each other. Escondido's first squad read like a club team's all star lineup. Vista's players rarely found themselves out of position on defense, and their offensive attacks were precise, usually producing excellent opportunities for shots on goal.

Momentum in the game had shifted wildly from one team to the other. Each squad enjoyed periods of supremacy, but the goalkeepers had kept the game close. After fifty-five minutes of play, the score remained tied at one goal apiece.

Diego's coach called time, waving his players to the sideline.

"Only five minutes left, boys," he said. "We need a score. I don't want this thing ending in a shootout."

"What's the play, coach?" asked Ricardo.

"Conor?" asked Morales, looking at the Irish kid, who shrugged his shoulders.

"Jose?" asked the coach.

"Let's play the fade. They won't know it."

"*We* don't even know it," said Conor.

"We know it well enough," said Diego. "Let's run it, coach. I'll come in behind Jose. Conor, you cover the middle."

"Aye," said Conor, smiling. "It might work at that."

"Alright," said Morales. "That's the play. Good luck, boys."

The teams met at midfield. Conor tossed the ball toward Ricardo, who held up his hand and called a fake play. Vista's defender came up to challenge him, and he passed quickly to one of his wingers.

Jose and Diego ran away from the play, fading close to the far sideline. Only one sweeper stayed with them, exactly what their coach had assumed when scouting Vista.

The winger fired the ball down the center of the field. Conor took it in stride, his cleats spitting grass as he left the Vista players behind. When the middle defenders began closing in, his feet flashed and the ball shot toward Jose.

Diego and Jose played the two man game better than anyone in the league. They almost looked like twins darting down the field together. Diego watched the defense form up in front of them. He waited patiently for his friend to draw them in. He smiled as he watched things unfold. The Vista players were reacting exactly as they'd hoped.

An eerie gust of wind rushed over the field. Jose disappeared right before Diego's eyes. The soccer ball bounced once and rolled away, drifting toward the sideline.

Everyone froze. Players on both teams stopped where they stood, afraid to take another step. Most of them looked to Diego, since he'd been closest to Jose when he vanished.

A woman in the bleachers screamed. Jose's mother, in shock momentarily, finally swallowed the reality of what had happened. Her only child, her beautiful son, had been taken by a force she couldn't comprehend. She shrieked again, tried to move, found she couldn't, then gripped the sides of her skull and screamed anew.

Moaning like a mother bear that had lost her cub, she finally pushed her way through the crowd and down the wooden steps.

As she tried desperately to reach the field, friends reached out, not to hold her back or help her forward, but merely to offer comfort.

She heard, saw, and felt nothing as she fought her way onto the grass. She ran to Diego, pleading with the Blessed Mother to bring back her son.

"¿Donde esta Jose?" she asked. "¿Qué pasó a él?"

Frightened beyond understanding, Diego looked to the sideline for guidance. A second later he watched as Coach Morales blinked out of existence. He turned again after hearing panicked cries from the Vista bench. Two of their players had gone missing.

Jose's mother embraced him, screaming her son's name again and again. She yelled into his ear, delirious, sobbing, hoping beyond reason that her pleas would be answered. If she bellowed loudly enough, perhaps the nightmare would stop.

Diego reached out, trying to hug and comfort his friend's mother. His arms collapsed against nothing. She'd disappeared just as her son had, in almost the same location. He felt one of her tears slide down his neck. His eyes went wide. He could still smell Señora Navarro's breath on his jersey. He became blind to everything, took off running in no particular direction, trying to get away from...

The soccer field and the stands erupted in chaos. One after another, people faded out of existence. It seemed as though an invisible giant was playing a cruel game, plucking players and spectators away from their world. People watched helplessly as someone close by them vanished. Not wanting to be next, they rushed in all directions, hoping to avoid the strange force that had taken their friends and family away.

Bodies slammed into each other. Frantic cries spewed forth, some asking their savior for help, others screaming for a path out of the stadium. The crowd surged toward the two gates, trying to punch through the openings like salmon squeezing up a small river.

The first few made it through unharmed. The rest cried out as the chain link fence bent outward, clinging to their clothing and skin like devilish fingers trying to hold them inside the haunted field.

Calls for order and sanity went unheeded. No one realized that the horror had ended, that no more had been taken by the unseen hand. They wanted out, away from whatever terror had descended upon them.

Only after escaping the field did parents and siblings turn and look for their families. Players, finally spilling through the gates, too shocked to shed tears, buried their faces in their mother's and father's arms, clutching them as if they were infants again.

The sobbing began after order had been restored. Ricardo hugged his father fiercely, repeating Jose's name. Two teams of eighth grade boys, so cocky around school, in classrooms, in front of girls, stood with knees shaking as blaring sirens approached.

Back in the stadium, one player sat on his team's bench. With eyes closed and fingers laced behind his neck, he held his head between his elbows. He'd spoken to Diego about strange things, but even with all he'd experienced, the scene he'd just witnessed made his skin ripple like the wind.

"Breathe," he whispered softly. "Just keep breathing."

He listened, hearing tires screeching as cars swerved and slammed against curbs in front of the school. Doors opened. Megaphones blurted out orders. Officers and emergency personnel began attending to the players and their families.

Conor exhaled, slowly unfolding his body. With his head held high, he opened his eyes. Everything seemed serene, as if the match had ended without incident.

He leaned forward to stand, but quickly seated himself again. Another rush of wind, icy and surreal, passed through the stadium like a ghost escaping a prison. Sensing him, the spirit shifted, heading in his direction. It passed over him, around him, trying to move through him. Conor felt the frigid strands, the skinny fingers, trying to grasp his soul.

It released him, leaving him behind, as if discarding something it didn't desire. Conor swore he'd heard a voice moaning its frustration.

He stood, looked to the sky with tear filled eyes, and uttered a phrase he thought he'd left behind for all time.

"Mind of the Creators."

Diego found Ricardo sitting on a bench next to his parents. Medical personnel had a blood pressure cuff wrapped around his bicep. A young nurse stuck a thermometer in his ear. A second later he removed it and tapped the result into an i-Pad. A police officer had crouched down next to him. As softly as she could, she peppered him with questions.

"Do you remember where you were when it started?"

"No se," said Ricardo. "On the soccer field I think."

"Were you close to your friend, to Jose?"

"No, it was my job to play decoy."

"Did Jose say anything before he disappeared?"

"Nada. He was there and then he wasn't. That's all I remember, I swear."

The nurse removed the cuff. He input more data before moving on to another player. The officer stared at Ricardo for a moment, deciding whether to question him further. She touched his arm, and when he looked at her, she smiled before walking away.

Both teams had huddled together after finding their families. On the field they fought furiously, but here, in the aftermath of the attack, they found comfort among each other.

"Ricardo," said Diego, slapping his friend's hand and hugging him fiercely. He turned to Ricardo's mother and father, embracing them as well.

"Are you all right?" asked Diego.

"Si. Shook up, that's all."

Diego acknowledged his friend's discomfort. He gave him the time he needed.

"What happened, Diego? Where's Jose?"

"I don't know."

He saw the look in Ricardo's eyes, the same frightened stare everyone else showed. The police had no answers.

"Son," said the officer to Diego. "Do you feel up to answering a few questions?"

Diego turned. He recognized her from the horse club last year. He didn't like her much, but he realized she had a job to do.

"Sure," he said. "What would you like to know?"

The officer opened her mouth and then disappeared, like a balloon popped by a pin.

Players and parents, finally growing comfortable after the episode on the field, panicked as people began vanishing again. All along the streets surrounding the school, people poured out of homes, screaming that family members had disappeared without warning. Cars crashed in the intersection bordering the school. A crowded city bus slammed into a concrete barrier in front of the entrance, shattering windows and spilling passengers.

Diego looked at Ricardo. His parents had disappeared. A second later his friend was gone.

"Run!" he screamed. "Everyone run!"

Diego watched as they ran for their lives. Some kept going. Others blinked out of existence like victims of a bizarre prank.

The area around the school fell into turmoil. No one knew what to do. None of them could understand, they only knew they didn't want to be next.

Conor came around the corner and saw Diego. Their eyes met, two boys terrified beyond belief.

"Go, Diego, go home," said Conor. "Go to the market, go anywhere, just get away from here."

"Where will you go?"

"It doesn't want me."

"What doesn't?"

"The demon, or spirit, or whatever it is. I felt it, on the field, after everyone ran away. It grabbed me, then let me go."

Diego squinted at his friend. Three people ran behind Conor. Two of them vanished without a trace.

"Go, Diego!" shouted Conor.

CHAPTER TWENTY-ONE

All he could think about was his parents and Esteban. None of them had come to the game, but he'd heard about people on the streets and in homes disappearing. For all he knew his family was gone.

He lived six miles from the soccer complex. He didn't register an inch of it as he ran. Looking in every direction, he waited for others to vanish as he raced by them. He prayed silently for his family. If any of them had been taken...

With his chest heaving, he ran up Jed Road toward his home. He saw people drifting about his neighborhood, some openly crying, others calling names out loud.

"Diego, have you seen Alonzo?"

"Where is Lucia? Have you seen her, Diego?"

"My cousins, where are they?"

He had no answer for any of them. Turning up his driveway, he held his side while limping toward his home.

"Papa! Mama! Esteban!" he cried.

Esteban cracked the front door open. He peeked through the slit, saw Diego, and yanked it wide.

"¡Hermanito!"

He ran out onto the driveway and grabbed his brother. Diego collapsed in his arms. Esteban dragged him into the living room, where his father sat staring at the television. His expression told Diego everything he needed to know.

"Where's Mama?" he asked.

His father's eyes never wavered. A female reporter stood in front of the Escondido city hall. She looked serious enough, but spent far too much time adjusting her clothing and brushing strands of hair over her ear.

"We're here at city hall trying to determine exactly what's been happening. So far the mayor's being tight-lipped. A representative has come out twice to say only that his honor is conversing with law enforcement, emergency, and medical staff to try and sort out what's been occurring today."

An anchor broke in. "Tiffany, can you tell us anything about other areas of the country?"

"Yes, Brian," she said, brushing her hair back again. "Apparently the phenomenon isn't confined to north county San Diego. Every southwestern state is suffering through an identical crisis. As far as we can tell, hundreds of thousands, if not millions of people of Latino descent have disappeared since this afternoon."

"Jesus Christ," whispered Alvaro.

"Dad?" said Diego.

His father made the sign of the cross and looked at the ceiling.

"Papa!" screamed Diego, kicking the ottoman in frustration. "Where's Mom?"

His father continued mumbling as he looked at the screen in horror.

"We don't know, Diego," said Esteban. "She left the senior center to try and make your game. No one's seen her since."

Diego felt his insides bubbling up into his throat.

"The police found her car in a ditch, not far from the soccer compound. There's been no sign of her."

Diego ran into the kitchen. He never got close to the sink. The vomit splashed on the stove, the floor, and his socks. He didn't realize until that moment that he'd run all the way home without his cleats on.

Esteban came in and grabbed his shoulders. "Papa's in shock, Diego. We have to stay here with him, make sure he's okay."

"Mijo?"

It was his father's voice from the living room. Diego didn't bother to clean himself. He ran into his father's arms, sobbing like an infant.

"Mama," he bawled. "Oh, Mama."

Alvaro held him in his huge arms. He rocked him back and forth like he used to when he was a little boy.

"Don't worry, Mijo," he said, suddenly rational again. "We'll find her."

Esteban sat behind his father, staring into his brother's eyes. Without blinking, he sent his message loud and clear. Wherever Magnifico was, they needed him now. He was the only one who could help them, the only one who could possibly understand the sinister magic that had catapulted their community into a living hell.

Diego saw Esteban's plea, and in his brother's eyes he saw the answer. The Mexica. Satadon. The conquistadors. The sixteenth century.

"I'm going to my room for a while, okay Papa?"

"Okay, Mijo. Don't leave the house, though. I need to know that you're safe here, with me."

"I won't, Papa."

He slipped away from Alvaro's arms, flipping his head toward his room. Esteban followed him. As they walked silently down the hall, they heard Tiffany on the television, talking to the mayor of Escondido.

"What plans do you have to protect the people of Escondido, Mr. Mayor?"

"Well, after discussing the issues at length with the police chief, the fire chief, the office of emergency services, and the Red Cross, our plan is to coordinate their efforts to ensure the safety of our citizens."

"Can you be a little more specific, sir?"

"I'm sorry, but I just can't right now. We're obviously dealing with something beyond our comprehension, and I want to make certain our emergency personnel are prepared to deal with any contingency."

The mayor turned and hurried off, back toward the safety of city hall. He obviously wanted nothing to do with the press.

"That was Mayor Al Hebed, commenting on the frightening events that occurred and are still occurring all over San Diego County."

The anchor chimed in again. "It appears this phenomenon isn't confined to the United States. Huge numbers of Mexican citizens, and Central and South American citizens, have also disappeared."

"Our hearts go out to everyone in those countries," said Tiffany, "and anywhere else in the world where this horrible event might be transpiring." She tucked a stray strand behind her ear. "Back to you, Brian."

"Where's Magnifico?" asked Esteban.

"On the sun, I think," said Diego, pulling his socks off. "That's where we left him, anyway."

"We need him back here, and I mean now. If Mama's gone, there's no telling who else might have been taken."

Diego's senses went numb. He couldn't see clearly as a thought formed in his mind. It danced around a bit, trying to signal him.

He pushed Esteban aside and grabbed his cell phone. His hands were shaking so badly he dropped it. He blew the sequence three times trying to check his text messages before Esteban took it from him.

"Who?"

"R-Racquel."

"Jesus. You haven't heard anything yet?"

"Please," said Diego.

It seemed like a month before his brother spoke again.

"She's left sixteen texts for you. The last one was less than five minutes ago. I'd say she's all right. Why don't you..."

Diego snatched the phone and dialed her number. When she answered he almost fainted.

"You're okay?"

"Yes," she said. "I've been out of my mind with worry."

"My mother's gone."

"I'm so sorry, Diego. How's your Dad?"

"Not too good."

"No one in my family's been taken, not yet anyway."

Esteban shot his hands in the air impatiently.

"Racquel, where are Estrella and Magnifico?"

"I don't know. You were with me the last time we saw them."

"And Jenna? Have you seen her?"

"Not since we left the library. What's going on, Diego?"

He heard the fear in her trembling voice. "I don't know, Racquel, but I'm pretty sure about one thing."

"What's that?"

"We were right about Satadon and the Aztecs."

CHAPTER TWENTY-TWO

"Misterioso," said Magnifico. "Fly to earth immediately. Bring Diego and Racquel back here at once."

"My lord, why not use a portal? They could be standing before you in a second."

Magnifico continued, as if Misterioso hadn't spoken. "Don't let them argue. You will collect them and return to Sol without pause. Do you understand your instructions?"

"It will be done."

"Estrella," he said, turning to his mate. "Check with the Spirits of the Sun. Ask the elders to join our counsel. We will meet in the outer chamber."

"My lord?"

"Carry out your orders, my Lady. I haven't time to explain."

"What's happened, my lord?"

"Satadon has begun his attack. It is as we feared. The ancients are with him."

She turned without a word and left.

Magnifico pushed his wings frantically, lifting his body away from the sun. He turned and began flying parallel to Sol's surface. Closing his eyes, he summoned a spell of supersonic speed. Soon, he stopped flapping his wings, allowing the magic to rocket him around the sun.

Dipping his head low, he opened his jaws and roared so loudly his body shook. He held his speed and his voice, telling the Sol Dragones that something horrible had occurred. They would know it was a signal to gather at the appointed place. Those that had conduits were ordered to bring them. Dragons without conduits or guides would attend in a separate pack.

When Magnifico felt certain his message had been received, he released the spell. With his speed decreasing, he turned upside down and glided through the flames. In past times he'd done his best thinking within the brilliant fires of the sun, but on this passage his mind registered only confusion.

The ancients? How could it be? And if they were to awaken, then why align themselves with Satadon?

What of Diego's people? Have they been taken forever? Are they dead? Are they being held in a ghostly prison by some mystical force only the ancients understand? Will Sol be able to bring them back? Will he use my dragons as his army, or is the magic of the ancients beyond even us?

Forms began to appear in the flames around Magnifico. They called to him, indicating their readiness for battle. As their numbers increased, their leader turned upright again, soared in front of them, and led them to the outer chamber.

"We're wanted on Sol," said Sullivan.

"Yes," said Jenna. "I hear Estrella calling me. I'd rather try and find Diego and Racquel. I fear for them, for all their people."

"We can't change what's happened. Maybe the Sol Dragones have a solution, or a strategy."

"Perhaps there is nothing anyone can do."

"Sol has power we cannot fathom. I doubt even he understands the magic Celestina can wield."

The two conduits joined hands. Sullivan drew Jenna close. He kissed her forehead, her cheek, and then tipped his face slightly lower. When his lips touched hers, they both slowly disappeared.

Hundreds of dragons, conduits, and guides shuffled around the outer chamber. No one had emerged to call them to order, so they spent their time talking, questioning, and trying to understand exactly what had happened on earth.

Jenna and Sullivan appeared at the rear of the chamber. They greeted those close by them, then asked after Magnifico and Estrella's whereabouts.

"They haven't left the inner chamber since we arrived," said Misterioso. "But these two have been waiting to see you."

Racquel slid down the dragon's tail and ran to her conduit. She fell into her arms, hugging her fiercely.

"It's all right, dear," cooed Jenna. "Everything's going to be all right."

"Are you coming down, Diego?" asked Sullivan, looking up along Misterioso's monstrous back.

Diego leaned down on the shoulders of the giant, multicolored dragon.

"That's okay," said Sullivan. "I'd feel better up there myself."

"No one is safe, it appears," rumbled a deep, familiar voice from behind Misterioso. "Not anywhere."

Magnifico looked up at Diego. "The broad back of the largest of the Sol Dragones might seem the safest place for you, Guide, but I assure you, when Cortés's soldiers find the right person and kill him or her, it won't matter where you sit or where you hide. You'll disappear as quickly as everyone else."

"Hernán Cortés?" asked Racquel, "The captain of Spanish conquistadors?"

"Yes," said Magnifico.

"He's not the one leading them," said Diego.

Magnifico whipped his head around, glanced at Estrella and then back at Diego. "What?"

"Satadon has shifted the lines of history. Francisco Pizarro, the man who conquered the Incas, is in the Mexica lands with the Dark Lord. I saw him in the vision I told you about, but it didn't register until the day we were in the library. Something was there in his cabin. I don't know what exactly, but it seemed like a spirit."

"Satadon," said Estrella.

"There can be no doubt," added Misterioso.

"It must have been him," said Magnifico, "for that's precisely what's happened. Satadon is with your Captain Pizarro in the year 1519, when the Spanish conquistadors wiped out the Mexica nation."

"For what purpose?" asked Sullivan. "The Aztecs were destroyed by the introduction of European invaders. Why would Satadon alter history by changing commanders?"

"What if by doing so he'd be able to insert a subtle change?" asked Jenna.

"Yes," said Racquel. "Some type of genetic progression that would move forward through every generation for the next five hundred years."

"Very good, Guide," said Estrella.

"Satadon has changed history," said Magnifico, "but in a way we'd never have guessed. He's decided not only to destroy the Mexica people, but also threaten every possible descendent of theirs for all time."

"But why?" asked Misterioso.

The question floated softly above the flickering flames. He looked down at Sullivan, then at Diego. Jenna's eyes followed his, then Racquel's, Estrella's and finally Magnifico's.

"I fear the strategy is also an act of revenge for the battle in the Rift. Satadon is truly evil, and he would annihilate an entire race of people to satisfy his bitter soul."

Misterioso allowed his body to lose its color. Both he and Diego faded into Sol's fire.

"Amusing," said Magnifico, "but hardly a solution."

"But I'm still here," said Diego, after sliding down Misterioso's tail and regaining his former appearance. "So many have died, why haven't I been taken?"

"Obviously, Pizarro's men haven't found all of the people yet," said Magnifico. "And I wouldn't be so certain that those who've disappeared have died. That must be why you and Racquel are still with us."

"But my mother is gone. Don't I have her blood?"

"That is proof enough that those taken in Satadon's purge might not be dead. If your mother had been eliminated, you wouldn't be standing here."

"That's why only certain players disappeared from the soccer game." Diego looked down, remembering his friends. "Jose and Ricardo are gone."

"I am sorry, Diego," said Magnifico. "Both of their parents must have been taken. As I said, though, they may still be alive. That is something Sol and Celestina haven't been able to determine."

"Then we have to find them, all of them, I mean everyone who's gone."

"People are still disappearing," said Racquel.

"The Mexica people scattered when the conquistadors came for them," said Jenna. "Their warriors fought bravely, but against a trained army with cavalry, armor, and an alliance with another tribe, they were quickly defeated.

"But there must be thousands that have escaped into the forests and hills surrounding Tenochtitlan."

"That's the only reason the two of you are still with us," said Magnifico.

"Pizarro will hunt their ancestors down if he is under Satadon's spell," said Sullivan.

"And when he finds them, he will kill each of them without pause," said Jenna.

"Then we don't have much time," said Racquel.

"What do we do?" asked Diego.

"The obvious thing," said Magnifico.

"Don't play with me, dragon. My mother's missing, and you can't tell me whether or not she's dead. What are we going to do to get her back?"

"An interesting choice of words, Guide," said Magnifico, "because we're going back in time to get her back."

CHAPTER TWENTY-THREE

"We need guides," said Magnifico. "We have young dragons that are willing to fight, but I won't bring them to battle alone."

"Guides cannot be summoned so quickly," said one of the elders. "You know this yourself, Magnifico, so why would you ask?"

"We have no time. We must leave as soon as possible."

"Even if we could locate the appropriate guides, we'd need to bind them to their dragons. Their souls must be connected in order for them to function as one being."

"I am aware of that, grandfather," said Magnifico, "and under normal circumstances I would never ask for an exception to the ancient code. But with the all due respect, we ask..."

"I understand, Magnifico, and I answer with equal if not greater admiration. Guides and dragons have been carefully matched since the turning of the first sun. If that process is disturbed in any way, there's no telling what the consequences might be."

"I understand." Magnifico bowed low before the ancient spirit. "Your wisdom, your way, our way."

"Take the dragons you have and their guides, and go with our blessing. Know that you travel in the light of the sun, and whoever flies within the light will find their way to victory."

"A third of our force has been denied to us."

"Those without guides?" asked Estrella.

"Yes," said Magnifico. "The spirits will not create the pairings without the appropriate amount of time."

"Nonsense. Sol and Celestina could alter their compositions to adjust for the shortened training period."

"There must be some reason. They've never led us astray in the past."

"We'll take the dragons anyway. They will serve as our free fighters, without guides, just as ours did during the battle in the Rift."

"The Rift existed in space, my love. This time we'll be trapped inside earth's atmosphere."

"We must find a way. The young dragons are fierce and strong, and they itch for battle. We'd be foolish to leave them behind."

"I will not develop a strategy that goes against what the Spirits of the Sun advise," said Magnifico.

"Maybe you won't have to," said Diego, walking up behind his dragon.

"*You* have a plan?" asked Magnifico, mocking him.

"I have an idea," said Diego. "It might not work, but it's worth a shot."

"Tell us what you hope to do," said Estrella.

"Yes, please," said Magnifico.

"Racquel and I need to get back to earth, right now."

"You're counsel is needed here."

"My counsel? I'll have to remember you said that."

Magnifico burped a large, orange cloud of flaming smoke.

"You need all of your dragons to fly, don't you? Then let us leave and go to earth and talk to some people."

"I'd rather you stay here," said Magnifico.

"He's worried about you, Guide," said Estrella, "but he's too proud to let you know."

"Quiet, woman," said Magnifico.

"If what we've spoken of is true, it won't matter where I am if my father's ancestor gets killed. You need an army, and you can't take the young dragons unless they have guides, or at least riders, right?"

"And you're going to find them?" said Magnifico. "Where?"

"Never mind where, just get me back to earth. I order you to take Racquel and me, and I mean now."

"Misterioso!" boomed Magnifico. "Heed my words!"

"At your command," said the giant dragon.

"Take Diego and Racquel home, immediately."

"At once, my lord."

"Become invisible the moment they are aboard, and don't leave their side for a second once you've delivered them to their destination."

"I understand," said Misterioso. "How will I know when you'll need me to return to Sol?"

"Follow your instructions, dragon. If I have further orders, you'll hear of them."

"Why not send us through a portal?" asked Diego. "You said time is important."

"Don't be a fool, boy. For all we know, Satadon has flooded the portals with spirits. They could be looking for you everywhere."

"But..."

"Go with Misterioso or stay here on Sol," said Magnifico. "The choice is yours."

"Come, Diego," said Misterioso. "Up you go." He snatched the guide by the collar and hoisted him up onto his shoulders. "Where's that pretty girlfriend of yours?"

"With our conduits, I think."

"Hold tightly to each other," said Misterioso, as he punched through the earth's atmosphere. A frozen field began forming at the dragon's nose. Spreading around the huge shoulders and torso, it created an impenetrable barrier that protected Diego and Racquel as they rocketed around the planet.

Diego buried his face within Misterioso's scales. Racquel nestled hers in Diego's side. Together, the three of them penetrated the highest part of the sky.

"It's incredible," said Racquel, after lifting her head and opening her eyes. "Look Diego, you can see the Americas."

As Diego watched the continents grow nearer, they flew directly over a squadron of F-22 Raptor air force jets. He wondered if their technology would be able to spot a camouflaged dragon and his two passengers. *Now that would be an interesting battle.*

After another twenty minutes, they cruised over the middle school. A few students were milling about in the quad, hanging around the tables, waiting for first period.

"Perfect," said Diego, pointing to a spot by the soccer field. "Just drop us there and you can go."

"You heard my lord. I won't leave your side. I'll die before I let anything happen to you."

"Fine. Just try not to knock over a school bus."

"Diego," said Racquel. "Apologize!"

"I'm sorry, Misterioso. If you hadn't shown up in Vipero's lair a year ago, we might not be alive. I appreciate your protection."

"No need to apologize, Diego. After all, you're only thirteen years old."

"And how old are you, dragon?"

"In your years, it's hard to fathom. But if I had to guess, I'd say somewhere close to three hundred thousand years old."

"Wow," said Racquel quietly.

"Yea, wow," said Diego.

"I suppose I've lived half my life. If I see another span equal to the first half, I'll die happy."

The first bell sounded in the school yard.

"We have to go," said Racquel. "Will you stay here and wait for us?"

"If you need me, call, and I'll be by your side in an instant."

CHAPTER TWENTY-FOUR

"Órale," said Diego to Rafael and the others gathered around the tables.

"What's up?" said Rafael, tossing his head back a little.

"Listen," said Diego. "We only have a second, so I want you to spread the news. Tell everyone to meet behind the gymnasium at lunch today."

"Why?" asked one of Rafael's teammates.

"You'll find out then," said Racquel. "Please, just come, all of you, especially you guys," she said, pointing to Rafael and his buddies.

The second bell sounded. The students scrambled, running to their first class. After what had happened during the last few days, it was a welcome relief to have order in their lives.

After a quick lunch in the cafeteria, over a hundred students gathered behind the gym. They sat or lounged around, waiting for Diego or Racquel to step forward. Some fiddled with their cell phones, but mostly out of nervousness.

Diego walked through the group, touching as many as he could along the way. Racquel followed behind him, giving her fellow students the same encouragement. They'd all been through an awful experience. They needed a plan, but what they longed for was security.

"Thanks for coming," said Diego. "We're sorry about what's happened to your families. I'm worried about Jose and Ricardo. My mother's missing, too, and I'm pretty damn scared. I wonder if I'll ever see her again."

He lowered his chin, sucking in a breath before continuing.

"How many of you have lost someone you love?"

Arms began rising around the group. Within a minute every student there had a hand up. Some were openly crying, others held fear in their eyes, almost all of them had that far away look of lost children. They were caught in a nightmare they couldn't escape. They wanted their mothers and fathers to tell them it would be okay, but in most cases, one or both parents had disappeared.

"What if I told you that you could do something about it?"

"Don't mess with us, Diego," said Rafael. "My mother's gone, and my aunt and uncle, too. So are all my cousins."

"He's not joking," said Racquel. "There's a way we can all help, a way that might scare you even more than what's happened so far."

Everyone quieted down. Lost eyes regained hope. Bodies straightened, a few students shared muffled comments.

"So," said Rafael. "What's the deal?"

"It'd be better if we showed you," said Diego.

"Don't run away, any of you," said Racquel. "You're about to meet a friend of ours." She glanced at her lookouts, who gave her thumbs up. "Misterioso, if you please."

The students heard an unpleasant grumble in their midst. Many of them stood, preparing to run from another spirit that might snatch some of them away.

"Stay calm," said Racquel. "Please, do you think I would harm any of you?"

They settled, and behind a girl most had known all their lives, a dragon nearly twice the size of the gym appeared. Its skin glittered with every color known to them. Its scales and expression left them speechless, frozen where they stood.

"This is one of the Sol Dragones," said Racquel. "His name is Misterioso, and he's here to protect us, all of us."

As well as he could, Misterioso bowed his huge head. As a group, the students carefully moved forward.

"There are hundreds of dragons who live on our sun," said Diego. "A lot of you met one of them two years ago when I won that writing contest. Remember the dragon statue I won? He came to life, his name is Magnifico, and he's their leader.

"I'm his guide, kind of a buddy for him. Racquel is a guide also, to a dragon named Estrella. Estrella is Magnifico's mate."

"We're called upon from time to time to ride with them," said Racquel. "It's incredible."

"Most of the dragons on the sun have guides," said Diego, "but there's a group who don't, not yet anyway. The elder spirits won't allow these dragons to go into battle without them, and there's no time to find any. I told Magnifico I could probably find some riders."

"How can you ride something that big?" asked Rafael.

"It's weird at first," said Diego, "but with a little practice it gets easier. The bad thing is we don't have a whole lot of time for everyone to get used to it."

"You've all seen horses, right?" asked Racquel. "All you have to do is find a scale that feels like a saddle. Then you find another one to hold onto, like reins."

"You," said Misterioso, motioning to Rafael. "Climb up my tail and sit on my shoulders. Show the others it can be done."

"Go on, Rafael!"

"Get up there!"

Other students began shouting encouragement. Rafael looked at Racquel, who smiled at him. He caught Diego's eye next. His friend nodded toward the dragon.

Rafael walked over to Misterioso's tail. He carefully stepped onto it, about six feet from the tip. He crouched, grabbed the small scales for balance, and then walked the rest of the way using his hands and feet in a crab-like motion. He got to Misterioso's shoulders and squatted, plopping down on a huge scale. He grabbed three or four scales in front of him, selecting one to balance himself. He looked out toward the other students.

"¡Jinete de dragón!" called a student.

"¡Viva Rafael!" shouted another.

One of Racquel's lookouts whistled sharply. She held four fingers, indicating that four adults, whether security, coaches, teachers, or whatever, were coming their way.

"Misterioso!" she cried. "Disappear, now!"

He vanished, as did Rafael.

The lookout signaled again. They were coming straight for them. When they turned the corner to investigate the informal gathering, one of them might walk right into the dragon.

"Hold on, Rafael!" she shouted.

"Misterioso, fly!" said Diego.

With no warning, Rafael was launched into the air beneath fifty thousand pounds of dragon. He shouted, but no one heard him. In seconds he'd been rocketed high into the sky. The fact that he hadn't reappeared was the only way the others knew he'd managed to stay aboard.

"Hello, Diego," said Coach Carlyle.

"Hey, coach."

"What's everyone doing out here?" asked Principal Ibrahim.

"Just hanging out," said Racquel. "We're a little freaked out, and we wanted to be somewhere alone together."

"I think that's a great idea," said Ibrahim, "and I don't mind at all. Just let us know where you're going to be, okay? You all had us pretty scared for a while."

"Sorry," said Racquel.

"And I'm sorry, too. We've all been through something terribly frightening."

"Does anyone know what happened?" asked a student. "Do they know anything?"

"I'm afraid not," said the principal, "and people are still disappearing. Not as fast as before, but it hasn't stopped."

"We're just glad all of you are safe," said the coach. "We're happy you're here, but don't let me catch any of you out here after lunch. I want your butts in your fifth period classes when the second bell rings. Clear?"

Almost all of the students nodded. They liked Coach Carlyle. The few that weren't nodding had their noses tipped to the sky, as if searching for something.

"We'll leave you kids alone," said Ibrahim. "I'm always around if you need me."

"Me too," said Carlyle.

They turned and walked back toward campus. They'd barely cleared the far side of the gym when the students began to hear Rafael's screams.

A second later a thick gust of wind ruffled their hair and clothing. Rafael's voice rang true and clear as Misterioso banked hard and returned to the gathering. None of the students could see him yet, but they heard fear and excitement in his panicked cries.

The lookouts signaled Racquel again.

"It's all right, Misterioso," she said.

Like a special effect in a movie, the huge dragon materialized before their eyes. Rafael also appeared, gripping the scale with all his strength.

"You ride well," said Misterioso, "for someone with no training."

Rafael half slid and half fell from the dragon's back. Several students helped him stand after he tumbled to the ground.

"How was it?" one of them asked.

"Was it hard to hang on?" asked another.

"Would you do it again?"

"Can I ride next?"

Racquel walked over to Rafael. She hugged him fiercely. "Thank you, oso grande, you showed everyone it can be done."

"Órale," said Diego. "Muy bueno."

Over a hundred students crowded around Misterioso, touching him, asking questions, hoping to be the next. The dragon took it all in stride. He was as much a showman as Magnifico, and he didn't have to keep up an image of leadership among his kind.

"You'll all get your turn, I promise," he said. "Maybe not with me, but each of you will have a dragon of your own."

The students exploded in conversation and laughter. The

excitement among them couldn't be contained. Thirty minutes prior, they'd been wondering what had happened to their world. Now they felt hope, and not only that, they'd get to rescue those they loved.

"Listen," said Diego. "Everyone, please listen."

"Hey!" shouted Rafael. "Shut up for a minute!" When the crowd settled, he looked at Diego and nodded.

Diego smiled. "Thanks." He turned to the students. "We only have two minutes until the first bell for fifth period. I want you all to swear to something. Promise me right here and now that you won't tell anyone about this.

"It's more serious than you know. There are evil spirits lurking about, listening, looking for those who would try and help our people. No one can know about Misterioso, or the other dragons, or that you will fly with them.

"We'll leave sooner than you think. Be ready, because when the dragons come to earth, they'll find you and expect you to leave with them. Don't think about which dragon belongs to what person, just run up the tail of the nearest one and get ready to fly."

"Where are we going, Diego?" asked Rafael.

"Yes, at least tell us where," added a few others.

"Back in time, to the year 1519, to the lands of our ancestors, the Mexica."

"And then?" asked Rafael.

"We're going to destroy the soldiers of España, the Spanish conquistadors."

CHAPTER TWENTY-FIVE

"No, Conor, we cannot interfere."

"You won't do anything? Even after the story I just told you? They need our help."

"What they need, they will receive from Magnifico and the dragons of the sun. He is a worthy commander."

"What if they can't win?"

"If the situation were so dire that we felt certain every dragon and guide would perish, we still could not help them. This is their world, Conor. If I or any of the other Champions crossed over, there would be consequences."

"You came to earth to find me."

"No, others performed that task. I found you on one of our worlds. That posed no danger."

"Every one of you came to earth to fight the killer corridor, remember? Even the creators helped."

"The power of their presence prevented the disaster I describe."

"What could happen?" asked Conor. "What's the *worst thing* that could happen?"

"The reincarnation could be in jeopardy."

"So?"

"If the soul of the first warrior became unstable, there's no telling what might happen. He might disappear and never return. He could turn to evil. A thousand other possibilities exist.

"Interference in Diego's world could cause unspeakable damage to the time flux created by the destruction of the killer corridor. Portals could become so distorted they would be unusable.

"Is that what you wish, Conor? After what you learned during your travels with me, are you still so selfish?"

"Is it selfish to want to help others in their time of need? Did you not teach me to forget yourself and help your friends?"

The golden cougar knelt next to a blazing silver portal. Large enough for the cat to step through, the wall with the sizzling membrane in its center seemed alive. It looked as though it breathed as steadily as the cougar sitting beside it.

He had come at Conor's summons, and against the wishes of his mistress. The last time any of them had visited earth, it almost meant the end for Conor's world. If the first warrior hadn't prevailed over Nemelissi, earth would have been wiped away from the stars. Soon afterward, the glade of Champions and the realm of the creators would have met the same fate.

"Yes, of course," he said, "but your eagerness to help Diego blinds you from the truth. If we take part in this battle, the system you helped stabilize could fall into chaos."

"Everyone in the inner element died," said Conor. "There's no one left to threaten you."

"And we wish to keep it that way."

"I'll command you to help me. You know who I am, and you can't refuse me."

"I know who you were, but Trolond Tar commands me now, as he does with all our brothers. He is first warrior, not you."

"But he *is* me!" said Conor, his voice shaking.

The cougar flared his wings to their full width. He stood, as big as a tank, dwarfing Conor, who stared at him defiantly.

"Yes, he is, and can you imagine what would happen if the two of you suddenly appeared together in the same world, at the same time? You *were* him, Champion, but he is himself now, and no one can change that. You are my brother, and always will be, but Trolond Tar is first warrior of the Crossworlds, and we follow him."

"I won't let my friends fight alone. If I have to take a dragon of my own and fly with them, I'll do it."

"That will not be allowed."

"Who's going to stop me?"

"Try and be guide to one of the dragons of the sun and find out for yourself."

Conor kicked a rock a couple of dozen yards. "If you didn't want me to help them, then why did you bring me here?"

"Don't be difficult," said the cougar. "Take hold of yourself. What you ask cannot be granted. I won't sacrifice an entire system of planets for one boy and his dragon. If Diego and Magnifico cannot claim victory, them it's in the stars that they fall in battle."

"No!" shouted Conor. "I'll help them. I'll find a way. Go back to the safety of the Crossworlds. Give my regards to the Lady of the Light."

The cougar turned toward the blazing portal. "If that is your wish, then go with my blessing. But I warn you, do not use the magic you acquired during our journeys in the Crossworlds. Nothing from our system can be used to help the Sol Dragones."

Conor ran to the golden cat, catching him before he entered the portal. "I'm sorry, Purugama, I'm worried about my friends. I've heard your words and I won't forget them."

The tail came around Conor's backside quickly and silently. He never had a chance to deflect it. The tip smacked the back of his head hard, tossing his hair over his forehead like a set of girl's bangs.

"You are as you always were, Conor. I miss our time together." The big cat blinked, slowly. "Believe me, I'd help if I could."

With that, the three thousand pound cougar tucked his wings into his body and jumped through the membrane. He disappeared without a sound, and soon after, the portal folded itself up like a sheet and vanished.

CHAPTER TWENTY-SIX

"Hear me!" roared Magnifico. He looked out at a sea of dragons and guides. They stood within Sol's flames, some of the guides mounted on their dragons, others standing close by them.

They didn't spar amongst themselves, didn't talk or laugh. Their focus lay with Magnifico. He'd signaled an emergency meeting, and even with few details, they all knew a serious situation had developed.

"We must ready ourselves for battle. Satadon has released a spell so powerful it travelled through time to attack Diego's people. His goal is to kill Diego, here, in this time, by wiping out his ancestors in the past. He doesn't care about the millions who've disappeared, they merely served his sick desire for revenge for our victory in the Dark Rift.

"He's succeeded with his plans. Many have been lost, but Diego's people are cunning. Hundreds have fled into the jungles surrounding their cities, and with luck, they will elude the soldiers. We must prevent them from completing their mission.

"Sol has agreed to help us find our way. If we're lucky, we'll be able to sneak up on the soldiers prior to their attack and prevent it before it begins. If we can stop Satadon before his plans succeed, perhaps none of what has occurred on Diego's world will take place.

"I won't mislead you. Satadon is not our only foe. He has recruited the ancients as his allies."

The dragons stirred. Their guides did their best to calm them, but they, too, became uneasy at the mention of the all powerful creators.

"Some of you may be wondering if we're being led into a trap," roared Magnifico. "It may be so, no one can see the future, but nevertheless, we must do our duty."

Magnifico looked out, watching his dragons regain their strength. Their courage could not be questioned.

"Are you with me?"

The hall exploded with roars, snarls, and growls. The guides joined in, screaming along with their dragons.

"Go," said Magnifico. "Prepare yourselves. We leave at the eclipse."

Huge swaths of dragon wings filled the great hall. It looked like a cave of bats suddenly spooked from their sleep. The guides continued their cheers, mixing them with orders for their dragons.

Magnifico looked over to a smaller group, a troop of younger dragons huddled together. Hurling a blast of flame in their direction, he pounded over to them. They gathered around their lord, anticipating their assignment.

"I'm sorry, my brothers and sisters," he said, his head held low. "You must remain here, on Sol. You may not join this battle. The elders have forbidden it."

Protests rose up from nearly all of them. They argued with Magnifico, or amongst themselves, but all expressed their passion to join the Sol Dragones.

"We must be allowed to go," said Noralon, stepping forward in front of the others.

"My brother speaks for everyone," added Nobalon, Noralon's twin.

Shouts of support went up around the group. They would not be denied.

"We'll carry the first wave," said Valiente. "Honor us by letting us die serving you."

"Yes," said many of them. "Let us serve Diego, and you."

Magnifico held his wings high. "You are brave, my dragons, but my answer remains. The elders have spoken. Sol and Celestina agree with them, as do I, reluctantly. We will not risk valuable warriors before they're ready to be paired."

Dozens of eager eyes wilted in front of Magnifico. The young dragons felt defeated, but they would never disobey their lord.

"I'm sorry," said Magnifico.

"Of course we're going," said Sullivan. "I won't stay here and let Diego go up against Satadon, much less the ancients."

"And Magnifico?" asked Jenna.

"He can handle himself."

"I meant he can watch over Diego."

Sullivan kept strolling through the flames. He lost his train of thought for a moment.

"Nathan."

"What?"

Magnifico, Diego, Satadon, the ancients, remember? Are you still with me?"

"I'm sorry, my love."

"What troubles you?"

"The elders. I don't understand their decision. Why would they leave their fastest dragons behind, even if they're without guides?"

"That's why you're going?"

"Of course. Even at full strength, Magnifico's forces will be outmatched."

"How can you be so sure?"

"The ancients created the universe. How can anyone expect to counter that kind of power?"

"And you're sure they'll join the battle? Perhaps the Sol Dragones will be against Satadon alone."

"The Dark Lord?" asked Sullivan, "the one who killed the other Rift Lords? Is that all we should worry about?"

"You don't think he could destroy the Sol Dragones by himself, do you?"

"I know he turned Vipero against his own brother. I know he gave him powers far beyond that of an ordinary dragon. It's possible he gave his powers to Vipero so he could defeat Magnifico."

"If that's the case then we've nothing to worry about," said Jenna. "Vipero is dead. The Dragons of the Dark Rift are gone forever. By your logic, if Magnifico defeated Vipero, he defeated Satadon."

"It isn't that simple, and it doesn't matter. I'm going. They might need me."

"If they have a need for you, it will be here, in your altar room. You know this. What haven't you told me?"

"Nothing," said Sullivan. "You know everything I do."

"Can't I convince you to stay?" she asked, draping her arms around his neck. "Nathan, we're together after so many years apart. Are you really so eager to run away?"

"Jenna, please don't ask me to stay."

"Then let us never be separated again. If you feel you have to do this, then I'll go with you."

"There is great danger there, of a kind we can't comprehend.

This is a culture even Diego's people don't fully understand. There may be magic there that Satadon has mastered. He could use it against Magnifico and his dragons."

"All the more reason we should be there," said Jenna. She drew him close. "Where you go, I will follow. I won't take no for an answer."

CHAPTER TWENTY-SEVEN

"Fool!" screamed Satadon, spitting the word at Pizarro. "Many of the people have escaped. They must be found at once!"

"My soldiers have searched for days," said the captain. "The jungle is possessed. It grabs their arms and legs every time they try and make progress. If you want them found, find them yourself."

"Burn the entire forest if you must, but destroy them. Millions have disappeared from Diego's world, but the most important objective remains. He has survived, in fact both guides still live. Until their ancestors are killed, you will not rest."

"If a person wished to hide themselves in that forest for all time, it could be done. They could be miles beyond it by now anyway, for all we know. I won't sacrifice more men to look for people who may be lost to us forever."

Pizarro turned to leave. As he reached for the key to unlock the cabin door, his hand sagged, the bones and nerves dissolving. He watched in horror as his fingers wilted, dripping flaming pieces of skin onto the wooden floor.

His uniform collapsed around him. He leaned his head back, shrieking when his skin became drenched with liquid fire. Watching the ceiling of his cabin spinning above him, he felt his body bubble into a pool of stinking flesh. What remained supported only his face, leaving him the ability to see, hear, and talk.

"Say the word, Captain," said Satadon, "and I will complete the spell. I still need you, or I'd have disposed of you long ago. Do not anger me, though, or I'll blink my eyes and let the rest of you seep into the well of this ship."

Pizarro glanced at the cross over his bed. He thought of Juliana, his lovely wife. His life suddenly had no meaning without her, without her happiness. Nothing that happened to him could be worse than hurting those he loved.

If he obeyed the spirit he'd tied himself to, he might never be rid of it. Satadon would haunt him forever, always demanding something, perhaps someday even a member of his family as payment for assistance with his current voyage.

His mind ran wild, thinking of every possible conclusion to his predicament. He could find no peace, nothing made any sense. He scolded himself for his weakness.

In the end the love for his woman won him over. He worshipped her, and he would die to ensure her happiness. He'd been led back to his ship after ordering the attack. He had stayed, waiting for his men to return with word of the Mexica people. In between reports, he'd knelt obediently before the cross, praying for hours on end, asking his Lord to deliver him from his horrible mistake.

"I grow impatient, Captain," hissed Satadon.

"I'm busy," said Pizarro. "Let me think."

Satadon whispered a few words.

Pizarro began feeling the wood beneath his eyeballs. His ears had nearly disappeared, and only his lips remained if he dared speak anything other than what Satadon wished to hear.

"It will be done," he said.

"What exactly will be done?" asked Satadon, his voice seething.

"We will hunt down the rest of the people."

"And when you find them?"

"They will be destroyed, I swear it."

A moment after his last spoken word, Captain Pizarro felt the ship beneath the bottom of his feet. With his body restored, his uniform replaced, he turned once again toward the door. He wrestled with his key momentarily before inserting it into the lock. Once the latch had disconnected, he pulled the heavy door toward him.

"Captain," said Satadon.

Pizarro turned.

"Not another word of defiance. I will have my vengeance, with or without you."

"Whether you complete your hellish mission or not doesn't concern me. I have selfish reasons to obey you, and I will do so for those alone."

"I am pleased, Captain. You will have your chance right now. A rowboat approaches with your latest report. You will return with your crewman and see to the battle personally. Take whatever measures you need to achieve your goal, but make certain it happens. I won't be lenient much longer, and the next time you anger me, it isn't you who will suffer."

Pizarro whipped his head around, prepared to warn the spirit not to harm his crew. His words stalled when he saw an image burned into the wall of his cabin. Juliana cowered in a corner of their home. A living fire danced around her, touching her now and then before receding. Her screams rattled his mind, drained his anger, leaving him defeated.

"Someday, Satadon, the Blessed Mother will stomp you with a bare foot the way she did your father. I only hope I live to see that happen."

"Swallow your useless threats, Captain. Obey my orders or I assure you your family will suffer horribly."

The door to Pizarro's cabin slammed so hard the latch bounced before springing open again. Satadon peaked through the gap and watched the captain disappear onto the quarterdeck. After assuring himself that Pizarro would do his bidding, he focused his energy on the temple of Huitzilopochtli. In seconds, the Asesino de mar floated aimlessly on its anchor, vacant of all life. The spirit holding the lives of all of Diego's people, even those floating in a timeless void, had departed to begin the second phase of his plan.

CHAPTER TWENTY-EIGHT

"Come, Diego," said Misterioso. "It is time."

Diego walked up the dragon's tail, hand in hand with Racquel. Once seated on the heavy scales, he looked down at Rafael.

"We need you, hombre," he said. "The rest of them will follow you."

"They'll come," said Rafael. "You heard them."

"I saw their courage with all of us gathered together. When the dragons arrive and each of them has to choose, then you'll see who has the guts to jump onto one of them."

Rafael stood alone, having answered Diego's call to meet him after school. "I'll make sure they're ready. I won't mount my dragon until the last one of them is aboard."

"Gracias, oso valiente," said Diego. "I know one dragon that will be glad to fly with you."

"Bye, Rafael," said Racquel. "We'll see you in the sixteenth century."

Rafael waved once as he watched Misterioso turn invisible. As the giant dragon lifted off the ground, the wind from the huge wings nearly blew him off his feet. He smiled, feeling a flutter of fear dancing in his stomach. Soon, he and a hundred schoolmates would depart on the journey of a lifetime. He had strength, of course, and he would lead them, but he would never tell anyone how scared he felt.

As Misterioso approached the sun's surface, Diego saw Magnifico, Estrella, and a small army of dragons and guides assembled and ready to depart. As soon as he landed, Diego ran and climbed aboard Magnifico.

"We're still without the young dragons?" he asked.

"Nothing has changed, Guide. Are you ready?"

"Wait a minute."

Diego turned and looked at Estrella. Racquel sat astride her neck, poised and ready. He stared at his girlfriend, almost seeing her for the first time. She looked older, like a woman, a warrior woman who'd seen many battles.

She smiled and waved, instantly becoming a thirteen year old girl again. Diego waved back, then held his hand high for all the dragons and guides to see.

"For my people!"

One by one, the dragons roared as they soared away from the sun. The guides waved to Diego, some nodding to him solemnly, telling him they would fight to the death to reverse the horrible events that had befallen his family and friends.

Estrella and Racquel roared over Diego's head, missing him by inches. Diego ducked quickly as the golden tail mussed his hair. He smiled, knowing Estrella would never harm him. Still, the tip of that tail would knock him unconscious before he ever hit the ground.

"Always playing around," said Magnifico disgustedly.

"Maybe she knows something you don't," said Diego.

"Like what?"

"A little laughter relaxes you, gets rid of the nervousness."

"We can rejoice when the battle has ended. Until then, she needs to focus on her responsibilities."

"Don't be a grouch," said Diego.

A volcano exploded underneath him. Magnifico wrenched his body away from the sun, using his powerful legs as springboards, his immense wings as whips. In seconds he'd launched himself miles from the surface.

Diego never had a chance. Head over heels backwards and thrown from his dragon's shoulders, he felt the hot wind of the sun's flares tickling his skin as he rolled and pitched back toward Sol.

A second later, a scaly tail slapped him lightly. He turned the opposite direction, flipping wildly with arms and legs askew. He had no idea where he was, or where Magnifico had gone.

He heard the unmistakable snarl of his dragon, close and then far, then nearby again. The swooping winds from Magnifico's passes tossed him around like a doll dropped onto a highway.

The tail came around again, catching him in midair and tossing him lightly onto Magnifico's back. Diego scrambled to find a scale to grip. He closed his eyes and felt around as Magnifico darted this way and that, trying again to knock him off his shoulders.

Finally he managed to grab a large scale, scoot himself up, and wrap his legs around Magnifico's strong neck.

"What the hell was that all about?" he asked, angrier than he'd ever been at his dragon.

"Rather amusing, wouldn't you say?"

"Oh, please, don't even try and compare that to..."

"I *am* feeling quite relaxed," said Magnifico, interrupting his guide. "I'm beginning to understand what you meant about Estrella's antics."

Diego shook himself, trying desperately to clear his mind. He felt a splitting headache coming on.

"¡Idiota!" he screamed. "When are you going to grow up, and when will ever you stop screwing with me?"

Magnifico flew as fast as he could, using the whistling in his wings to drown out Diego's complaints. He turned his huge, scaly head and looked at his guide. He smiled, throwing a blast of flaming ash toward him.

Having collected himself, Diego ducked and let the cloud speed by him. He did the only thing he could do, he spit on Magnifico's head.

"Feel better, now, estúpido?"

"As I said, I'm feeling very calm."

"I'm thrilled," said Diego.

"Good, now prepare yourself. Sol has given me the correct flight pattern. We will trace the limits of the sun three times before flying directly into its center. When we come out the other side..."

"If we come out."

"Don't joke about that," said Magnifico.

"Just trying to relax."

The huge red eyes turned toward Diego again. They squinted, giving him a look that froze the blood in his veins.

"That will be enough, Guide."

"Agreed," said Diego. "Go on."

"Forget it," said Magnifico. "Just hold on, and keep your fist raised so the others can follow us."

They sped by the other dragons, moving ahead of them and soaring to the right, back toward Sol. Diego held his hand high. He clenched it tightly, and within seconds a sparkling fire surrounded it. It burned so brightly the back of Magnifico's head glistened. Diego saw the creases and cracks in every scale.

He turned and saw Racquel and Estrella following close behind. She'd lowered herself close to her dragon's head, and Diego could see her whispering something. How she heard a word Racquel said was a mystery, but then so much about the Sol Dragones puzzled him.

The other dragons formed a tight group behind her. Their guides saw one thing only, the sphere of flame Diego held above his head. As they flew ever faster, the beacon would be the only way they'd be able to follow Magnifico.

Diego's dragon uttered a short spell. He tucked his wings and let the magic consume him. Rocketing toward Sol at supersonic speed, he led his dragons to their destiny.

Three times they circled, hundreds of dragons that looked like tiny dots against the vastness of the sun. After the third loop, Magnifico activated a frozen field. Turning directly away from Sol at a speed unknown to the ancients, he roared past the appointed distance and banked hard back toward the sun. His dragons stayed with him perfectly, their guides watching Diego and giving them direction through their mind links.

As he entered the brilliant light, Magnifico felt his soul bursting through the source of all life. For billions of years, Sol's spirit had burned ferociously, giving heat and warmth to worlds orbiting around it. He looked straight ahead, hoping to see the wonders encased within the powerful spirit. He saw nothing but purity, and in that virtuous place where all life began, he roared until his voice cracked like a crystal shattered by sound.

Although his muscles ached, Diego held his hand high. The others would need the symbol of their journey, for it was the only light that outshone the sun. Gripping the scale on Magnifico's shoulder, he dipped his head low, praying silently for deliverance.

He didn't feel an overwhelming heat, didn't imagine they'd end up burned to a crisp, like ashes dispersed within the endless mass of the sun's center. Only one thought repeated itself over and over in his mind – please let us reach the other side safely, and at the right time in history.

A pair of sunspots converged at the exact moment Diego and Magnifico burst free into the stars surrounding the sun. Like a hive of angry bees chasing an intruder, the rest of the dragons emerged from Sol's brilliance.

Diego struggled to keep his hand above his head. He yelled until his throat burned, hoping to replace the pain in his arm with another sensation. He held the side of Magnifico's scale as the giant dragon banked hard, turning back toward the sun. He matched Diego's voice, roaring continuously, greeting his army as they appeared in the unsoiled blanket of stars. He never blinked when Estrella banked toward him, twisting at the last second to soar so close Diego and Racquel could have touched fingers.

Magnifico decreased his speed, coasting back and forth in front of the sun, checking the last of his dragons as they popped into view and joined the formation. When he felt certain all had survived the journey through Sol, he flew through the group until he found Estrella.

"Have we made the passage successfully, my lord?"

"We'll find out soon enough. Look below us, my lady."

The solar system surrounded the sun, and Estrella followed his line of sight until she saw a tiny speck, the third planet, earth.

CHAPTER TWENTY-NINE

"Sergeant Cardona!" barked Pizarro.

"Sir!" he answered, surprised to see his captain away from the ship.

"What is the status of our pursuit?"

"We've cleared the forest to the south, sir. Our soldiers are setting fire to the east and west of us."

"That will leave only the north, and the mountains beyond?"

"Yes. They'll be trapped, unless they have caves we haven't discovered."

"Let us hope for our sake they don't."

"Sir?" asked Cardona, confused.

Pizarro shook his head. "Nothing, Sergeant. How long before the people are flushed into the hills?"

"Hard to say. It depends on how thick the forest is. At best, twelve hours, but it could take more than a day."

"Assign as many men as you can, Sergeant. I want those fires raging as soon as possible."

"Shall I send a man for you when we've broken through?"

"No," said Pizarro. "I'll stay here with the troops."

Cardona gave his captain a puzzled look. "We could be here all night, and well into tomorrow. Certainly you have more important duties than overseeing a brushfire."

Pizarro shifted his eyes, giving his officer a look no crew-man ever wished to see. He peeled off his jacket, tossing it on the ground beside him. After looking around, he found a reasonably comfortable rock. He sat, flicking his eyes at Cardona again.

"It will be done," said the sergeant. "I'll see to it personally."

"The strangers set the forests on fire," said a Mexica sentry, after returning from his assignment.

A tall, broad shouldered warrior nodded once. He looked up, sighting his eyes in all four directions. He watched huge plumes of smoke decorate the sky to the south, west, and east. A smaller, thinner wisp began rising from the north, directly behind their position.

The warrior worked his hand through a mane of dense, dark hair. The top had been tied with a leather band, but the rest fell loosely about his shoulders. His cheekbones seemed cut from granite, framing a sturdy, handsome face. The coffee colored eyes missed nothing, and a hawk-like nose inhaled the scent of the putrid chemicals the Spanish had used to fuel their assault on the forests.

A few hundred people huddled around him. Most squatted close by, arms slung over thighs, their breath coming in short bursts. A few days ago they'd been living peacefully, trading, gam-ing, raising their families, and listening to the teachings of the high priests of Huitzilopochtli.

The invaders had come swiftly during the night, butcher-ing their friends and families without mercy or conscience. The Mexica warriors had fought the enemy bravely, but before dawn's light appeared chaos had replaced the tranquility they'd known for centuries. Their city lost, their homes raided or destroyed, the people had followed whoever called them, running for their lives into the very forest they now saw disappearing before their eyes.

The warrior stood before them, a jaguar skin draped over his shoulders. He gazed down into the valley, to the magnificent city his people had occupied for generations. It seemed serene, beautiful, untouched by the horror inflicted on it.

"The hills are our only choice," he said.

"We will be trapped," said a man standing at the back of the crowd.

"The soldiers will overrun us," said another.

"Would you stay here and die?" asked the warrior, turning back to address the people, "squatting before them like a monkey demanding food?"

"We can do nothing," said the first man. "We will die whatever we decide."

A woman clutched a crying child. She rocked lightly, trying to calm her daughter. Her eyes never left the auburn gaze of the warrior standing before her. She'd placed all her faith in him, whatever his decision might be.

"Some of us must die," said the warrior, "so others might live."

Many voices spoke at once. Some supported the warrior's position. Others rose in defiance, blaming him for giving them no means of escape. He'd led them into the forest, beyond the safety of the city, where others might have protected them.

"He has kept us alive!" a man shouted.

"For how long?" questioned another. "We will all suffer the same fate as our brothers and sisters, only with more time to wait until the end."

"Quiet, please," said the warrior softly. His eyes showed how weary he felt, his distress over their loss. What he hoped to propose weighed heaviest on an already tormented heart.

"Chimalli," he said, nodding to a young man in the middle of the group. "Take two hundred of our people and make for the hills. Climb as high as you can, as fast as you can. Don't look back for any reason. It is up to you to save them."

Chimalli rose and bowed. "I am honored, great one, but how am I to choose who will come and who will stay?"

"How can anyone choose?" shouted an angry man sitting in the rear. "Who will say? You, Acalan? We need Moctezhuma's wisdom."

"Moctezhuma is dead. We are all that remain of our people."

Voices exploded into another round of heated discussion. Acalan allowed his people the time they needed to vent their pain. He looked again at the woman rocking the baby, which had fallen asleep in her arms.

She rose without disturbing the child. Walking up to Acalan, she smiled and nodded before addressing the crowd.

"I will stay with you, hero of the people. If it will save another's life, even one of us, I will stay and try and convince the invaders that we are the last, and after they slaughter us they can leave this place with whatever they came to steal."

Acalan knelt before her, touching his forehead to her elbow. "Teyacapan, it is you who are *my* hero," he said with eyes closed.

He rose, staring at those who previously quarreled about his plan. "Go, then, any of you who are weaker than this fine woman. She holds a child in her arms, and knowing what will become of her and her innocent daughter, she chooses to spare you with her courage."

He spat on the ground before his feet. "Who among you can match her bravery?"

One by one, squatting men rose and walked forward. They touched the woman's shoulder before standing next to her. Before long, half the assembly had split into a group behind Acalan.

"Teyacapan," one of the men said. "Go back with the rest. You have helped our people regain our strength. May your daughter receive your courage as she grows to womanhood."

She looked to Acalan, who nodded, smiling at her. With her daughter in her arms, she walked back and sat down quietly.

"We will walk part of the way into the low hills," said Acalan, waving his arm at the group behind him. "The rest of you will run to the mountain behind Chimalli."

He removed his jaguar robe, draping it around the young man's shoulders. "May the strength of Tezcatlipoca be with you, Chimalli, as you lead our people to safety. Go, quickly, my son, the fire rages ever stronger in our forest."

Acalan embraced Chimalli, before holding him at arm's length. He looked into the young man's eyes, injecting the fierce bravery of the warrior into his heart.

"Come," said Chimalli, waving to his people, "to the mountains and beyond."

Those that hadn't volunteered to stay gathered what little they had and stood. They ran as well as they could, following Chimalli toward the hills. They focused on the jaguar pelt, rippling behind their leader as he ran. Soon, a vision appeared before them, a giant cat, black as night, with the faintest hint of jaguar spots flashing in the sun's light, guiding them to the mountains. He turned once, his immense head the size of a man's body, and growled his defiance of the men who'd invaded his lands. He turned back and bounded up the first few rocks, disappearing toward Popocatépetl, the great mountain beyond the city of Tenochtitlan.

Captain Pizarro wiped his forehead with the lace cloth his wife had given him the morning he sailed to the Americas. Refolding it, he caressed his neck, moving it around his shoulders softly. He let his head droop, stretching his knotted muscles. Closing his eyes, he inhaled the stench of the burning rainforest.

"Sergeant," he said softly. No answer came.

"Sergeant Cardona!"

He looked up and saw no one, no living being at least. In Cardona's place swirled the rancid mist of the spirit that controlled his every move. The fire seemed to vanish, although Pizarro could still sense it. The forest, what remained of it, faded somehow, as did the sky. Satadon controlled his vision, and the voice that floated from the mist was the only thing Pizarro heard.

"I have sent him to collect your soldiers, Captain. You will return to your ships at once."

"Are you insane?" asked Pizarro. "We're hours from our goal. The forest will soon burn itself out. We'll be able to hunt the rest down and kill them. That's what you ordered me to do!"

"I am giving you new orders, Captain. The guide and his meddlesome dragon have somehow appeared in the stars above us. They will be here shortly."

"A dragon, here?" asked Pizarro, snorting. "If such a thing even existed, how would you expect me to fight a dragon?"

"There will be hundreds flying out of the heavens by the time you and your men reach your ships. I would begin now if I were you."

"Hundreds? What kind of madness is this? Dragons, here, in our world, and they've been sent to attack us? I don't believe it."

"Look upon me, Captain Pizarro," said Satadon. "If someone had told you a year ago that a bodiless spirit would appear before you, speak to you, bring you halfway around the world, give you new lands to conquer, and threaten your life if you disobeyed, would you have believed them?"

Pizarro gazed at the shifting smoke. The eyes appeared and vanished. The voice had poured forth from the mist, with no organ to carry the sound.

"I'll summon the men at once," he said.

"Run to the shoreline, Captain," said Satadon. "You will find the last rowboat waiting for you. Everyone else is aboard. They've been given their orders. They await their Captain."

"What orders? I gave no such command. Who would dare give orders to my men, Cardona, another officer?"

The silence unnerved Pizarro. He almost demanded an answer. His mouth didn't respond, though, as he gazed at the mist.

Satadon reshaped himself quickly, first as Huitzilopochtli, then as one of the Mexica nobles. Finally, the shifting smoke settled, and Pizarro gazed in wonder at a mirror image of himself.

"How?" he said. "How is this possible?"

"It is a reality you cannot understand, Captain, just as your mind won't accept the thought of an army of dragons descending from space at this very moment.

"I could have killed you the first moment I saw you in Spain, but I needed you to control your men, as I do now.

"Go, Captain, your crew awaits. The dragons will be upon you moments after you arrive."

"I'll fight your sky demons for you, for all the good it will do. They'll destroy my ships and turn my men to ashes, and then they'll find this city in seconds. If it's you they're after, I pity you, spirit. Perhaps my God won't have to waste his time with you after all."

"Aim your cannons at the sky, Captain. Fire your weapons as you would at any enemy. And don't concern yourself with me. I lived long before dragons came into existence, and I'll live to see the last of them die."

CHAPTER THIRTY

The Sol Dragones penetrated the atmosphere, falling into a cloudless sky above the Americas. Magnifico sniffed the hideous scent of the fires before getting close enough to see them. He pulled up, telling Diego to signal the others.

After settling his army in the sky, he flew through the ranks until he found Estrella. Racquel gave Diego a curious look as their dragons floated next to each other.

"What is it, my lord?" asked Estrella.

"We are too late," he spat, turning his huge head toward earth's surface. The anger and frustration poured through his scales like steam from a geyser. "The smoke can mean only one thing. The Spanish have already launched their attack."

"No!" cried Racquel.

"We came all this way," said Diego, a blank expression on his face. "Jose, Ricardo." His breath caught in his throat. "Mama."

"Strike at their ships, my lord," said Estrella. "Perhaps their war has just begun. We must continue, even if only a shred of hope remains."

Diego heard Estrella's comment as if it came from a dream. It took a second, but it jarred him from his trance. "Yes, we must attack now, before anything else can happen."

Magnifico floated silently among his dragons. He considered every thought carefully, eyeing Racquel's expression the entire time. He saw the pain she felt, and also Diego's, reflected in her eyes.

"Sol Dragones!" he roared, "to the ships below!"

Nathan Sullivan descended from a sphere of light. He faced the stairway of Huitzilopochtli's temple. Jenna followed, holding his finger in one of her own. She trusted the transport, it had never failed before, but she desired the physical connection.

"Tenochtitlan," she said, "the great capital of the Mexica empire."

"It's deserted," said Sullivan, glancing all around him at the stunning architecture. Expansive islands rimmed the temple area, each brimming with homes, agriculture, or beautifully groomed pathways connecting the communities. Neither of them spoke for some time as they gazed upon the remarkable city.

"Have we come during a festival? Why are there no people here?"

She couldn't answer. Her finger fell from Sullivan's, and then her body crumpled. She collapsed, falling to her hands and knees in the dirt. She retched, her insides splattering the ancient soil. She knew what had happened, but it wasn't her mind that had told her. Her soul had doubled over, taking her stomach with it.

"The people," she cried, spittle dangling from her lips. "All of them, gone, dead."

"No," said Sullivan. "I don't believe it." He ran to the city walls, leaving his mate behind. After nearing the entrance, he regained his mind and turned back.

"Jenna," he said, reaching down, touching her shoulder. "Can you walk?"

She stared, breathing shallowly. "Yes, a second, please."

Captain Pizarro ran through the smoldering jungle, slapping the charred remains of leaves and branches aside. When he could, he held his hand over his nose and mouth, lest the sour scent overwhelm him. These respites lasted only seconds, for it seemed that every few steps the soil would slide out from under his feet.

At times he fell, failing to brace himself against a tree or the ground quickly enough. He cursed his God, Satadon, his queen, and his mission, anything that might take his guilt from him. He had failed everyone, mostly himself. His greed had blinded him from the simplest of truths, that a life with his family, no matter how meager his income, was worth a thousand kingdoms of earthly wealth.

"Damn!"

He swore again, stopping suddenly. Ripping a dead branch from its trunk, he hurled it through the smoking remains.

"Damn you, spirit, show me the way if I'm to save my men."

He grabbed the medallion dangling around his neck. He wanted to rip it off and toss it away as well. Something held him back, a voice, an impulse, a part of him only he could speak to, his deepest, most secret place, the one he kept locked away from the world.

Gathering himself, he closed his eyes, rubbing the medallion and asking for guidance. Breathing slowly, evenly, letting his mind rest, he waited for an answer. It came in the beautiful face of his beloved Juliana.

His shoulders fell, the crease between his eyes softened. She smiled at him, letting him know that whatever happened, she forgave him. She would love him always and eagerly await his return.

Pizarro's eyelids rose. He saw the same stinking, scorched

forest before him, but panic no longer ruled his mind. Glancing at the sky, then at the ground, he began walking toward the coast. The shadows of the smoldering trees confirmed her direction, and he started running toward his ships, toward a reunion with her. He smiled, certain he would see his family soon.

"It can't be possible," said Sullivan. "All the people, wiped out, down to the last child?"

He and Jenna had raced through the city entrance, running hand in hand down stone hallways, along lengthy canals, into marketplaces, temples, and vast amphitheaters.

"The Sol Dragones didn't arrive in time," said Jenna, "if they even made it through Sol's time portal."

"You don't think…"

"They could be anywhere, at any time in history. For all we know they travelled into the future, or perished trying to get here."

"Sol would never allow it," said Sullivan. "He loves Magnifico. The dragons are as dear to him as children."

"And yet they aren't here, and they obviously didn't stop the slaughter."

"There must be an explanation."

"Come Nathan," she said, "follow me to Coatepec. Perhaps we'll find answers there."

She led him back to the largest market in the city. They looked above the walls, toward the highest structures, the sunlight nearly blinding them as they searched the great city.

Jenna squeezed Sullivan's hand. "There, the tallest temple with the openings cut into the wall facing us. That must be it."

She dashed away, pulling Sullivan along behind her.

Pizarro stopped, placed his soaked palms on bent knees. He spat, spraying his beard, his clothing, the ground at his feet. Lungs heaving, he spat again.

After a lengthy break he straightened, twisting his spine as far back as he could. He wiped his face with a filthy hand, squeezing his beard, ridding it of any surplus sweat and saliva. He pushed both hands through his hair, gliding his fingers through the gristly strands. His sleeve served as a towel for his forehead, whether the brass buttons scraped against his skin or not.

"Capitán!"

The voice made no sense at first.

"Capitán Pizarro! Call out if you hear my voice."

My fatigue plays tricks with my mind.

"Capitán, it's me, Sergeant Cardona. Answer if you can."

A light appeared in the gloomy tunnel. He shook himself, clearing his head. "I'm here, Sergeant! Follow my voice. Find me. Help me through these Godforsaken wilds."

Pizarro stumbled, knees wavering, his mind gone. He grabbed a sticky trunk for balance. Screaming like an infant, he gave his men the signal they needed to find him.

"Capitán," said Cardona after weaving through the jungle toward him. "Thank the Blessed Mother we found you. We thought you'd disappeared."

The men around Cardona visibly relaxed. Their captain may be harsh, even cruel at times, but they knew their only chance to return home stood before them. Many reached out, hoping to touch him, to make sure they weren't pinning their hopes on a ghost.

"As did I, Sergeant. Now listen carefully. Send your men back to the ships." He looked up, past Cardona, at the men surrounding him. "Run as if todos los diablos de España are at your heels, waiting to snatch your souls from you. Return to our fleet and prepare for battle."

"Capitán?" asked Cardona, knowing the Mexica had been all but destroyed.

Pizarro ignored him. "Tell the weapon masters to haul the light cannons onto the main deck and point them at the skies above our ships. Fill them with chain, the longest links we have, the kind we use to splinter the masts of enemy vessels.

"Load every rifle and crossbow in the armories. Lay them across the decks. Tell every soldier that after they fire one, they're to toss it aside and grab another. Assign men to reload the discarded weapons. Find those with the swiftest, nimblest fingers. They'll need to be quick as the wind, have nerves of iron, and courage beyond definition."

For the first time in fifteen years of service, Cardona saw fear in his captain's eyes. "Sir, I don't understand…"

"Blast you Cardona! You men, run as you've never run before. Return to the ships and carry out my orders. The sergeant will guide me back. Send one man to the shore with a rowboat. We'll be back on the Asesino de mar as quickly as we can."

The search team took off through the forest. Fear drove them, fear of their captain, but more than that, the fear they heard in every word he spoke.

"How do you know this is the correct location?" asked Sullivan, pointing to different areas around Tenochtitlan. "I see similar structures surrounding this one."

"If this temple housed your god," said Jenna, "wouldn't you build others to confuse anyone trying to find your most precious place?"

Sullivan counted six more around the city, two pyramid shaped, and four more capped by rectangular frames. They were arranged in a sequence, a pattern arrived at, yes, mathematically. Every one of them seemed like…

"Jenna," he said, grabbing her shoulder, turning her so she faced the other structures. "There's something about these temples, the way they reflect the sun's energy."

"I don't feel it, but perhaps you can sense things I can't." She turned, walked to the entrance, then turned back. "Are you coming, Nathan?"

Sullivan stared a minute longer. He wanted to burn the image of the sequence into his memory so he could ponder it as they searched Huitzilopochtli's temple. Raising his eyes, he glanced at the blazing blue sky.

He reached out, hoping to take Jenna's hand. His fingers scraped against rough stone, and he walked headlong into a solid wall.

Stunned, he raised his hand to his forehead, wiping blood onto his fingers.

He heard Jenna's muffled screams from inside Coatepec, the Hill of the Serpents.

CHAPTER THIRTY-ONE

"Settle yourselves," said Misterioso.

The young dragons jostled for position around their leader. They wanted to show courage, prove their worth, move to the front of the pack, so Misterioso might see them. More than that, they were young, and teenagers never sat still very long.

When they learned they'd be joining the battle after all, and that Misterioso would lead them through the sun, they could barely contain themselves. It was all they could do to keep their excitement from the spirits of the sun. They'd shot into the stars above Sol, careening about like bottle rockets gone wild. Most of the males went mad, sparring with each other to see who would blaze the first trail behind Misterioso. A few of the most eager had to be carried back to the sun and placed in the care of Sol.

The female dragons relied on cunning as well as strength, usually defeating any male they flew against. One in particular showed an incredible gift for battle. Misterioso kept an eye on her, watching her send foe after foe away in shame. He'd seen her during early training periods, when barely past childhood, she'd held her own against older, much stronger dragons.

"Zephyer," said Misterioso. "With me."

The slightly built dragon floated toward Misterioso. The cobalt blue scales shone brilliantly, a sign of humility.

"My lord."

"You will guard my flank. Never leave my side. I will depend on you for my safety."

"I am honored to serve you. If I am to die protecting you, I will do so gladly."

"Let us both honor Sol by returning safely." Misterioso looked forward again, scanning the crowd of anxious dragons.

"Furtivo,"

No one answered his call.

"Furtivo!" he roared. "Blast you into a million galaxies, come forward this instant!"

With the whistling roar of a volcanic fissure, the flames behind Misterioso parted. He didn't have time to breathe, much less react. A bolt of dragon fire bore down on him so quickly he barely turned his head before it exploded against his shoulders.

Zephyer took off after her cousin. Twisting and turning, mirroring his every move, she caught his tail in her jaws. She bit down, hard, and Furtivo squealed with pain and delight. He raced around the training grounds, swinging this way and that, trying with everything he had to send her spinning into space.

Zephyer bided her time, allowing Furtivo to believe she was helpless. She waited until he dipped low toward the rest of the dragons. At the last second she reared up, flapping her wings madly.

Misterioso jumped into the air and caught Furtivo as he tried to sail by him. With Zephyer holding his tail and Misterioso's jaws clamped around his neck, Furtivo's wings couldn't hold him aloft any longer.

The three dragons crashed into the dense flames. Misterioso flattened out on the surface, while Zephyer and Furtivo bounced once and then lay still.

The others inched closer. They knew none of them were dead, but they wondered about their injuries.

"Oh, Zephyer," said Furtivo, laughing like a hyena, "how did you ever catch me?" He rolled over, ripping his tail and neck away from the two dragons. He laughed again, holding his belly scales and squeezing his eyes shut.

Misterioso slammed his tail down. "We leave for battle soon, and all you have on your mind is mischief?"

Furtivo rolled to the other side, trying to hide his smile from Misterioso. Even with this tactic, his shaking body gave him away. He finally turned and faced his leader.

"I apologize, my..." He exploded into a series of uncontrollable giggles again. "My l..."

"Never mind him, my lord," said Zephyer. "If he weren't such an asset in battle, I'd advise against taking him with us."

"Unfortunately, we need him. His fondness for folly will blind the enemy to the rest of us. They'll use whatever weapons they have against him, leaving a clear path for us to follow."

Misterioso turned toward Furtivo and blasted him with enough fire to melt a mountain. The laughter continued, but only for a moment longer. When the inferno died down, the young dragon stood, facing his leader.

"Are you finished?"

"Sorry," said Furtivo, a smile creasing his scales. With all his strength, he smashed his face into a look of solemn attention.

Misterioso coughed harshly, mourning the poor child that would ride the clown into battle. A cloud the size of a circus tent blew forth, billowing against Furtivo. "If you can hold a serious thought for more than a second, I'd like you to watch my other side."

"As you command, my lord."

Zephyer glanced sideways at her cousin, waiting for another round of laughter.

"The rest of you will follow at our heels. Do not fall away from your formations. Fly together. When we reach the center of the sun, you'll have only each other to serve as escort. If you lose sight of your brother or sister once we enter the time portal, you could be lost forever.

"I would mourn the loss of any of you," said Misterioso, "but we must watch out for our young riders from earth. They are not experienced guides. It will be your task to train them in our ways during the journey.

The dragons stirred, unsure of their ability at so young an age.

"We will not be the cause of their death!" he roared. "Serve Magnifico, Estrella, and the suns who gave you life. Place yours before the children who've volunteered to ride with you into battle."

Misterioso looked out at his troops, his first command as one of the Sol Dragones. *Children only,* he thought, *but eager and ready to serve.*

"Have you heard all I've said?"

Furtivo sang out before the other dragons. He stood proudly, at attention, next to Misterioso. He looked across his back at Zephyer. She was family, and while he'd give his life for the new guides, and for Misterioso, he'd sacrifice anything to save her.

She looked over, smiling. She wondered which child would accompany him. Hopefully a boy or girl with a sense of humor, or the pairing might not last.

Blinking her eyes, she extinguished the thought and pushed everything else from her mind. She could see Misterioso straightening himself, saw the look on his face, the determination in his eyes. Her cobalt scales flashed once. He switched his coloring to match hers, then, as if saving it for another time, shifted from blue to a dozen other colors before settling on his favorite.

The young dragons, the future warriors of the Sol Dragones, saw their leader, a multi-colored dragon, the first and possibly the last of its kind, rise before them. More than twice the size of any gathered around him, he spread his gigantic wings to their full width.

"Zephyer, stand ready!"

"I'm here, my lord."

"Furtivo!"

"At your side, always."

Misterioso turned his huge head and addressed the young dragons. "You are trainees no longer. From this moment forward you are members of the Sol Dragones, protectors of Sol and Celestina, and of all worlds beholden to them.

"Fly with me, dragons of the sun!"

CHAPTER THIRTY-TWO

"¡Christo!"

Captain Pizarro blinked. He pulled the telescope away and rubbed his eyes, then looked up again. Closing his left eye, he placed the scope lightly against his right.

"Brace weapons," he ordered.

"Brace your weapons!" shouted the mate.

Prior to Pizarro's arrival, the soldiers, although confused by their orders, had heaved the cannons on deck and elevated the muzzles so they pointed toward the sky. They'd lashed them down tightly with mooring ropes, then slapped wet sandbags around the base of each cannon. Not even a direct hit from an enemy vessel would have dislodged them.

"Top off the touch holes."

"Top off holes!"

At each cannon, one man gently upended a powder horn, filling the touch hole to the point of overflowing.

One sailor had been assigned to the bowsprit and poop deck of each galleon. The orders passed over the shallows from boat to boat. Within seconds, over two hundred and fifty cannons peered skyward.

Rifles and crossbows littered the quarter, gun, and main decks of all seven ships. Soldiers, dressed in full armor, pistols rammed into thick leather belts, searched the world above them. Seeing nothing but bright sun surrounded by a crystal blue sky, they relaxed as a soothing breeze passed by.

Pizarro gazed through his telescope again, still unsure of what he saw. The spirit had promised, and his eyes confirmed the vision, but still...

"Take this," he said to his mate. "Hold your tongue, I don't want the soldiers unsettled."

"Capitán?"

"I need to know I haven't gone insane."

The mate removed his hat, placing it on the ship's wheel. "Where should I point the lens?"

"Look above us, damn you."

Craning his neck back, the mate positioned the scope over his eye. Closing the other, he turned the focus wheel and scanned the sky.

Pizarro waited, eyes closed.

"My God!"

Thirty thousand feet above Pizarro's fleet, Magnifico dropped like a spear from the stars above him. Estrella, wings tucked in attack position, streaked alongside him.

Diego and Racquel glanced at each other. They gripped their scales with hands strengthened by many flights. With hair flattened by the winds, eyelids fluttering, and cheeks flapping, both of them smiled as best they could.

The guides and dragons trailing them flew silently. At times a dragon would shoot a look at his brother or sister, perhaps to encourage, maybe to advise. The guides kept their eyes on the ocean, and in the direction Magnifico took them.

"Insert cords."

The mate opened his mouth to relay the order. A scratchy, nearly silent plea tickled his captain's ear.

Pizarro jerked his head around.

"Insert cords!" he yelled, cupping his hands around his mouth. He looked to the bowsprit to make certain his man had heard him. He saw the reaction, the heave in the man's stomach, and the response of the sailor on the poop deck of the next ship in line.

Hundreds of men scurried into position. Those manning the cannons covered their ears, all except the one standing over the fuse. They'd been trained in their craft, yet still almost half had lost their hearing in previous battles. Cannon fuses flashed instantly, sometimes giving enough time for a soldier to draw his hands back, sometimes not.

"What are they, Capitán?" asked the mate, recalling the tiny dots he'd seen in the sky.

"If I told you, you'd think I was mad, and then yourself for believing me."

"Please."

"Dragons, Señor Aritza, they are dragons, and they'll fall upon our fleet by the time you remember the meaning of your name."

Ship's mate Aritza turned away from Pizarro, a look of terrified disbelief marking his face.

"Prepare to fire," said Pizarro.

Aritza crossed himself and looked to the heavens.

"Prepare to fire!" he yelled.

Magnifico shot five flaming streams, all in different directions. The Sol Dragones divided their forces instantly, executing his battle plan perfectly. Estrella and Racquel veered right, taking a hundred dragons with them. Three other dragons split away from the main group, leaving Magnifico and Diego with enough of a force to draw the fire of the galleons.

They dropped below twenty thousand feet, resembling a pack of falcons speeding toward prey. Diego bent the scale back and wrapped his forearm around it. He dragged the fingers of his other hand through the air, feeling the warmth of the fire gathering in his palm.

At ten thousand feet the monstrous, oak galleons became visible. At a thousand feet Magnifico pulled up, taking his attack group in a wide circle. He wanted to see the ships, smell them, listen for any sign of enchantment.

"They're made of wood," said Diego. "Only the decks and masts contain iron casings."

"It may be only wood," said Magnifico, "but Jenna said it's heavy oak, cured and aged. It will not burn readily, as another lighter wood might."

"The sails, then," said Diego, holding a ball of fire in his hand. "We'll disable them if we take the wind from their sails."

"Look below you, Guide. Do you see any cloth billowing in the breeze?"

"I can't tell from way up here."

"I assure you, the captain has taken every precaution. If his sails aren't stored away below deck, then they're furled tightly to the yardarms. I'd stake my life on it."

"Then we burn the ships with dragon fire."

"That easily?"

"The wood doesn't matter. Dragon fire will melt iron."

"What of Satadon," said Magnifico. "Have you forgotten his part in this battle?"

"He came to strike at me," said Diego, "to kill the descendents of the Mexica people. If he kills me before I'm born, the battle at the Dark Rift could be in jeopardy."

"Everything could be," said Magnifico, "but enough talk. We're in position. Prepare yourself, Guide. We get the first pass."

"Stand ready," said Captain Pizarro.

"Stand ready, men!" barked the mate.

Like trumpets sounding the charge, the roar of a hundred dragons shook the seas surrounding the galleons. Even though ready to abandon ship and dive overboard, Pizarro's men stayed true. Those standing aside the cannons held swatches laced with gunpowder, ready to light and slap against the fuses. The feel of the material against their skin calmed them, the knowledge that they had them boosted their courage. Their eyes, as were the eyes of every sailor and soldier aboard the galleons, stared in horror at the demons falling from the sky.

Captain Pizarro had heard enough. If he let the dragons get any closer, his men would never hear the order.

"Fire all cannons," he commanded.

"Fire!" shouted the mate. "Fire cannons!"

Dozens of powder swatches touched iron. Chains sixty to eighty feet long exploded from the barrels, shooting into the sky like eerie metal fingers. Nineteen cannons lost their footing, injuring a score of Pizarro's soldiers. Replacements quickly moved into position, pushing the heavy guns back into place. Other soldiers stood ready, aiming their rifles skyward.

Three hundred yards above the ocean, Magnifico veered away as soon as he heard the rumble of Pizarro's cannons. The dragons in his squadron followed his line precisely.

"Look!" shouted Diego.

Magnifico turned. He roared a warning that came too late. The chains designed to bring the dragons down from the sky had come alive.

"Satadon!" cried Magnifico.

The cannons should have produced a shot heading straight into the air, easily outmaneuvered by dragon flight. After blasting away from the galleons, the chains shifted their pattern, taking off after the Sol Dragones as if controlled by a magician's wand. Their speed increased as well, they'd approached the dragons' tails in seconds.

Diego held on as Magnifico executed every move he knew, with his dragons trailing close behind him. Dipping, twisting, hurtling toward the heavens, nothing shook the living iron coming ever closer to his forces. With a manic thrust, the chains shot forward, curling at the tips.

Ten dragons fell from the sky, their wings crumpled within the iron links. The sea burst in wide circles, welcoming the dragons as they crashed onto its surface. The guides, pinned to the scales by the heavy chains, could do nothing except beg their dragons to dislodge themselves and take to the sky again. The huge beasts struggled mightily, tails slapping the ocean. Knowing the end was near, they did their best to keep their backs above water, so their guides might have a chance to escape.

"Hold on, Racquel!" screamed Estrella.

Magnifico watched her dive straight for the drowning dragons. "No!" he roared. "Keep away!"

She neither acknowledged nor obeyed him. Their brothers and sisters flopped about in the ocean, struggling, sinking. She sped toward them, taking her force straight to the sea.

"Reload!" bellowed Pizarro. His mate repeated the order, shouting until his throat burned.

Their courage boosted by what they'd seen, the soldiers manhandled the cannons. They swabbed the barrels before sliding in charges, cloth wadding, more chain, and more cloth. They pushed each of these down with a rammer. The touch holes were filled, cords inserted.

"My God," said Pizarro. "How many are there?" He stared at a sky filled with dragons. They'd exhaust their armaments well before they brought down half of them. Turning back to the main deck of his ship, he saw his men awaiting his order.

"Fire, damn your souls. Fire at will!"

The mate, with what remained of his voice, relayed the order. Similar to battles in the open ocean, the ships' cannons exploded in sequence. Pizarro heard the reports, deafening at first, then becoming quieter as the weapons down the line sparked.

The chains reacted quicker this time. They jumped from the mouths of the cannons, targeting Estrella's forces in seconds. They changed direction instantly, accelerating into the sky toward them.

Estrella managed to dodge volleys from the first two ships, but the remaining attacks left a thick chain wrapped tightly around her tail.

"Can you fly, dragon?" shouted Racquel, turning to see Estrella struggling to shake it free.

She responded by lifting both of them away from the sea. She turned, awkwardly, and watched the chains crumple a dozen of her dragons. Cheers came from the soldiers as they fell helplessly, collapsing into spouts of whitewater spray.

Magnifico dropped down ahead of her remaining dragons. A dozen fireballs shot from his mouth, blasting the deck of the Asesino de mar. The soldiers that hadn't dived for the hold were blown fifty feet from the vessel, dead before they made contact with the water. The huge ship rocked and then stilled, held in place by her heavy anchor.

Pizarro knelt by his mate, frantically ripping the sizzling clothing from the man's skin. The fire seemed as alive as the chains. Once in contact with its prey, it burned through clothing like tissue paper. It attacked nerves and muscles, as ship's mate Aritza was now discovering.

"Blast you," shouted Pizarro. "Take the pain, act like the man you are."

He dumped a pail of seawater of Aritza's naked body. His mate screamed anew, his neck straining with ungodly suffering. Pizarro ripped his coat off and draped it over him, covering the flames. In the midst of cannon fire, dragon fire, and thoughts of his family, he dropped onto the man. He would crush the fire with his weight, if his God willed it.

Aritza lay still, staring at the skies he'd hoped to navigate as captain of his own vessel. Pizarro lifted his coat, then quickly replaced it. He vomited at the shocking sight of what remained of Aritza's body.

He dragged a shirtsleeve across his face, tossing the bile aside. On his feet an instant later, he vaulted onto the gun deck, hitting it at a full run. He danced through cannon fire, his eardrums popping. Within seconds he heard nothing. He saw the flashes, though, and the courageous and terrified looks on the soldiers' faces.

"Muskets!" he yelled as he reached the bowsprit. "Crossbows!"

The sailor manning the station screamed the order to the next ship, then turned back, awaiting further instructions.

Magnifico came around again, this time with reinforcements. Half of his and Estrella's dragons flew with him. He'd checked her progress with the chain, saw she couldn't navigate, and ordered her to the skies above.

"I've as much right to this fight as you!"

"Will you sacrifice your guide to exercise that right?" he'd snapped, swerving in front of her and knocking her from her flight line. "You have no rudder, dragon, away with you!"

He took a long look at the ships. He had no idea where the bewitched chains were, but at least he couldn't see them anywhere.

"Close ranks," he ordered. "Follow my path until we're right on top of them."

The guides and dragons cheered their leader. The dragons folded their wings, the guides held their scales, leaning into the drop.

"Valerian!" ordered Magnifico.

"Here, my lord!"

"Fly like the gulls of this world, barely an inch above the water. Soar like lightning and draw their fire."

"My lord!" shouted the dragon, nodding to her guide, who notched her heels into the stiff scales at the base of her wings. She wrapped her arms around the huge scale in front of her, bowing low.

"Taragon!"

He swooped in, silently settling just ahead of his nose.

"Follow your sister. Take whatever path you wish; I trust your judgment. Blast the sky above those ships with everything in your belly and get out of there. We'll be dropping in right behind you."

Unlike Valerian, he descended without comment. Turning away, he floated down softly from the heavens. Also unlike his sister, who sped toward the ships like a rocket, he took his time, evaluating every aspect of his assignment.

Pizarro held the telescope to his eye. The dragons had retreated, the men giving a rousing cheer he saw but couldn't hear. His eyes still worked well, though, as did his mind. He watched patiently.

"Steady, men," he said. "Ready your weapons."

"Rifles at the ready!" shouted his new mate.

The surface of the sea rippled beneath Valerian's advance. Unlike the seagulls that floated aimlessly along, hoping to spy a meal swimming close to the surface, her sleek body screamed across the water, a living missile in dragon form, wings tucked, eyes wide open.

The Asesino de mar shot toward her, rapidly coming into view. Valerian turned on her side, holding one wing aloft like a shark's fin. She grinned, watching the soldiers train their weapons on her.

The muskets erupted, the bullets shifting shape and course immediately. They raced after Valerian like pellets exploding from a shotgun cartridge.

"Cease fire," said Pizarro.

The mate shouted the order. As the command was repeated, soldiers on every ship set their guns aside. Those on the Asesino de mar rushed to the starboard rail. They gripped the stiff oak, leaning far over the rail, hoping to get a glimpse of the streaking dragon. They saw only a shadow lacing the water as she blew past the stern.

Valerian turned again, increasing her speed. Her guide rolled with her perfectly, now able to see the remaining ships just by looking down. Their speed prevented her from focusing on a single vessel, so she glanced past her dragon's tail. She leaned farther in, slapping Valerian on the side, asking her to fly faster as they left the haunted bullets behind.

Two hundred crossbows suddenly appeared over the starboard rails. The soldiers loosed their arrows when they felt the dragon was closest, following an order issued earlier by their captain.

They shot forward, missing their target easily. Then they turned, like the bewitched chains before them. Now flying as a single pack, they raced after her, magically controlled by Satadon's power.

"Valerian!" screamed Taragon, dropping straight down from the sky. He inhaled, signaling his guide he intended to fire. The young alien, a disciplined rider from the Andromeda galaxy, grasped the steering scale in one hand. He raked his fingers through the air, pulling a huge sword of dragon fire from the elements.

Taragon arced down from the sky, flames bubbling in his

throat. His guide threw his fire at the Asesino de mar, a distraction to give his dragon a clear lane.

Taragon shifted his eyes to his sister a split second before releasing his fire. He poured his breath toward every ship in the line, praying to Sol that Magnifico would save Valerian.

Half of Pizarro's men had rearmed their crossbows. The other half hefted the muskets, aiming them toward the demon falling from the sky. The captain watched as the giant dragon bellowed, sending a billowing cloud of fire streaming toward the ships.

"Hold!" he shouted. His crewmen and soldiers nervously stood fast, their fingers shaking against firing pins. The order went down the line, freezing the men in their boots.

Pizarro watched the flame fill the sky. When it began to balloon instead of streak, he knew he'd guessed correctly. Whoever commanded the dragons understood warfare tactics very well.

"Weapons skyward!"

Magnifico blasted through Taragon's flame with over a hundred dragons on his tail. Another fifty veered toward the ocean a hundred yards off the Asesino de mar's port bow. They would try their best to save those who'd fallen during the first pass.

Something bothered Magnifico, but he couldn't pinpoint it. The decks of the boats seemed too calm, too void of movement. It was as if they'd already buried them in flames, killing everyone on board.

"What is it, dragon?" asked Diego. "You're as tense as a newborn pup."

"I'm not sure. Something troubles me enough to pull up and cancel the attack."

"Then do so and reconsider. We can always return."

Magnifico glanced over at Estrella's dragons. They'd reached the others, some of whom still flopped about in the ocean. Half had died, but he knew the dragons aloft would sacrifice themselves to save even one of the living.

"Hold on, Guide."

Pizarro saw everything and heard nothing. The loss of his ears seemed to increase the excitement of the battle, especially now. He leaned out of the bowsprit, checking the men he could see on the other ships.

"Fire all weapons," he ordered.

"Fire!" screamed the mate, a big man with a booming voice.

Hundreds of arrows and bullets shot skyward.

"Turn!" screamed Diego.

Magnifico was still watching the rescue operation when Pizarro's soldiers discharged their weapons. Without looking back, he veered right so hard he almost lost Diego. The other dragons followed, their guides in perfect harmony. Four hundred feet above the vessels, a streaking army of dragons soared by.

The arrows and bullets matched the dragons' moves flawlessly. A second before, Diego, Magnifico, and the others had been ready to destroy everything. Now they were flying for their lives, feverishly swooping and swaying, trying to shake the haunted weapons.

The arrows disappeared in a streak of supernatural speed.

Fifty dragons fell from the sky, crashing into the ocean like giant boulders shaken from a cliff face. Their guides splashed down with them, some lucky enough to land on top of their dragons. The others died instantly, smashed to a pulp underneath tons of heavy scales.

Magnifico soared skyward like a rocket, straight up, trying to stay free of the remaining arrows. He never once glanced back to check on his forces.

"Down, dragon," shouted Diego. "Look at what's happening. Turn and fight!"

He tucked his body tightly beside his dragon. Two dozen arrows shot by, missing his head by inches.

Magnifico did as ordered. At five thousand feet he dipped and turned, flapping his wings furiously. He looked around and saw the arrows roll right behind him.

Reaching out with huge claws, he batted the arrows aside. Six stuck in his wing, but the others, momentarily stunned, became an easy target. With a searing blast he fried them where they floated. Nothing remained, save a sickly mist of a foul color he'd never before seen.

He groaned, letting the wing that had taken the hits sag. Tucking the other one, he let himself fall toward the ocean.

Diego took one look at the wing and knew instantly. Keeping a solid grip, he crawled along Magnifico's back until he reached the damaged wing. He grabbed the spine, inching his way down the leather covering. After reaching each arrow, he found the tip and ripped it through the tough skin. Magnifico shrieked when the first one came loose, nearly jarring Diego off his wing. He remained silent as his guide removed the others, waiting patiently for the ability to fly freely again.

Without a word of thanks or a moment's delay for Diego to climb to his shoulders again, He shook the injured wing a few times, then tucked it into his body. Dragon and guide fell from the heavens, the remainder of his force trailing silently behind.

Magnifico scanned the sky. No dragons flew above the ships. Those bearing the chains of the first attack run floated in the water, bobbing aimlessly. At eight hundred feet he drew up, floating softly, his eyes trained on the scene below him.

"C'mon," said Diego. "Why are we waiting here, there may be someone we can save."

"There is no life except for the soldiers on their ships," said Magnifico.

"What about the guides? Some of them could be treading water down there. We can't leave any of them behind."

"The guides are dead, Diego. They stayed with their dragons, trying to save them. They gave them the last beat of their hearts. It is the way of the bond."

"You don't know that. You can't tell from this height. Fly lower, I want to see for myself."

The scale slipped from Diego's fingers. Upended and tossed aside, he fell helplessly toward the sea. When he did manage to hold himself steady enough to scan the scene below, he saw that Magnifico had spoken truly. He heard the delighted screams of the soldiers, but nothing else. He saw the dragons, even in death such beautiful creatures, floating in the sea around the ships.

He watched as the men continued to fire rounds into the bodies of the Sol Dragones. Before he realized it, he'd drawn a huge ball of dragon fire from the sky.

Wrenched from his fall by a fist of gigantic claws, his flame burned to nothing as Magnifico raced to safety, taking his guide with him. He gave no orders, no instructions, and offered no condolence for the fallen. He merely flew, dragging what remained of his forces behind him. The other two attack groups, those that had stayed aloft awaiting orders, joined with him. Less than two hundred fifty dragons and guides escaped the salty grave of their siblings.

"My lord," said Estrella, limping through the sky beside her mate. The chain had tightened around her tail, cutting into the small scales. Gusts of wind brushed away the oozing blood.

Magnifico said nothing. He flew without expression or feeling. He hadn't uttered a word since grabbing his guide from the sky.

Diego sat, thinking, putting himself in Magnifico's place. Half of their forces lay dead in the ocean. They had no defense against Satadon's spells. The puny weapons of the Spanish had, with the Dark Lord's help, become lethal.

They would attack again, he felt sure of that. He knew Magnifico was pondering strategies, he could almost feel the mental machinery churning away beneath the scales.

For now, his dragon needed to think, to hold off his grief, pack it away for a later time. Diego rested his head on Magnifico's body, slapping his scales lightly, just to let him know he understood.

CHAPTER THIRTY-THREE

"Jenna!"

Sullivan had run like a madman from the sealed entrance to Coatepec. After locating the quickest way to another door, he'd dashed across the grounds as if chased by the dead lords of the Xibalba. Twice he slipped, falling hard on the grainy pathway. The second time his shoulder took the full impact as he crashed against a stone wall. Even though aggravating an old injury, he never cried out or stalled his pursuit. Up in a flash, he ran as fast as he could, limping and holding his arm.

"Jenna, can you hear me? Say anything, scream, tap a stone with a fallen rock, anything. Please, Jenna, for Sol's sake, let me know you're alive!"

After reaching the other entrance he bolted through the doorway without a moment's thought. Not once checking to see if his way out had been sealed, he ran down hallway after hallway shouting Jenna's name. At a dead end, he finally succumbed to exhaustion and pain.

"Jenna!" he bellowed, blinking back tears.

He stood, hands on hips, waiting for his breathing to slow. Closing his eyes, he practiced a calming trance he'd learned decades ago.

Breathe in for seven seconds.

Hold for seven seconds.

Breathe out for seven seconds.

Hold for seven seconds.

He performed the sequence seven times, until his body and mind joined with his heart and soul. Having stilled himself completely, he listened.

He heard no whimper, no cry for help, no tapping of any kind. The temple lay completely silent. His mind raced away from peacefulness, rushing in a dozen directions.

She's dead.

Satadon's taken her away.

I'll never see her again.

My love, please give me a sign.

"Away, Nathan," said the voice of Satadon in his mind, "or I'll toss what's left of her body to the animals."

"Open the temple door, Satadon," said Sullivan, "or are you afraid to face me."

A sickening laughter battered Sullivan's ears. He slammed his hands against them, yelling as loud as he could.

"You are afraid! You're weak, too weak to face anyone yourself."

"Come to Huitzilopochtli's temple. You will see her there. The doorway has been reopened."

"I don't believe it."

"Come, Nathan. We await you."

CHAPTER THIRTY-FOUR

Over the burned forests they soared, until they reached the hills where they could see Popocapetl, the smoking mountain beyond Tenochtitlan. Still flying silently, Magnifico lowered his eyes, scanning the ground below him.

He turned, and the Sol Dragones turned with him. Like a flock of giant prehistoric geese, they flew in formation over the mountains.

"There," said Diego, pointing ahead to Magnifico's left, "people, climbing through the hills."

After warning Estrella to watch for treachery, Magnifico dropped from the sky. He soared over the small group of hikers, seeking their leader. When he saw a strong warrior staring up at him, he looked ahead for a suitable place to land.

"Acalan," they screamed, cowering under the giants flying above them. "Save us!"

"Wait," he said, calmly. "Do not be afraid. Look at who they carry on their backs."

The people looked at the guides, their eyes drawn to the peculiar aliens riding atop some of the dragons. Fear gave way to awe when they saw Diego and Racquel sitting astride the largest of the pack.

Magnifico floated ahead of the group, maybe fifty yards, before settling among the bulky rocks in the hills. Estrella followed his example, landing softly on an outcropping close to Magnifico. The rest of the dragons perched where they could, hundreds of them, wings fluttering, jaws whipping around, tails curling and unraveling.

"Diego," said Magnifico. "The warrior will be upon us in seconds. I think he'd be more relaxed talking to you than to us."

Diego looked back at Racquel, pitching his head toward the Mexica people. She slid off her dragon's shoulders and followed him along the stone pathway. They hadn't walked a hundred steps before they saw the warrior coming up a rise directly ahead of them.

The leader held up his right hand. He and his group stopped just shy of the crest. They stood, waiting, every eye glued to the girl and boy walking toward them.

"Diego," said Racquel, "look at that man's face."

He didn't even answer. He hadn't breathed since the man held up his hand. He stared, and the warrior stared back. It was as if Diego was looking at his brother Esteban.

"Hola," said Racquel, smiling brightly, full of friendship. "¿Como esta?"

Acalan tilted his head. He couldn't answer, but somehow he knew the two children meant him no harm. He smiled, the smile of a jaguar that hasn't made up his mind about an intruder.

"What do we do now?" asked Diego.

"I can't make him understand," said Racquel. "A smile's only going to go so far."

Acalan suddenly drew back, hands raised, eyes wide with fear. The people turned, running back the way they came.

"Tell your people we mean them no harm," said Magnifico, his huge head appearing over the crest of the hill. "I will speak with you, Acalan."

The warrior heard his own language coming from the dragon. At first he felt it must be more of the Spaniard's magic, but as he looked into the hooded eyes and saw they never blinked once as he made his promise, he called his people back to the hill.

"I am Magnifico," he said, bowing to Acalan. He turned to Diego. "Stay with the people. It's up to Racquel and you to calm them. Let them know they're safe with us."

Diego half nodded as Acalan walked by him. They locked eyes, and Diego felt certain the warrior's thoughts matched his own.

Acalan walked beside Magnifico, giving him a wide berth. The dragon's heavy feet thumped the ground beside him, grainy clouds of soil shooting away with each step.

Soon the warrior saw hundreds of dragons, some huge like the black god next to him, some quite small, and most somewhere in the middle. Every one of them looked like skilled hunters, with their massive talons and jagged teeth easily visible.

A golden dragon, beautiful, gentle, walked forward and addressed him, speaking in the ancient tongue.

"Greetings, Acalan," she said, bowing low before him. "We grieve for you and your people during this horrible time."

She grimaced, bowing again. Acalan saw the rusted chain slung around her tail.

"With your permission, may I examine your injury?"

"The chain is bewitched," said Magnifico. "Every time we try and remove it, it comes alive and winds itself tighter around her scales. She's in great pain, we cannot allow it to stiffen again."

"With your permission?"

Reluctantly, Magnifico nodded.

Estrella laid her head down, laying her claws within her teeth in case the pain became too much to bear. "Proceed, warrior."

Acalan walked the length of her body, then around her tail. He placed two fingers on the crusty iron and watched it move inward an inch. Estrella sucked in a breath, held it for a second, then exhaled.

"Move away, Acalan," said Magnifico, "the spell is too strong."

"Nonsense," said Estrella. "We know as much about the Mexica as they know about dragons. I trust you, Acalan. Remove the chain."

He walked slowly along her right flank, dragging the same two fingers along her scales. When he reached her ear, he touched it, massaging it lightly. He felt her pain, and in doing so, he knew where to place his hands. Moving along her huge head, he rubbed her chin, her nose, her other ear, then he placed his cheek against her neck. Closing his eyes, he inhaled slowly, found her rhythm, and exhaled with her, until Estrella's claws fell away from her mouth.

She closed her eyes. Breathing subconsciously, she became Acalan. She'd never felt so relaxed.

"You may open your eyes, now, lady dragon," said Acalan.

"Awaken, Estrella," said Magnifico, "Look upon the magic of the Mexica people."

She did so. For a few seconds she didn't recognize herself, where she was, or with whom. Then her tail twitched involuntarily. She waited for the biting pain, and when nothing registered, she immediately woke and whirled around. The links rested on the ground beside her, lifeless, without magic. Her tail, bruised and bleeding, felt considerably better.

She turned back, thrilled. She was so excited by the lack of pain, a blast of smoke shot through her teeth toward Acalan.

"I'm sorry, warrior," she said. "I am *most* pleased. My mate spoke truth when he talked of your way."

246

"No magic removed the chain," said Acalan. "You let it fall from your tail."

"Do you mock me?" asked Estrella.

"Mock *you*, you who are powerful enough to crush me where I stand?"

"Then how..."

"The chain drew its power from you. Every time you tensed, or whenever anyone tried to pry it off you, your fear and pain gave it the energy it needed. All I did was calm you, let your heartbeat match mine. Together we relaxed. One by one the links fell from your scales."

She looked at Magnifico. "Is this true?"

"I watched them tumble off myself."

"Thank you, warrior, you truly are a mysterious and unpredictable people."

"My pleasure," he said, bowing.

"Now," said Magnifico, "to more pressing matters."

He turned and walked up the hill, joining the other dragons. Estrella followed, with Acalan walking beside her.

"Taragon," said Magnifico, as he walked through the boulder strewn mesa, "make a seat for our honored guest."

Acalan stopped when he looked at the red dragon, smaller than the rest, but equally as deadly. He looked at the black, unblinking eyes, unsure whether to take another step.

Glancing up at Taragon's guide, his nerve withered even further. The alien's eyes matched his dragon's, black as night, mysterious, stunning. The alien sat astride Taragon, two arms crossed and the other two resting lightly on the scales. Acalan flicked his eyes to Magnifico, then to Estrella, who comforted him with her soft voice.

"Do not be afraid, warrior. We know you've seen strange things today, but believe me, we're here to fight for your people, not to harm you."

"Yes," said Taragon. "Come, I would be honored if you sat next to my guide."

Acalan shook his head. *First gigantic, fierce creatures, next, strangers with different bodies, and now I'm to sit and calmly talk with all of them?*

He took the alien's hand, who he would discover was named Icoron, and climbed Taragon's shoulder. He sat uncomfortably, looking at all the dragons. He turned to Icoron, not sure how to greet him.

"Do not smile, Acalan," said Magnifico. "It would be an insult. Instead, close your eyes as you tilt your head back slightly."

Acalan did as instructed. After opening his eyes, he watched Icoron repeat the gesture.

"Taragon is the fastest of all our dragons," said Estrella, "and Icoron is the most gifted guide in their ranks. They've never been touched in any of our battles."

Acalan stared at Icoron, then shook his head. He looked at Estrella in total disbelief.

"Magnifico," she said, glancing at Acalan.

The leader of the Sol Dragones spoke. "We are the dragons of the sun." He lifted a huge paw, pointing it up into space. "Your sun. It is where we live, where we've been for thousands of years.

"The boy, Diego," he continued, tossing his head back toward the crest of the hill. "He is my guide, and we are here to help him and his people."

"He is my people," said Acalan. "I can tell when I look at him."

"Good," said Magnifico. "You are his ancestor, and he is a descendent of yours from five hundred years in your future."

Acalan turned to Icoron, who closed his eyes and tilted his head back.

"The Spaniards who've invaded your land were not alone. An evil spirit traveled with them, and it is he who is the cause of everything that's happened. Because of him we've lost half our force."

"Did you see, my lord?" asked Taragon. "The arrows and bullets, when they left the weapons, they looked small, harmless. A second later they grew much larger. The arrows became poison tipped spears, the bullets cannon shells. That's why so many of us fell after Valerian drew their fire.

"The dragons," he said, blinking back tears, "they were dead before the ocean took them."

Magnifico cringed, his eyes closing as he prayed to Sol. "I swear by everything that's in me, Satadon will…"

He reared up, looking back toward Tenochtitlan. "Sol's creation, no!"

"What is it?" said Estrella.

"Diego," roared Magnifico. "Ready yourself!"

"Tell me," screamed Estrella. "Don't leave me wondering!"

"Nathan's inside the temple. He intends to attack the Dark Lord – alone!"

CHAPTER THIRTY-FIVE

"Satadon!" shouted Sullivan, his voice shaking with fury. "I know you're here. I feel your presence. Come out and face me, or do you fear a lowly conduit!"

The interior of the temple lay in complete darkness, a stark opposite to the dazzling sunshine beyond the entrance. The faces of the Mexica Gods, cut into the stone walls, seemed to come alive as Sullivan walked by each one. The eyes followed his every move, hungrily waiting for the moment when he would pass a little too closely.

It wasn't the shadows that disturbed Sullivan. The dank wetness tickling his skin unnerved him. It seemed Satadon had taken control of the temple's environment. He'd changed it to suit his purposes, and to unsettle anyone foolish enough to challenge him. The temple had become Satadon's body, the interior walls his essence, the putrid, sticky moisture a living pool, waiting to attack and destroy invaders.

Sullivan heard the entrance being sealed. The stone crumbled around the opening, then built itself back up, as if the body were re-growing a limb. He turned his head, closing his eyes. He listened as the stone deities breathed and chanted around him.

"Satadon!" he bellowed. "Are you ordering your demons to do your work for you? Will you let them kill me? Are you so weak that you won't even face me yourself?"

Sullivan screamed the name of the Dark Lord again, commanding him to come forward.

"I am here, Nathan," said a soft, menacing voice. "I have waited many years for this moment."

"You're a coward," said Sullivan, sensing an evil spell meant to cripple him. He chanted his counter spell, creating an impenetrable field around his body. He waited as Satadon's foul magic dropped into the sand, dissolving harmlessly at his feet.

"You betrayed your own kind in the Xibalba, led Vipero to his death, and now you've killed an innocent woman who never did you a moment's harm." Calling his magic back to him, he stepped over the remains of Satadon's spell.

"Face me!"

"Was she dear to you, Nathan?"

"She was everything to me."

Satadon spat his next words. "Then she *served her purpose*, conduit."

"You heartless monster," breathed Sullivan. "She meant nothing to you. If you'd left her alone your plans could have proceeded without interference. Killing her didn't change anything. You did it for spite, nothing else."

Sullivan felt a freezing cloud swarm over his shoulders and back. Two rigid hands gripped his arms, holding him where he stood.

"I did it because I knew it would bring you here, into this temple, where you'd be foolish enough to challenge me."

"May the fifth sun silence you forever."

Sickening laughter erupted within the temple. Sullivan tried to jerk his arms up to cover his ears, but found them locked to his sides. He screamed, trying to drown out Satadon's voice. His eardrums burned inside his head, bending, twisting under the overwhelming assault. A last round echoed around the temple before slowly fading into the carefully etched images.

Sullivan shook his head. He heard nothing but a high pitched tone, but he felt Satadon's presence close by.

"Are you afraid of me?" he asked. "Do you have to keep my arms locked to my sides so I can't strike at you?"

"You bore me, Nathan."

"Then do your worst, spirit."

Sullivan surprised Satadon by breaking one of the dark lord's most powerful spells. He crouched and turned in one motion, knowing Satadon was a coward and would attack from behind. He thrust his hands forward and closed his eyes.

A hundred beams of concentrated light shot forth from his fingertips. They quickly fanned out, blasting the interior of the temple. The heat of a hundred suns soaked every crease, leaving Satadon nowhere to escape.

The Dark Lord roared as Sol's relentless power seared his spirit. His cries blasted the dust from the walls of the temple. He curled within himself, trying to shield himself from the sun's brilliance.

Sullivan's body convulsed. He sent the awesome power forward again before turning and running down a long hallway. He felt Satadon racing through the darkness, his fury hotter than the sun that had scorched him. Turning corners as fast as he could, he ran wildly amidst the ancient stone carvings.

He turned one final corner and bounced off an unseen stone wall. Carefully feeling the symbols, he ran his palms over certain sets. Jenna had burned the images into his mind many times, instructing Sullivan to let his hands dance within the markings until he could recognize them with his eyes closed.

The walls shook with Satadon's rapid charge. He couldn't focus, his mind faltered, his fingers trembled, and the sound of the Dark Lord's spirit scraping against the stone confused him.

He felt the temple come to life under his palms. At the same time, he breathed a spell he'd practiced for years. The stones began to separate. Sullivan smiled, he knew the battle would last a little longer. If he could force Satadon to deplete his energy, he might have a chance.

Within the intricate arrangement of deities, a doorway emerged. Sullivan stepped through without delay. Almost crushing his foot, the living rock shifted back to its original position behind him.

His hair scraped against the rough stone as he leaned against the wall. Slowing his breathing, he listened for Satadon's advance. Closing his eyes and hearing nothing, he smiled, thinking he might have left the evil one behind.

The stones exploded, slamming him against the far wall. Nearly unconscious, he looked at a swirling mass of filthy smoke slithering down the hallway toward him. Sullivan saw two eyes floating within the mist. Both stared directly at him, a sick voice spilling from the cloud as it approached.

"And so," said Satadon, "we come to the end."

He spit blood at the twisting vapor, now settled immediately in front of him. "You'll meet your end, you soulless devil. Diego will destroy you."

"The guide?" Satadon squealed with delight. His laughter echoed up and down the hallways of the temple, battering Sullivan's senses.

"He is nothing, an afterthought, a peon. When Magnifico brings him to me I will crush him as easily as I did your lovely mate."

Sullivan screamed until his throat cracked and bled. He'd waited a hundred lifetimes to find Jenna again, the only woman who'd ever captured his heart. After her there'd been others, companions only, but through everything, Jenna had always been a light in his mind, a reminder of something his training master once told him.

"If you want to find the woman of your dreams, Nathan, stop searching. Sol has selected a match for every being under his care. She is already with you, within your heart, as you are within hers. Live your life, give to others, strive to be your very best, and one day, the spirit of the universe will see fit to bring the two of you together."

His senses left him. He said her name again and again, and as he did, he called forward a spell he was told never to use.

Diego ran full out, matching Magnifico's takeoff speed perfectly. He vaulted from a rocky ledge, grabbing his steering scale in mid-air. Swinging his leg over the huge neck, he sat and tucked his feet in tightly.

"What is it, dragon?" he asked.

"Nathan."

"He's in trouble?"

"He may already be dead."

Diego ran full out, matching Magnifico's takeoff speed per-

"Die, Nathan," said Satadon. "Die most horribly."

Sullivan whispered the final words. The temple reeled as a shock wave blasted through the Mexica lands. He saw the dark lord rear back, swiveling his eyes wildly as he looked for new enemies.

"Even you wouldn't be that foolish," he gasped.

"They're coming for you," said Sullivan. "What remains of the Xibalba has already passed through Tenochtitlan. They are here, and you are the one they seek."

"You have condemned yourself, Nathan. They will move through these stones like air, grabbing anything in their way and killing it."

"No, Satadon. You killed them and took their power. They're coming for you and you alone. You killed Jenna, and now you will join her in the afterlife."

"Imbecile," said Satadon. "By the time they arrive I will be far from this city."

A second quake thundered through the temple, and then another. After the third time, the entrance to the temple crumbled.

Magnifico hovered above the top of the temple. With his wings holding him aloft, he kicked his legs out one at a time, bashing the entrance to rubble.

Within minutes nothing remained. A hole at the top of a huge pile of pebbles served as the entryway.

"Let me go in," said Diego. "I'll find him and bring him out."

"And you'll do nothing more than that," said Magnifico. "Promise me you'll go in, get Nathan, and return."

Diego had already hopped off his dragon's back. He kicked away a few rocks around the hole. "You could have just burned away the door, you know."

A blast of steam shot from Magnifico's nostrils. Every bit of loose rock and clay flew from the top of the structure.

"Hurry, Guide. We still have another battle with Pizarro's ships."

Diego carefully stepped into the darkness. He descended two flights of stairs and found himself in a darkened chamber. Using his finger, he scratched a bolt of dragon flame from the air, giving himself a torch. He found a third stairway, then a long hallway ahead.

"Mr. Sullivan!" he yelled. "Nathan! It's me, Diego."

⌐∥⍁⌐⌐

"No, Nathan," said Satadon. "*He* is here. Your foolish guide has come to save you."

"Diego!" yelled Sullivan. An instant later his body froze. A tear squeezed from his eye. He watched helplessly as the swirling vapor backed away a dozen feet.

Satadon began spinning. The smoke whirled madly, the eyes disappeared into the mist, sucked inside by the Dark Lord's command.

Sullivan felt his body being drawn toward his enemy. At three feet away, he watched as a hole opened within the whirling spirit.

Satadon spun at a blinding speed, except for the strange opening that appeared in the middle of his essence. Sullivan, still unable to move, saw the bizarre occurrence with frozen eyes. Suddenly, as he understood Satadon's intent, a chill swept over him. He screamed through lips that never moved.

⌐∥⍁⌐⌐

"Stay down there, Diego!" Magnifico roared.

Without plan or direction, the giant dragon lashed out at the temple. With wings, forepaws, legs, and jaws, he knocked huge chunks away from the stone structure. Enraged, he grabbed on with powerful hind claws and slammed his massive head against the rock.

Satadon released Sullivan from his spell. All the same, the conduit could do nothing except float in awe of the Dark Lord's power.

"Yes, Nathan, you forgot in your rage that the ancients are at my command. It was they who created your spell, as they did with all spells, all dragons, and all suns. They alone hold power over life itself, and it is they who have turned your spell against you."

The endless abyss of the Xibalba opened before Sullivan. Within Satadon's spiritual essence, a wormhole had appeared, and even at its small size, Sullivan saw his ultimate destination. He would join with the energy of the eleven lords Satadon had destroyed. He saw them, their faces, their teeth and claws, their eyes, so hungry for a soul to devour.

Magnifico floated above the shattered remains of the temple. He inhaled quickly, deeply, feeling his belly fill with explosive oxygen atoms. He mixed them with his insides, preparing to melt the rest of the structure.

Diego rounded a corner inside the stone walls. He stopped suddenly, his breath catching in his throat. Looking on in horror, he saw his conduit disappearing into a murky haze, first his stomach, then his chest and legs, his feet, and finally his head. One arm reached out as what remained of his face vanished inside the horrible fog.

Diego called out, knowing it was too late but still wanting to say something, do something for his conduit, his friend and escort for the last three years. Sullivan had taught him how to fight dragons with their own fire, and Diego had done nothing to save him.

A moment's thought passed, then his fingers scraped against

the dank air. A dazzling sphere of flame boiled up in his hand. He flung it at the Dark Lord, blasting the vapor all over the temple. If he couldn't help Sullivan, he would end his suffering and kill the Dark Lord at the same time.

Again and again he drew the magical fire. He used his rage, even his hatred as weapons, energy to fuel the dragon fire as he hurled endless missiles at his enemy.

He immediately switched to the frozen field when Satadon thrust his own flame at Diego. Vipero's fire was a matchstick by comparison, but Diego held his ground. He was determined to strike a fatal blow, to repay Satadon for everything he'd done, here in this time, to his ancestors, and back home, to his friends, his mother.

When he thought of Alejandra, tears fell onto his hands. The frozen field erupted in a jet stream of fantastic power, blasting Satadon through the seams in the wall behind him. Diego stalked the Dark Lord, saying his mother's name as he sent the power of an interstellar comet surging forward.

Satadon's smoky spirit flattened against the stones. The Gods of the Mexica inhaled, pulling the Dark Lord deeper within their temple, the real temple, that which lay within their souls.

The ancients roared, peeling Satadon away from his death. Diego flew across the inner sanctum, crashing against the stones on the far wall. He saw a dozen faces streaming toward him, every one of them glowing with venomous hatred, and to his horror he saw Sullivan's within the group. His held the most terrible expression of all, a soul changed from gentle to evil. Diego reared back, plastering his body against the stones.

A massive fist crashed through the temple wall. Magnifico ripped the roof off the inner chamber, bellowed at the Dark Lord, at Sullivan, and at the ancients for aligning themselves with evil. In one motion he scooped Diego up and blasted the area with dragon fire, melting the stone like butter. A second later he was up and away from the ruin, Diego's body sagging in his claws. His wings tossed the two of them everywhere, with no set pattern, should the ancients wish to strike. He would not let it end here, not after everything Satadon had done. Over the burned forest they flew, back to Acalan, his people, and Estrella.

⌐⌐⌐

When she saw Diego dangling like a corpse in Magnifico's claws, Racquel screamed his name and ran underneath his dragon. Stumbling many times, cutting her legs in a dozen places, her eyes never left him as she followed Magnifico's path.

He set Diego down on a semi-flat area amidst the rocky hill-side. Acalan moved to assist him, as did Icoron, but Racquel beat both of them to his side.

"What happened?" she panted.

"He fought the Dark Lord," said Magnifico.

"The fool," said Estrella, quickly lowering her eyes when Racquel snapped her head around. "I'm sorry, Guide."

Icoron grabbed Diego's shoulder and head with his right arms. "He seems to be breathing, at least. His skin is cool, a sign of shock in humans I believe."

Racquel dropped down beside him, hugging him close, trying to give him as much warmth as she could.

"Estrella," said Magnifico. "Nathan is dead."

Her eyes flashed. "How?"

"Sucked into the Xibalba. There are twelve lords walking the Dark Road again."

Her forepaws rose, an involuntary movement. She twisted her neck, trying to push the words from her ears. What sounded like a compressed growl escaped her jaws.

"Why would he act so irrationally? A *dragon* would fall standing against Satadon alone."

"Jenna," said Magnifico. "He believed she was dead."

"How do you know this?"

"I sensed it. That's why I called to Diego and left so quickly. I could feel his rage as if it burned my own skin."

"He's coming around," said Acalan.

"Mr. Sullivan!" shouted Diego, fighting Icoron's arms. "Nathan, he's one of them!"

Racquel popped up onto her knees. "It's alright, Diego. You're safe now."

"But Mr. Sullivan!"

"Nathan is dead, Diego," said Magnifico. "Accept it."

"That's it? You saw what Satadon did to him and you stand there talking as if nothing happened?"

"Your dragon speaks truth, young warrior," said Acalan. "Honor the fallen by fighting bravely to avenge them. Fight the enemy, not each other."

"Let me help you sit up," said Icoron.

Diego looked at the alien, remembering him from the battle. He allowed him to grasp his hands and arms at the same time. He looked at everyone, finally finding Racquel's concerned but smiling face.

"Are you okay?" he asked, throwing his arms around her.

"Yes. One of the chains found Estrella's tail, but Acalan removed it."

Diego turned and looked at the Mexica warrior. Acalan stared, then smiled.

"You look exactly like my brother," said Diego.

"Then I am fortunate. Your brother is a warrior among your people, in the future?"

"Not exactly, but my father served in the army when he was younger."

"What is the army?" asked Acalan.

"Later," ordered Magnifico, frustrated and angry. He rose, looking around at his dragons. "Sol Dragones!"

"My lord?" asked Estrella, "so eager to attack?"

"Nathan gave his life foolishly, but he weakened the Dark Lord. If we've any chance of defeating his magic, it's now."

Racquel was up on her dragon's shoulders before Magnifico finished speaking. She blinked her eyes at Icoron, tipping her head back as she did so. The alien returned the gesture, then ran to Taragon and mounted his dragon.

"Valerian!"

"Yes, my lord."

"Scout the ships in the bay. Return to me in the sky and give me your report."

She turned and spoke to her guide in a language Diego knew he'd never learn. The creature, a lizard with hands, feet, and a stubby tail, answered her. Her scales, although smaller, seemed to mesh with the stronger scales on her dragon. Valerian leapt from the rocks in one quick thrust, and the lizard aboard her never slipped an inch. She almost looked like a part of Valerian's body.

"Come, Diego," said Magnifico. "Clear your mind. We will mourn our loss later."

Diego grabbed an ear, pulling himself up onto Magnifico's neck.

"Taragon!"

Icoron jumped aboard, slapping Taragon's side as he seated himself. He grabbed his horn and shook it for luck.

"Take a dozen of our fastest dragons. Pick those you've trained yourself. You will draw fire again, but this time you must destroy the enemy's weapons."

"It will be done, my lord."

"Icoron," said Magnifico.

The beaded eyes turned toward him.

"You must set the example for the others. If one dragon falls, you all fall. If the enemy's weapon reaches one of you, all of you will be blown from the sky. Do you understand?"

The Andromedan blinked, tipping his head back.

"If you see the end coming, don't try to save part of your force. Turn and sacrifice yourselves, but make the enemy pay dearly."

The mesa went completely silent. No one spoke – not man, alien, or dragon.

Icoron blinked, but this time he bowed. When he raised his head he slapped Taragon again. The red dragon flashed once and exploded from the ledge. Eleven dragons, sleek, lethal, and battle ready, took off after him. Their guides leaned into the thrust, feet and hands tucked into the scales.

Chapter Thirty-Six

"Capitán!" shouted a sailor as he bobbed back and forth in the crow's nest of the Asesino de mar. "The dragons, they're aloft again."

"Where?"

"Six degrees to stern!"

Barely able to hear his crewman, Pizarro hopped up to the quarterdeck. Leaning over the starboard rail, he looked skyward. A dozen streaking bullets screamed toward his ships. Many more followed, but at a much slower pace.

"Ready all weapons."

The order bounced from ship to ship. The soldiers prepared to fire, confident in their ability to fight the sky demons. They'd turned them back once, burying a good number in the sea.

Cannons were braced, the touch holes filled and ready. Crossbows and muskets lay strewn about the decks. There were so many, men would trip over them as easily as fire them.

"Come at us, devils," said Pizarro.

At ten thousand feet, Valerian spun down through the wispy clouds, watching her brother lead his squadron toward the ships. As he sped away from the main force, she let herself freefall toward Magnifico.

"Your report, Valerian," he asked, after she took her position beside him.

"They've had the time to prepare for an all out attack," she said. "They still have over a hundred cannons, at least."

"What about smaller weapons?"

"They seem to be well stocked. I'd estimate six hundred guns, maybe four hundred crossbows."

"Where?" said Magnifico, talking out loud. "Where could they have gotten so many small arms?" He thought of the Dark Lord, hoping he hadn't regained power so quickly. Staying out of range was impossible when bullets and arrows lived and breathed.

"Pass the word, Valerian. Assume attack formations."

Icoron grasped Taragon's scales with all four hands, pulling hard so his dragon would know he was ready. He wedged his feet into the small scales by the wings. If he wanted Taragon to turn right or left, he'd apply the correct amount of pressure with either foot. A tip of one toe meant a slight adjustment. If he stomped on the wing, Taragon would turn in a flash.

Icoron glanced behind his dragon's tail. The others flew with him perfectly, as if they shared one mind. He blinked and bowed. The others answered with their own custom, offering total commitment to the mission.

He signaled Taragon. The pack turned, plummeting a thousand feet straight down. Icoron watched the boats increase in size as they dropped.

Rings of fire flashed on the decks, the cannons bursting with charge and chains. Dragons and iron rushed toward each other, a game of chicken the Sol Dragones had perfected centuries ago. At the last second, Icoron kicked down with his right foot and pulled hard.

No one but a guide could have survived that much G-force. Eleven dragons followed in sequence, leaving the living chains grasping nothing but air.

The iron links faltered for a moment, then shot forward like lightning bolts. The ends curled, metal fingers reaching out, hungry for dragon tails.

Following Icoron's command, Taragon shot straight up, eight dragons right behind him. Three had been caught, the chains winding tightly around the dragons and their guides. They fell, tumbling toward the ocean, squirming, trying desperately to escape.

The alien let loose a howl that echoed across the sky. The pain in his voice rolled over the lands like a tsunami.

Taragon understood, executing a twisting loop that put him face to face with his dragons. He saw in their eyes what he felt in his heart. Giving his own thunderous battle cry, he dove straight down, directly toward the ships.

⌐⌐⌐

"Estrella," said Magnifico. "It is time. Taragon is clearing a path. We must not delay."

"I am ready, my lord." She gave her instructions, then told Racquel to hold on tightly.

"Valerian!"

"Ready, Magnifico!"

Taragon spread his wings wide, a signal to his squadron. Eight dragons, four on either side, became a deadly battle group. Their view of the ships grew each second, and when the weapons exploded, they split into a triangle formation.

Icoron took his force straight at the Asesino de mar. Spears and cannon shells tore into his dragons, but most became disoriented in the torrent of fire he and the others hurled at the ship.

A crossbow spear slammed into Icoron, ripping one of his arms off. Howling, the alien grasped Taragon's scale even tighter. He turned him toward the mainmast where most of the cannons were stationed. Taragon roared mightily, dragon fire streaming from his nose and mouth as they crashed headlong into the ship. The other two dragons followed a second later, the heavy oak erupting beneath their huge bodies. A massive ball of flame consumed the Asesino de mar, killing everyone aboard.

After watching their beloved captain get sent to a sailor's grave, the soldiers rallied. Their weapons found the second group, musket shells blowing them to pieces before they could damage their ship.

Two of the dragons in the last group died in midair, their huge bodies thumping against the heavy ocean. The third found her way through the spears and shells. Spinning like a kite without a tail, she shattered the bowsprit, stem, and foremast of the second ship. It floundered, sinking steadily. The men who could dove overboard, tearing off their armor and swimming through the flames toward another of their boats.

Magnifico dropped out of the heavens, a messenger of death waiting for his chance to strike. Fifty dragons followed his lead, with another fifty trailing Estrella. Valerian stayed behind with over a hundred dragons, ready to polish off what they left behind.

"Their weapons are depleted," said Magnifico.

"They're soldiers," said Diego. "Those who can are reloading right now."

Magnifico looked at the ships. Two were gone, five remained, and all had fired enchanted weapons. He didn't like it, but Taragon and the others had done as they were ordered, sacrificing themselves to give them a clear lane of attack.

"Draw your fire, Guide," he said. "We're going in."

Fifty dragons swept around behind the ships. Flying low and fast, the water beneath their wings rippled as they raced toward the galleons. Magnifico looked up once, seeing Estrella leading her force toward the vessels from the opposite direction. He would reach the ships first, drawing most of the fire onto himself and his dragons.

His force split in half, sending a score of dragons streaking by both the port and starboard rails. Small arms fire rang out, the crossbow bolts and musket bullets instantly changing form. Most of Magnifico's pack turned away from the ships, arcing toward open sea or the mountains, depending on where they flew. The Dark Lord's weapons took off after them, leaving the ships vulnerable to attack.

Magnifico appeared from below the starboard rail, hovering beside the third ship like an angel of death. He snarled at the soldiers, scattering them with scorching fire. His flame flashed, a hundred feet long, slicing through the deck and destroying the vessel's keel. The ship cracked open like a plastic toy, the sides shifting before breaking apart.

Diego saw a dozen soldiers standing their ground on the

forecastle. With crossbows braced against their shoulders, they'd fire at point blank range in seconds. He threw a fireball at their feet, and as they jumped to find clean footing, he drew a larger flame into his palm. Reciting a spell Sullivan had taught him, he yelled his conduit's name as he tossed it.

One sphere became six, and before the soldiers could react, the flaming bullets exploded against what remained of their vessel. Those who weren't killed instantly drowned in the ocean, knocked cold by the impact.

Cannon fire tore into the ship. While waiting for sailors to reload their weapons, the soldiers on the next two ships had gone below to man the heavy cannons they couldn't move to the main deck.

The ship blew apart beneath Magnifico's wings, erupting in a barrage of oak splinters. The huge dragon pumped his wings forward, driving the two of them away. He protected Diego perfectly, taking the impact of the explosions into his body.

"Get aloft, my lord," shouted Estrella, sweeping by the sinking ship. She held her eyes high, refusing to look at his bleeding body. "Magnifico, there are a hundred wounds at least, open and bleeding. Get aloft, or I'll take you there myself." She looked at Diego. "See to his injuries, and don't allow him to rejoin the battle until he's ready."

Diego nodded, his eyes flashing to Racquel. Her eyes met his, and Diego felt the concern prickling her soul.

Disgusted, Magnifico pushed his wings hard, sending his body straight into the sky. "You will tend to me, Guide, and the second I'm well, we're returning to finish this fight."

Estrella turned back toward the ships, eyes wide with wonder. Dragons flew everywhere, some in organized packs, some alone, all of them engaging the enemy. The Spaniards fought bravely, fiercely holding off a force more powerful and deadly than anything they'd seen racing toward them on the ocean.

The dragons seemed to be taking the worst of it. By confronting the ships directly, they met their weapons head on. She watched the fiendish chains wrap around her sisters, dropping them into the sea like fishing lures falling from the side of a pier. Three of the larger dragons slammed into the deck of one ship, crippling her beyond repair. Sailors and soldiers alike tossed themselves overboard rather than get sucked into the coral reefs by the vessel's descent.

She almost cried, watching them, then she grew angry. Flapping her wings furiously, she flew toward the few remaining boats.

"Let us die as well, dragon," said Racquel, "if that will save another of our kind, and my people in the future."

Estrella opened her mouth to respond. What she saw falling out of the sky stopped the words cold.

Misterioso rocketed out of the sun's light, bellowing the ancient call of the Sol Dragones. Leading a pack of young dragons, with Rafael sitting tall on his shoulders, he turned toward the ships without slowing. It seemed Taragon had personally trained each of them, they flew with such amazing agility.

Zephyer and Furtivo, each carrying a teammate of Rafael's on their shoulders, aligned themselves so perfectly with Misterioso they looked like an extra pair of wings. The boys riding the three dragons held the same stare they did when facing an opponent in a game, until Rafael, seeing the battlefield below, gave each of his friends a devilish grin.

Valiente, with Lea aboard, curled beneath Misterioso. Taking a wide arc around her lord, she tucked her wings after feeling Lea's legs squeeze her sides tightly. She dropped a hundred feet straight down, leaving her rider's stomach high above them.

Noralon and Nobalon, holding Marco and his cousin Liliana aloft, snarled at Valiente's antics. Moving ahead to chase her, they fell back after hearing Misterioso's command.

"Stay with me, dragons of the sun." Dipping down a bit, he called to Valiente, summoning her back to the group.

Racquel squealed with delight as she saw her schoolmates leaning into their dragons, following their every move.

"Go, Estrella, fly!"

She joined the fight just as Misterioso came around for his first pass. His rider looked frightened and excited, but he held his seat as well as any guide with months of training under his belt. The young dragons followed their lord without hesitation, making her swell with pride. The elders would have their say when they returned to the sun, but for now, there was a battle to win.

Dragon fire shot forth from all directions, bathing the ships' crews in blistering death. The weapons continued to fire, now completely controlled by the Dark Lord. Chain, spears, and cannon shells blasted away from the decks, whether they raged with fire or not. The great ships groaned, bobbing in the sea like harbor buoys.

Valerian looked upon the slaughter from a thousand feet above the bay. Gathering her force around her, she would end it and save what dragons she could.

CHAPTER THIRTY-SEVEN

Magnifico winced as Diego yanked another jagged piece of timber from his scales. Standing in a vast pool of blood, he looked down, watching the new wound pour more of his insides onto the ground.

"Stay still," said Diego. "There are two more big ones. Once I get those, you can start sealing the wounds. Then we'll see if you can fly."

"I'll fly," said Magnifico. "My dragons are dying out there, I can hear them, and I feel it every time one of them falls."

"You can't help them if you bleed out. Let me get these, then you can burn your skin to close the wounds."

Diego grabbed onto another huge piece of wood. With hands so full of slivers he could barely squeeze them together, he pulled, hard, but the stick held fast. He swore after looking at fresh streaks of blood coming from between his fingers and thumb.

Fifteen minutes later he'd removed the last one. There were hundreds of small splinters in Magnifico's skin, but it would take days for him to pull them out. They had to get back to the battle, and he had to get back to Racquel.

"Alright," he said, panting. "Go ahead."

"Stand back, Guide."

Magnifico shot a focused stream of fire that sizzled like a welder's torch. Rolling back on his hind legs, he smothered his body with it, working diligently to stop the bleeding. He cooked his scales for five minutes before retracting the flame.

Flapping his wings, he lifted himself slowly. A couple of the wounds broke open, the fresh blood staining his body.

"It will have to do," he said, landing and crouching in one motion. "Get aboard, Guide, we're needed at the bay."

Diego ran up his forepaw, grabbing an ear and flinging himself into his seat.

Magnifico crouched, grasping the ground with his talons. Just before vaulting away, he sensed something evil and powerful beneath his feet. He pulled himself into the sky, two hundred feet above the great city of Tenochtitlan. Looking at the temple entrance he'd destroyed earlier, he watched as it rebuilt itself, stone by stone.

"Look," said Diego, eyes glued to the same bizarre sight. "How can it do that?"

"Satadon," said Magnifico, "or the ancients, or both. Somehow he's convinced them to fight for him, and they're going to use the temple as their weapon." Magnifico floated over the city, watching something he'd expected to see but hoped he'd never witness.

The contour of the temple remade itself, the stones tumbling on top of one another as if the ghosts of the Mexica were notching them in place. Once reassembled, the doors to the temple emerged, carving perfect rectangles along the seams of the heavy bricks. Magnifico and Diego watched, mouths agape, as the largest entrance flashed once, an indication that its rebirth had been completed.

The energy field Magnifico had felt before the temple repaired itself suddenly surged beneath the city. The other structures flashed together, then joined the seventh in a planned sequence. One by one, they came into perfect alignment.

Finally, the temple entrances sparked at the same time. They seemed to feed off each other, glowing together like candles around an altar. They looked completely harmless, until the ground underneath Tenochtitlan began to shake. Suddenly, Satadon's wickedness exposed itself, and Magnifico understood his plan clearly. No doubt remained, the ancients, with their infinite power, had joined with the Dark Lord.

"By Sol's grace, don't let this happen!"

CHAPTER THIRTY-EIGHT

After watching Estrella and Misterioso take their dragons high above the ships, Valerian dropped out of a clear blue sky. She ordered attack formation as the vessels came into view. Tucking her wings, she felt her guide clinging tightly against her scales. She listened as the lizard spoke a few words, an emotional tribute for her brother.

The dragons in her command soared downward, a tight pack ready to strike a blow for Taragon and Icoron. They began spreading out, veering to either side, inhaling the fires that would send the last ships to the bottom of the lagoon.

Weapons thundered from the decks below as over a hundred dragons zoomed through the sky toward them. They shifted their flight patterns wildly, coming at the Spaniards from all directions.

The chain, spears, and shells chased them, and while a few fell under the onslaught, most of the dragons went untouched. Valerian shouted her brother's name, tearing through a ship's mast like kindling and lacing the deck with white hot flame. The men, those that weren't fried instantly, ripped off their armor as they launched themselves over the side.

Twenty dragons followed behind her, dousing ships with lethal dragon fire. The soldiers had no time to reload, nor did they have the desire. Their captain was dead, almost all their ships were destroyed, and killer dragons flew freely above them.

Suddenly, the sky cracked open, thunderstruck by a force unknown even to the five suns. The dragons circling Pizarro's ships, stunned beyond sanity, flopped about in the sky, trying to stay aloft.

Magnifico saw it happen the next time. A bubble of energy, dark, sinister, incredibly powerful, fractured the sky over the vessels. Every single dragon under Valerian's command died instantly. As she'd led them to battle, they followed her into the sea. The scene resembled a hundred starving pelicans, searching the ocean for food, all crashing into the water together.

"No!" cried Estrella.

"Away, Sol Dragones! Estrella, fly, my love!"

They flew frantically, soaring in all directions, but mostly away from the bay where the ships drifted about, a burning flotilla of death.

"The ancients, the temple," said Estrella. "Why?"

"We cannot know at this time," said Magnifico. "Get away. Lead what dragons we have left back to the sun. Take our young warriors away from this haunted ocean."

"Lead us away, Magnifico," pleaded Estrella.

He felt the energy building, getting closer. In seconds Satadon's mighty weapon would finish the rest of them.

"Don't argue!" he shouted. Then he softened his tone. "Go, please. You must take this responsibility, I beg you."

"I won't leave without you!" she shouted.

Racquel ducked underneath Estrella's wing when Magnifico's fire roared over the top of her dragon's head.

"Think of the others!" he roared. "Take our dragons home, they are all we have left!"

Estrella jerked her body into a turn, crying and furious at the same time.

"Come, Sol Dragones," she ordered. "We're beaten, we must save ourselves."

Misterioso almost objected, but he saw the anguish on his Lady's face. "We must follow, Rafael."

"Diego's back there, by himself. We can't leave him."

"He is with Magnifico, and it is by my lord's order that we retreat."

Rafael turned in his seat, watching his friend fly back toward the city. He faced forward again, making sure everyone from his school flew alongside him.

"We've got to find Satadon," said Magnifico. "We have to stop him, and we have to do it now."

"You just ran off our best chance of doing that," said Diego. "The rest of the dragons are on their way home. We need them here, with us."

"So they can be blasted from the sky like hummingbirds? I think not, Guide."

"And what can we do alone, by ourselves?" asked Diego.

"One dragon might fly where hundreds cannot," answered Magnifico. "Satadon doesn't have the power to crack open the sky. The ancients are here, with him."

"Then let's find them and stop Satadon."

"My plan exactly."

Magnifico and Diego raced over the wasted remains of the forest. With luck they would pass harmlessly over Tenochtitlan and find Acalan and the people. Magnifico knew they held the secret, the way to convince the Mexica Gods to come to their aid.

The ground buckled beneath them. Magnifico felt the energy swirling under the entire forest, but he stayed low so Diego or he could spot the warrior leading his people through the hills. The edge of the trees loomed ahead, and Magnifico looked at the gates of the city with apprehension. They only had to make it past the interior walls, then they'd be safe.

A voice screamed in his mind. Instantly, he pulled up and to the right, hard, feeling for Diego's small body on his shoulders. He hadn't lost him, and for a moment he allowed himself a second to congratulate Nathan on his training.

"Look out!" screamed Diego.

The tips of the temples had suddenly come alive. They no longer glowed gently, now they burned hotter than dragon fire. The energy beams strafed the sky, aiming for the guide and his dragon.

"Down, now!"

Magnifico followed his orders without pause. He would not allow the Dark Lord to…

"Go left, left!"

He barely made it through the turn before one of the beams sliced through the tip of his wing. Magnifico pulled hard to the left, then rocketed toward the sun. He dipped and rolled, falling back toward the haunted temple. Roaring with pain and anger, he passed over the city at top speed, baking the entrances with his fire.

All but the seventh darkened, seemingly extinguished by Magnifico's flames.

"That must be the main entrance," shouted Diego. "That's where the power originates."

Magnifico turned sharply over the city, coming around and aiming straight for the tallest structure. Diego drew a sword of fire and threw it at the murky doorway as Magnifico closed in for the kill. He opened his jaws wide, releasing a fire so blazing hot it burned the inside of his mouth.

The other six pyramids flashed. Controlled by the seventh, they banded together, sending one immensely powerful beam of energy at Magnifico. It tracked the leader of the Sol Dragones across the heavens, exploding against his chest with the combined power of a thousand suns. Blood splattered the sky, raining down on the city below. Magnifico nearly blacked out, but he grabbed Diego and wrapped his wings around him as they plunged backward over the walls of the city.

Into the forest they flew, crashing down amidst the charred stumps. Drawing whatever breath he could, Magnifico held on to Diego with all of his remaining strength. They slid over a hundred yards before slamming against a huge boulder, ricocheting to the right and finally skidding to a stop.

"Magnifico?" asked Diego. He heard no answer, felt nothing coming from his dragon, no sign of life at all. He squirmed as hard as he could through the blood, trying to free his body from the protective embrace. Sobbing as he repeated his dragon's name, he finally pried himself loose.

His dragon's tongue lay still, a dead muscle twisting out of slackened jaws.

"Magnifico!"

He ran to the eyes, grabbing a lid and yanking it up.

He jumped from the head to the body, laying against it, waiting for it to move.

"No!"

He pounded Magnifico's body with his fists, then lashed out wildly with his feet. He kicked him as hard as he could, again and again, trying to jar him back to life.

He heard the animal running before he saw it.

He turned, drawing fire from the air, waiting for his end. He would die a warrior, as his dragon had, as his ancestors had, five hundred years before he was born.

He watched as a huge cat, black as night, ran toward him on the very path Magnifico had cleared with his fall. He knew the species, a jaguar, but so massive the ground shook with its footfalls. Diego readied his flame as it approached.

It could run him down and kill him easily. Diego did the only thing his mind told him to do, he reared back and hurled the fireball with all his might.

The jaguar swallowed it whole, snatching it out of the air like a treat thrown by a zookeeper. It never even broke stride, and seconds later it pulled up next to Diego.

Its legs towered over him, at least seven feet at the shoulder.

He couldn't begin to guess its weight, but one look at its face told him everything he needed to know.

"Come," it said.

"Magnifico," said Diego. "He's hurt."

"He may have given his life for you. Will you dishonor him by allowing the Dark Lord to destroy you as well?"

"I can't leave him like this."

"If he is to survive," said the jaguar, "then it will be because of forces greater than us. Now come, we must leave. The power is building again. If a dragon as great as Magnifico can be put down by the temple, do you think you or I could live through an attack?"

Diego looked at his friend. Magnifico still hadn't moved. He wanted to run back and stay with him, to be there when he woke.

The pyramids flared, the beams shot forth, uniting again.

"Diego, we have to go, *now!*"

He looked at the huge cat. It had lowered its shoulder, giving him an arm to use as a ramp. He ran up the giant forepaw, settling in around its neck.

"Do you have a name?" he asked.

"I am called Ajur." With that, the jaguar began running toward the safety of the hills.

Diego turned, looked intently at his dragon. "I'll be back. I swear on the five suns I'll come back for you."

CHAPTER THIRTY-NINE

"The guide acted unwisely," said the elder. "His foolishness almost cost the lives of our next generation of dragons, not to mention a good number of his friends."

"He did what he thought was right," said Estrella. "He feared for his people and wanted to do what he could to help them."

Sol's fire had never glowed so weakly. Its spiritual strength seemed to scatter throughout the heavens. The inner chamber lay in complete darkness, a troubling sight to the elders who'd rested in the sun's flames for thousands of years.

After sensing Magnifico's fall, Sol had locked himself away inside his chamber, barring even Celestina from entering. His sadness had swept through the stars in a powerful wail of anguish, the mournful echoes battering the galaxy.

Estrella wouldn't listen to words of her mate's passing. She'd demanded an audience with Sol, and when turned away by Celestina, she'd sought out the spirits.

"At what cost?" asked the elder. "You're fortunate to have returned with Racquel. Hundreds of our finest dragons have been lost, including Magnifico."

"We don't know what happened to him, or to Diego. Sol hasn't been able to determine anything, nor has Celestina. She told me this herself."

"Is Magnifico here? Has anyone seen him, heard from him? Accept it, my lady, he is lost to us, and without him our future is bleak."

"That is why I've decided to return to the past, to find him and help him if I can."

"That will not be permitted."

"I'm sorry, grandfather, I must."

"And when we lose you as well? What will become of us then? Misterioso vanished as soon as he brought his rider back to earth. No one's seen him since. We can only assume he's already risking his life flying over the towers of Tenochtitlan, calling out for his lord."

Estrella dropped her head low, her shoulders sagging under the weight of her decision. Keeping her eyes directed toward the sun's core, she spoke.

"Magnifico is my mate, my lord, and my life. I won't leave him at Satadon's mercy if there's a chance he might be alive."

"If you follow this course," said the elder, "you do so without Sol's blessing. Neither he nor Celestina will be there should you call for aid."

"So be it," said Estrella. She looked toward the Spirits of the Sun, a gathering of souls Diego and Magnifico had returned to Sol years ago.

"Come, guide."

Racquel said her goodbyes. She ran to her dragon, placed her hands around the huge fangs of her lower jaw, and allowed Estrella to lift her up onto her shoulders.

In a cave deep within the mountains, Misterioso bathed Magnifico's body with his magical flame. With strength he didn't know he possessed, he'd half flown and mostly dragged his lord's body to the edge of the lake surrounding Tenochtitlan. There he widened the entrance to a cave he'd located earlier and pulled the cold, unmoving form into the depths. After reaching a large, secluded cavern where he felt safe from Satadon, he'd unfolded Magnifico's body against a rock wall.

Misterioso's fire receded into his lungs. He stepped close to Magnifico, breathing quietly, listening, hoping to hear a heartbeat. He blinked his eyes, looked from nose to tail, and spoke quietly.

"She's coming, my lord, I'm certain of it. Whatever life remains within you, cling to it fiercely. Estrella will be here soon."

Diego gripped the jaguar's neck tightly. He sensed the uneasiness in Ajur's spirit. Even as huge and strong as he was, his pace suggested a powerful fear of Satadon. He wanted to take them as far away from the temple as he could, as quickly as possible.

Dodging trees stumps and scattered, smoldering plants, Ajur soared over a huge boulder. Diego squeezed his hands, feeling the jaguar's fur press through his fingers. He was so focused on Ajur's head, he didn't immediately sense the shadows flashing by his eyes.

A massive tree swept by his field of vision, demanding his attention. He raised his eyes and felt the wind rush out of his lungs. He couldn't breathe, nor could he believe what he was seeing.

The conquistadors had burned the forests around Tenochtitlan. They'd left nothing, not one stick in their quest to wipe out the Mexica people. Diego turned his eyes left and right, looking at a forest so dense and lush he felt he must be dreaming again. It was a trick, another vision, and he expected Satadon to appear within seconds.

He snapped his head around at a sound coming from behind him. He couldn't see anything, but he saw the ferns that surrounded the giant trees fluttering.

Another sound tickled his ear. He turned quickly, looking right. The stripes of a massive tiger sparkled within the greenery. Another cat, gigantic, swift and nimble, sprinted through the trees directly ahead.

Ajur slowed, and when a lion the size of a small house emerged from the thick brush, Diego's grip softened and he fell from the jaguar's back. The ground slapped his left shoulder, then scraped his face as he rolled on the forest floor. He opened his eyes and saw an enormous tiger staring down at him.

"Not much of a cat passenger, is he?" asked the beautifully striped animal.

"Very little we can do to help if he's that clumsy," added the lion.

"C'mon," said a smiling cheetah that measured sixty feet from nose to tail. "Give him a break, he rides a dragon. He'll have us figured out in no time." The cheetah bent down and scuffed Diego's face, licking him with a coarse tongue.

Lying on his back, Diego stared, looking at each of the giant cats one by one.

"They'll all make friends with you eventually," said a voice hidden within the trees, "except for the tiger. I'd watch out for him."

"Rubbish!" said Surmitang.

"Who *are* you?" asked Diego. "Show yourself, spirit."

The dense fronds of a low lying palm tree parted.

"Irish! Christ, Conor, is it really you?"

"Yea, it's me. There's no spirit here, just the two of us."

Diego stared at his friend. Conor smiled.

As if waiting for his cue, a stunning, three thousand pound cougar stepped forward. He unfolded an enormous pair of golden wings, flaring them once and then tucking them against his flanks.

"You're safe here, Diego," said Purugama, after walking forward to stand next to Conor. "This is the forest of forever, and we are the Champions of the Crossworlds."

Translations:

Abuela es; la abuela es = Grandmother's

Bobo = Clown

Chiquita Bonita = Pretty little girl

Buen hombre = Good man

Chicas locas = Crazy girls

Chico amante = Lover boy

¡Christo! = Christ!

Comodín = Joker

¿Donde esta Jose? = Where is Jose?

Es muy bueno = It's very good

España = Spain

¿Estás bien, hermano? = Are you okay, brother?

Estás excusado = You're excused

Estúpido = Stupid

Extraño = Strange

Gato gordo = Fat cat

Gatos locos = Crazy cats

Gordo y satisfecho = Large & contented

Gordo y estúpido = Fat and stupid

Gracias, oso valiente = Thank you, brave bear

Hermanito = Little brother

Hijo/Hija = son, daughter

¡Jinete de dragón! = Dragon rider!

Joto = Homo

La cocina de mi esposa = My wife's kitchen

Lo siento = I'm sorry

Los dos maniquís = The two dummies

Manos grandes = Big hands

Mi amor = My love

Mi corazón = My heart

Mi pequeño amor = My little love

Mira = Look

Muchas gracias, Capitán = Thank you very much, Captain

No se = I don't know

Órale = Hey

Oso / El viejo oso = Bear / The old bear

Oso grande = Big bear

Pequeño hombre = Little man

Perrito = Little dog

Poco = Little

Diablito = Little devil

¿Que pasa?" = What's up?

¿Qué pasó a él? = What happened to him?

Quinceañera = One who is fifteen, One who is turning fifteen

Si, Mamacita, yo estoy bien = Yes, Mom, I'm fine

Te amo muy mucho = I love you very much

Todos los diablos de España = All the devils of Spain

Tres ángeles hermosos = Three beautiful angels

Un caballo = a horse

Un cerdo = A pig

¡Viva Rafael! = Rafael lives! Or Long live Rafael

LOOK FOR THE FOURTH BOOK IN THE DIEGO'S DRAGON SERIES IN THE FALL OF 2014.

CPSIA information can be obtained at www.ICGtesting.com
Printed in the USA
LVOW13s0111070214

372631LV00001B/7/P